PRAISE FOR *NIGHTSHADE*

"What a marvel. In *Nightshade*, Lynn Hutchinson Lee conjures a world of heat-hazed fields and white gardens where glamour beckons and danger moves just out of sight. Zelda's desire to be seen—by wealth, by power—meets the fierce love and warning of Romany women who know the cost. The prose is sensuous and exact, the folklore alive, the politics unflinching. This is a novel about work and hunger, inheritance and passing, and the thin veil between rescue and trap. I'll be pressing it into many hands."

—Oksana Marafioti, author of *American Gypsy: A Memoir*

"*Nightshade* is an evocative and surreal read, conjuring sun-soaked tobacco fields, laced through with dread and magic. Hutchinson Lee has crafted a compelling story of strong women, the snares of wealth, and what happens when the puppeteers themselves find they are no longer the ones pulling the strings."

—Anuja Varghese, author of *Chrysalis*

"Lynn Hutchinson Lee has created a gorgeous, swirling story about family and heritage and temptation in this novel. Centering on a Romany family working on a tobacco farm in the early 1980s, we become particularly close to Zelda, who is desperate for the ease and opportunity that she thinks will come when she leaves her family and seeks a life elsewhere. Puri Dai dances in and out of the story, having vivid dreams and sharing knowledge and warnings that will hopefully keep Zelda and the family safe. An interesting read about Romany heritage, thankfully written by a gifted author of Romany descent."

—Manda Barker, Raven Book Store

"Lynn Hutchinson Lee's moving story about a Romany family working in the tobacco fields of Southwestern Ontario during the 1980s is a tour de force. Matriarch Rhodie and her sisters and daughter fight to preserve their culture while struggling with poverty, sub-par housing, cheating supervisors, accidents, and more. The family's struggles are interwoven with descriptions of nature—plants, birds, and stars, crafted in a haunting poetic prose. Simultaneously prose poem and page-turner, *Nightshade* draws us into the lives of its characters. And the puppets! Grandmother puppet Puri Dai's voice infuses the novel with a gentle wisdom, as she attempts to protect both her wooden and human charges."

—Ursula Pflug, author of *Seeds and Other Stories*

"Lynn Hutchinson Lee's novel *Nightshade* gives a very rare and precious insight into a Romany family and community, their language and history, and I for one am so grateful it has been written. Reading the novel, the author's words come from a wise and very old nomadic tradition. For many of us in the disconnected twenty-first century, it is time to speak about our hidden Romany identity and heritage. Today, it is about being a participant in a global story. Reading *Nightshade*, I felt like I was coming home."

—Frances Roberts Reilly, author of *Parramisha: A Romani Poetry Collection*

Nightshade

LYNN HUTCHINSON LEE

PRINCE EDWARD COUNTY, ONTARIO

Library and Archives Canada Cataloguing in Publication
Title: Nightshade / Lynn Hutchinson Lee.
Names: Hutchinson Lee, Lynn, author.
Identifiers: Canadiana (print) 20250333597 | Canadiana (ebook) 20260100617
ISBN 9781998336272 (softcover) | ISBN 9781998336289 (EPUB)
Subjects: LCGFT: Novels.
Classification: LCC PS8615.U835 N54 2026 | DDC C813/.6—dc23

Published by Assembly Press | assemblypress.ca
Cover and interior design by Greg Tabor

Printed and bound in Canada on uncoated paper made from 100% recycled content in line with our commitment to ethical business practices and sustainability.

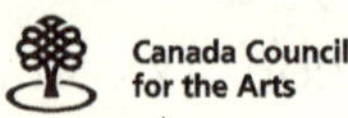

For the ancestors. For Lizzie, May, Lilly, Birchony, and Leonard.

For Rhoda and Bobby, who told me the stories.

For our remaining grandmother puppet, over one hundred years old, guardian of our family, and the beating heart of Nightshade.

You're glad you chose too much. You're too good at not enough.
So good you become completely invisible.

—CAREN GUSSOFF SUMPTION

1
Hooks

1.

Puri Dai the grandmother speaks.

A warning can be a shadow in a field, she says. A shadow waiting. It can be a kushti kauli ratti, a beautiful black night that holds all the loveliness and danger that could ever haunt you. It can be a black hole in the overturned bowl of the night, hidden behind a veil of stars. It can be a full moon. It can be a soft, defiled voice, a mokkadi voice: Come. It can be the mother voice: Watch out. Watch out for them gorjos. They'll get their hooks into you before you know it.

The warnings—her dark voice a ribbon unspooling in the air—the warnings are seeded all around us, just as a hundred thousand tobacco plants are seeded in the earth.

2.

When I was a girl, a little shey of ten, Buddy Watmore, an apple picker from north of Thorold, got out of jail for the third time and went home with *love* tattooed across the fingers of one hand and *hate* across the other.

Love and *hate* became my first road signs, the drom that led me from there to here. The second of my signs was *You are now entering Invisible.* Invisible is the transparent movable territory I carry with me as a snail carries its shell, moving with my family from town to town and farm to farm across the province. If I stood in front of trees, you'd see only trees. In a parking lot or a gas station or in a supermarket, you'd not know I was there.

I wonder what Buddy Watmore was trying to remind himself of with those tattoos of his. I keep asking myself, *What's with love and hate?* Sometimes I don't know who or what to love or hate. Can I love and hate at the same time?

And this life lived inside the shroud of Invisible: that would be thanks to my mother and the little I know of her early years in England, which come from stories about people seeing her in the road and telling each other, *Look out, here comes a Gypsy*, so she'd make herself small as an acorn. Murri dai, my mother, my small dark Rhodie, invisible.

★

Shifting from one foot to the other on this hot morning in the hiring shed at the edge of Mister Tormentine's tobacco fields, I couldn't have known that answers to my questions about love and hate and Invisible would unfold in the coming weeks. Instead, in that moment, a cold lip of air kissing the back of my neck, I was visited by Puri Dai's most recent warning, a tired one she'd delivered a thousand times before, about the full moon devil-man who moves without human feet through the night forests. With each new telling, her story changed, and now, with us having ended up somewhere between Delhi and Tillsonburg, it had shifted from forests to the local tobacco fields. As I waited, though, Puri Dai's story dispersed in the simmering air.

It was dark in there. No windows. Only a door. The shed smelled of tobacco and the hidden parts of men's bodies. Musselwhite, the low, squat foreman, and Mister Tormentine, the owner, stood and studied me with their heads angled back, arms folded over their chests. The hair of their forearms was bleached from the sun, and the muscles lay hard and impatient under their skin. In the heat, their eyelids were heavy with an unreadable gaze. My mother noticed. Both my aunties noticed.

"Ready for picking" was all Musselwhite said.

Mister Tormentine's head went up and down in slow agreement.

"We're here for the work," said Mam. She kept her voice small and her eyes down, like she always did with the gorjos.

If they knew what kind of people we were, would they still take a chance on us? Would we be accused when a tobacco knife went missing, or leaves from the drying sheds? Since we spoke English, and already lived in Ontario and weren't coming from away, and because we'd arrived in our own truck with our own things, they couldn't treat us like the other migrants. We had a few more rights. Which wasn't saying much, according to my auntie Lilly.

We stood trapped and waiting in that moment of sizing up, judging, guessing. Not that we weren't doing our own sizing up—it was a survival thing. Musselwhite's smile was comfortably cruel. I couldn't read Mister Tormentine. Tall, with a dark, thin scar angled across his cheekbone. *How would that scar feel if I touched it?* My aunties would call him too handsome. Was I the only one who saw a quick flare behind his eyes?

"It's gonna be hot out there," he cautioned, not looking at me.

Still leaning against the door frame, arms still crossed, the men looked like they might be figuring out how to get rid of us. They might've heard, then. *Watch out for them Gypsies.* Word had a way of getting around. I thought it would be almost a relief, having our identities out in the open. At least then we could be ready for whatever might come.

"I lost twelve men in five days," Mister Tormentine said. "That's how hot it gets." He looked over at me. "Girl's not under fourteen, is she?"

"Eighteen," said my mother in her small voice.

Musselwhite lit a cigarette. "Looks younger," he said. He gave a cigarette to Mister Tormentine. "We gotta check." He held out the pack to Mam and my aunties. I could tell they didn't like this invitation. It could be seen as a sly opening for something else.

"We don't smoke," said Lilly.

Mam stood and waited. We all did. That's the thing about our fowki, our people. We can wait. Mam frowned, and by the determined look of her I guessed that she was calculating possible tobacco wages. This calculation was meant to bring us closer to the flashing neon sign inside her head, the bright jittery lines that circled each picture in her dream of land, small house, garden, trees. I thought it was a disappointing dream. Mister Tormentine's house was probably big enough for five families. That was the house I'd be after.

"Okay," Mister Tormentine said. "I'll put you all out priming in the field because we're short, and the guys've been dropping like flies. Then, in a couple days, you two ladies," he nodded at Liza May and Mam, "are at the sewing table."

"You done the sewing before?" Musselwhite said. "Them tobacco leaves are no walk in the park."

"No kidding," said Lilly.

"I don't want no trouble in the field," said Mister Tormentine, drawing on his cigarette and sending a cloud of smoke out into the parking lot. "No monkey business."

"No," said Mam, "no trouble."

"The women aren't the problem," Lilly said between her teeth.

"Shhh," went Liza May, also between her teeth.

We kept on waiting in the hot wet dark of the shed, the air close and shimmering. I moved closer to the door, and when I looked across at the tobacco fields, the leaves bent and slid in the heat as if greased, and the asphalt of the parking lot pooled like water.

Musselwhite sat down behind the desk. He consulted a sheet of paper, then wrote in the margin. "I'm putting you girls in our executive suite," he said. The smile appeared again, mean as a sucker punch. My mother and my aunties and me, we all looked at each other. We knew we'd be going to a filthy room with mould in the corners and holes kicked in the wall and a shower that spat out brown water. "My guess is you're a family, 'cause you all look the same, except for young Green Eyes over here." He lifted his chin at me.

"Is there a key?" Mam dared to ask. The men gave her a look that said there was no key. This meant that during the day, while we were out in the fields, our family of puppets would lie inside unprotected. Lilly opened her big mouth to say something, but my mother stepped on her foot.

"So you got wheels," Musselwhite went on, looking out the door at our truck. "Good. You can get yourselves to work, then."

By this time, Mister Tormentine was looking restless. He went outside and lit another cigarette.

What happened next was like a dream billowing into a suspended moment: a sky-coloured car veered off the road and pulled up short in front of the hiring shed. The dream was a woman. She opened the car door and stepped out like a movie star, one slow leg at a time. Her hair was big and gold, a gold I knew from magazine hair. Skin white as the two o'clock summer sun, fingernails red, lips redder. Sunlight sparked off her jewellery.

"Hello, sailor," she called. "I was driving by." Her high heels picked their way across the asphalt to Mister Tormentine. "I just can't seem to keep away from you," she said to him.

"Trixie," said Mister Tormentine. There was an unsettled edge to his voice. "Trixie honey." He put his hands on her shoulders as if to keep her at bay. She looked out of place—all that gold out here on a simmering day at the edge of a tobacco field. She didn't fit in, but it didn't matter, because she shone. She, too, looked us over as we watched her through the hiring shed's door, then she leaned into Mister Tormentine, one leg bent, and kissed him, like in the movies. Everything about her was like the movies.

3.

On the way to Musselwhite's "executive suite," Puri Dai hears all she needs to know about this Trixie person. Overcome with the heat and the flies and laid flat with the other puppets in the back of the truck, she missed the whole show. Beside her, Zelda is going on about the movie-star name, white-gold hair, the ruby-blood lips, about the kiss in front of everyone, about the bracelets and ropes of sonnakai.

Trixie? What kind of name is that?

It's neither here nor there that Puri Dai didn't get to study the woman, because like the ant who waves her feelers before her, Puri Dai can determine at a distance the nature of almost any character or situation, and what she gets from Zelda's story is not good.

Watch out, she tells Zelda. Watch out for that sly raklie.

So we got hired, Zelda says, ignoring the warning. Mam and Liza May will be working at the sewing table and Lilly and me priming in the fields.

In the fields? Is that any place for a Romany shey, a nice Romany girl?

Puri Dai is horrified. She goes into another rant: The devil-man himself walks through them fields at night under the full moon, she tells Zelda, going up and down the rows, lighting one cigarette off the other. A chain-smoker he is, five packs a day, walking in a man's boots, but when he takes them off at night you'll see the cloven hoof. You watch out.

That's just your old story, says Zelda. She reminds Puri Dai that it's the 1980s now. The devil-man isn't even real.

Oh, he is, my girl, says Puri Dai, shaking her head. Not many see that devil, that beng, but I did: him coming through the dark forest under the full moon, gliding past the young tree I was carved from, the tree-memory still alive today inside this body of mine. And I froze, my shey. You may think I'm not human and nothing fazes me, but I have feelings. And the devil-man, my girl, you may laugh, but he's not just an old story.

Puri Dai remembers her young tree-self paralyzed by the dread of the moment. Not a leaf, not a twig could she move. And, being rooted in the ground, there was no escape as a tree. The memory sets her shuddering, as if the devil-man himself has once again appeared.

I remember him brushing my little leaves as he passed by, Puri Dai goes on. And the leaves, where he touched them, they withered and fell. There's a thin veil, my shey, between what's real and what isn't. It depends on how you see the world. Or, more likely, how the world sees you. When that devil shows up, you run like the hare and don't look back.

Puri Dai pretends not to see Zelda roll her eyes.

4.

The road wound us through the startling magic of the acid-bright tobacco fields, which went on and on till they met the sky. You'd think that with all the land's exposed flatness, other than a few dips and rises, there'd be nothing to hide. No secrets—you'd think. Everything wide open. I clung to the openness.

We ended up in the parking lot of a ruined motel with a battered sign that read *Crystal Beach otel*. There was no beach anywhere. Some of the windows further down the building were broken in places, cardboard taped over the holes. Missus Tormentine pulled in ahead of us and climbed out of the sky-blue car. "I'm Trixie Tormentine," she trilled, "but you probably already guessed." She must have done this a hundred times, shown tobacco workers into these death traps. "You'll be down here, at this end." She extended a long red fingernail. Her hand looked soft and boneless, as if Jell-O had been poured into a glove. Her mouth opened in a red smile. "So, girls, it's been nice meeting you," she said, fluttering her fingers and turning away, dismissing us, "but I really have to be off."

"We're not girls," Lilly hissed under her breath. "In case you hadn't noticed." Liza May frowned at Missus Tormentine as she got into her car. I watched. I wanted hair like that. I wouldn't mind long nails that said, *I don't have to wash the dishes or scrub the floors*; high heels that said, *I don't have to walk through the dust and dirt like them tobacco pickers do*. All that gold on her fingers, her wrists, around her neck. That sonnakai.

She tilted her head and turned to look at me from the driver's seat. Her eyes said, *You too could have all this*.

Trixie, I said inside my head as she pulled away. *Trixie honey*.

My mother's shoulders tightened. Her mouth went flat.

"She scares me," said Liza May.

Already, they didn't like Missus Tormentine. They didn't see the halo of rich light around her that I saw, nor the deeper, brighter light of privilege radiating off her skin. There's no telling, though, Mam always said. Them gorjos are always a tough call. Some are fine, some are not, and then there are the ones who go out of their way to do us harm. Lilly said my mother could figure them out at first glance, but Mam said no, Lilly had that deeper gift.

"'Trixie honey," Lilly cooed. She opened the door to a wave of bitter air, heavy and wet as a rainstorm. "Suck that mouldy air into your lungs, Trixie honey." I hated her mocking Missus Tormentine. "But you can get away from it," she went on, "can't you, Trixie. You don't have to live here."

The air seeped into my lungs. We pried open each window except for the smeared front picture window looking out over the parking lot. My mother opened a second door that led out back, and the air, swampy and thick, began to move.

What a filthy place. Its surfaces were shrouded by a sticky web of dust and grease. Six narrow metal bunks were crammed inside an alcove. A stove with duct tape over two burners and grease on the stovetop, a film of grease on the ceiling above it, and the oven door askew. A small, battered bar fridge, a leaking sink. Card table with four chairs. And the floor: almost black, with cracked vinyl tiles curling up from a thin subfloor. By the sofa, which looked to have most recently been used by a family of mice, was a gap deep and wide enough to trap your foot. I imagined a sickening chasm under the floor joists, bones and rodent bodies and unimaginable remains strewn across the earth. We'd landed in poor places before, but none like this. I wanted to cry, but I'd been taught not to cry when faced with such circumstances.

We brought in our soap and rags and vinegar and scoured every surface: walls, the ceiling, the bunks, cupboards, and windows, the dark corners. We shook out the thin, sour mattresses. I made circles across the floor with a soapy rag wrapped around my hand, and with each sweep I drew great peaks and valleys, imagining myself in a high meadow with tall grasses and flowers of many colours instead of here on my knees cleaning this dump across from Mister Tormentine's tobacco fields. But that's what our fowki do. Clean away the filth, the defiled. Restore the balance.

When the sun lowered itself over the trees, we stopped. Now, finally, we went out to the truck for the red curtains, and then the puppets, which we carried like sleeping children arriving home after bedtime. Their straw stuffing rustled; their wooden feet dangled from our arms. The long white hair of the old grandmother, our Puri Dai, brushed against my neck.

I took the puppets to the narrow back bunks, Young Chavo and Mr. Yesterday below, with Puri Dai, Morning Glory and Panni Mooi above. I brought their eyelids down over their wooden eyes so that they'd sleep.

The night was quiet now, except for crickets. We were in the deep, drunk heat of summer. The acrid-sweet perfume of the field washed into our room like waves from Lake Erie. I lay next to an open window, and the tobacco breeze moved toward me from the east and was met by a sudden perfume from the west. The two scents joined above my bed, the new one both heavy and light, and unbearably sweet. What did Missus Tormentine smell like? I closed my eyes, trying to picture her high pillow of hair, the hair that matched the necklace, the bracelets, the bright glinting sonnakai, the gold all around her. I tried to picture her buffed white hands, her rich-lady teeth, her head tilted toward us, leaning out the car window, her hand waving as she disappeared into the late-afternoon heat.

I half opened my eyes to the dark peeling room, to the medicinal smell of our soap, and the faint trace of mould under everything. Missus Tormentine could lift me into her world. How rough and ordinary I was compared to her, or even the raklies from the city. I imagined late mornings in a wide white bed, sun streaming through the windows, coffee served on a tray, a rack of high heels in a perfumed closet bigger than our whole sad room.

There'd been a time in my life when these things didn't matter because I'd never known they existed. Back when we lived in a rented trailer up in the Ottawa Valley for a year, on the road to the town dump, I saw beauty and poverty everywhere. My aunties had worked at the office in a lumberyard and Mam waitressed at a diner. We were as poor as everybody else. I liked the kids in my class at school and they liked me. Our trailer was fine; we didn't need a house. My mother was my house. She was my sun through the window, my moon over the fields. Every night she and my aunties pooled their wages in a coffee tin, and by the time we decided to move on, we had twenty-five coffee tins stacked in the trunk of the car.

Even back then, I think Mam saw her dream as a kind of signpost: this way to the piece of land, the little house, the garden, the trees. It was my aunties' dream too, although they didn't always go on about it, not the way she did. *Rhodie*, Lilly would always say, *are we nearly there yet? Not quite,* my mother would reply, never taking her eye off the prize. As I got older, she wanted the house on its piece of land to be my dream too. That was the problem.

★

In the morning, we explored the motel's parking lot. Mam and my aunties rushed to check out the green growth pushing itself up through the asphalt. "Look over here," they said. "Dik akai, dik at this." They ran their fingers over blue-flowered chicory, white yarrow, the wide-leafed plantain. My mother found St. John's wort everywhere. She picked fast, whispering to the plants, always leaving a few behind. Then she discovered vine after vine of black nightshade climbing the broken chain-link fence between the parking lot and the field. "Oh, Zelda," she said. "We got lucky." We spent the rest of the morning at the kitchen stove making black nightshade jam.

Just as the pot came to a slow rolling boil, Missus Tormentine pulled up, her brakes screeching, her high heels clacking across the parking lot. When she saw us watching her, she waved and swept off her sunglasses.

"Yikes," said Liza May in a whisper. "Dik at the raklie's yoks." Those eyes. They were brighter than the chicory flowers. They were like blue gas jets.

"She could burn a hole in a brick wall with them yoks," said Lilly.

Missus Tormentine swung a little suitcase. She marched up to our door and walked straight in. "Good gracious," she said. "I've never seen this place look so clean. You girls are professionals." My mother, eyes to the jam pot, made herself small and nodded. Liza May slipped out the back door.

"Not girls," Lilly said under her breath. "Women. In case you forgot." Missus Tormentine either didn't hear or pretended not to hear. I didn't mind her saying *you girls*. It was her way of being friendly. Intimate, even. She put the case on the table and lifted the lid to show us bottles of hotel shampoos, soap bars wrapped in paper, nail files, lipsticks, nail polish. "Just a little something," she said.

"Thank you," said Mam, without looking at the case. She kept stirring. It felt as if Missus Tormentine wanted something; Lilly would say it was written all over her face. Because of this gift, we would owe her, and the soft fingers of debt hung in the air.

Missus Tormentine looked brightly from me to my mother and back to me again. "My last girl took off," she said, "just like that. I need somebody over at the house, and it looks like I've come to the right place."

"Is this a job interview?" said Lilly, and Missus Tormentine laughed, clearly caught off guard that somebody like Lilly would ask somebody like her such a question. She seemed to need a change of direction, something to quiet the moment, so she set her sights on my mother standing at the stove. She asked what Mam was making.

"Just jam."

"Wow," said Missus Tormentine, "I never smelled jam like that." A little frown divided her forehead. "What's in it?"

"Berries," said Mam. She held up a spoon.

"Mmmm," Missus Tormentine said, taking the spoon and licking it. "Interesting." Nightshade jam isn't interesting. It's plain and ordinary—ordinary but wants to be flashy. "It's kind of like a mix between tomatoes and blueberries," said Missus Tormentine. "Can I try stirring it?" Mam handed her another spoon. "Oooo," trilled Missus Tormentine. "This is fun."

"Have you never made jam?" Mam asked.

"Never," said Missus Tormentine.

"Figures," said Lilly between her teeth.

Missus Tormentine stirred as if stirring was new to her. She lifted the spoon to let the jam, purple and slick, slide back into the pot.

"Wow," she said. "You should enter this jam of yours into the competition at the fair." Then: "Look at the time." She dropped the spoon. "Think about it." She was talking about the job again, I was sure. I heard the expensive quiet click made by the latch of her purse, the jangle of her keys.

She laughed. "Oh, I nearly forgot," she said to me, "this is for you." She handed me a heart-shaped bottle. *White Shoulders* read the rounded girlish writing on the label. "One dab behind each ear," she said, "every Saturday night."

I put Missus Tormentine's perfume in the suitcase where I kept my clothes. After she left, the cracked walls and torn linoleum seemed even more grim. My mother fished the spoon out of the jam and then began to shape a loaf of bread dough. Lilly fried eggs and green tomatoes. Liza May was still outside, fussing around the bird feeder she set up wherever we went. "Sparrows and a pair of house finches," she called through the window.

At supper, Mam said to me, "Why aren't you eating?"

"You gonna let all that hobben go to waste?" said Lilly, spearing eggs and tomatoes off my plate. She said I wasn't really there. She was right. Had I dreamt about Missus Tormentine all last night, her and that sonnakai of hers, all that glinting gold? It was almost too much, her impossible beauty.

"You'll not be working for that woman," said Mam later, dishing out more tomatoes from the frying pan. "Did you dik at that tikni little skirt of hers?"

"If she wasn't wearing underpants, you'd be able to see her mindj," said Lilly, and they laughed.

"I bet she puts the plates on the floor for her dog to lick," said Liza May.

"Mokkadi," said my mother.

I said nothing.

After supper, we went out back, where we found a weathered picnic table leaning to one side and six unsteady white plastic chairs. I brought out Puri Dai. *Puri Dai*, I thought. *This will be our new backyard for a while*. We sat looking up at the sheltering branches of the towering grandmother oak that stood in the yard, and beyond it to the darkening forest.

"I don't like them men from the hiring shed," said Liza May.

"They're men and they're bosses," said Lilly, "which is two counts against them."

"Looking at us like that."

"Ignore them," said Mam.

"I wish we could've gone to one of them smaller farms,"

said Liza May, "where the husband and wife and kids all work together."

"We're here now," said Mam. "We're staying."

"I bet they treat people better in them other places."

"We're staying," Mam said again.

The sky turned violet. We listened to the crickets. The sun dropped behind the trees and the heat settled around the walls. I was interrupted by an overpowering scent coming so sudden and rich and heavy I was almost afraid to breathe it in. "Grandmother," I said, "Puri Dai." Puri Dai's head shifted like the imperceptible turn of a leaf to the sun. "Puri Dai, do you smell it?" Puri Dai's nostrils widened.

5.

Puri Dai feels Zelda's mouth at her ear. She sees Zelda wave her hand to guide the air, and Puri Dai opens her nostrils to the night-flowering tobacco. Yes, she says, I smell it. Jasmine and something heavier. Maybe a scent from the old country, from the perfumed leaves of hedgerows and atchin tans, all those stopping places where they slept through the long nights. Puri Dai of wood and straw, canvas and wool, metal and string, brought over in a trunk across the bari panni, the giant water, under the giant sky. Crying. She was crying without tears, frozen with dread at being taken from her perfumed lands.

Here, now: the dark night, the crickets sawing away, and then the sisters interrupt it all by saying, "Time to turn in," and Puri Dai is carried to the far bunk. Zelda brings a hand to her eyelids and closes her eyes.

In the morning, they're on the road to the next town over. It's a lot of work rigging up the red curtains, but shows like this need to be flashy. The puppets are in top form today, and townspeople go crazy for the show. Puri Dai and Morning Glory clack their jaws around the tale of the devil who haunts the tobacco fields; the love that slides into hate; a water sprite played by Panni Mooi, our poor little water face, stabbed to shreds by a quiet, vengeful ghost. Mr. Yesterday is a terrifying devil, and Young Chavo, the ghost, needs to be more vengeful, but he's young and he'll learn. As they take their final bow, shivers scurry like centipedes up Puri Dai's wooden spine. Little do we know, she thinks, what may or may not unfold.

6.

Lilly dragged four of the plastic chairs around to the front of the motel, where we sat while she did her sewing. "We did okay yesterday, didn't we?" she says. "Them people didn't know what hit them, but they loved it anyway. What do you think, Morning Glory?" Morning Glory was silent. She was laid out flat on a piece of cardboard as Lilly measured her for a new dress.

"Panni Mooi wasn't happy," said Liza May, stroking Panni Mooi's face. "All that stabbing." Panni Mooi, slumped between Young Chavo and Mr. Yesterday, lowered her head.

"With them painted tears, she always meets a bad end," said Lilly. "It's in her DNA."

Lilly put Morning Glory's arms out to the sides and calculated the length of the sleeves and the distance from Morning Glory's wooden neck to her calves. Lilly could have used one of Morning Glory's old dresses as a pattern, but today she preferred the challenge of a fresh start. She said it kept her brain going in the terrible heat.

For the dress, Lilly'd been inspired by the green of the tobacco field across the road. Yesterday, I'd watched while she scampered over with her scissors and came back with a snippet of leaf. "I never chorred nothing, Mister Tormentine," she called out to the fields. "No stealing was involved! It was just a titch off your precious tobacco leaf, the size of a dime, and I bet you won't miss it." She took the snippet to the fabric store in town. The lady in the store called it avocado green, and Lilly thought it was the closest to the green she wanted.

Aside from sewing for Morning Glory, Lilly was passionate about books: the smell of them, the touch of the paper, the worlds they contained. She'd taught herself to read and talked often about her dream, which I felt was probably more attainable than my mother's house. What she longed for was a wall of books, and she didn't care where it might be. "A wall in any room," she liked to say, "anywhere. House, trailer, a shack in the woods."

Last week, when we were nearly finished at the strawberry farm outside Grimsby, she'd gone off and found a bookstore west of the farm, run by a woman called Annie. Lilly came back to the farm with an armful of art books. Those were the ones I especially liked, with paintings of red devils, lush nightmarish gardens, and portraits of girls standing on seashells, with their long hair covering the parts of their bodies that you weren't meant to see.

Aside from reading, Lilly liked to tear down the upper classes. She called them the booge-wazie. "What's the booge-wazie?" I asked her when I was still a kid.

"You'll find out," she'd said, "someday."

Now, Lilly was bent over her sewing, pins bristling from her mouth. She must have recalled my childhood question, because she shifted the pins to one side and said through her teeth, "Tormentine isn't part of the booge-wazie, but he wishes he was. And that mokkadi raklie, that wife of his, she is for sure." She looked up. "But forget about them people," she said. "We've got each other. And the puppets. We've got the puppets."

We loved the puppets. Morning Glory was Lilly's favourite, and she was shy for the most part, but when the time was right, she took on the gorjos. Sent them packing. She was more than a puppet. They all were. They spoke for us in words the gorjos didn't understand. They stood between us and the world. They were a circle of bison gathering round us while the enemy crept over the hill.

Lilly lifted Morning Glory to her knee and put a hand into her back. "So, Morning Glory," she went, "what do you think of your dress?" I heard the creak and pull of the gears and strings as Morning Glory rolled her eyes at Lilly, and then a louder rasp from other gears as her mouth clacked open and shut.

"Hard to say, the way it's looking right now," she cackled.

"But don't you like the colour?"

"I do," she said. "I like the green of all things. The leaves, the grasses, the frogs, Lake Erie at the shore. And especially the leaves of them tobacco plants over there."

"Tobacco plants? Really? Why tobacco plants?"

"Because next week I'll be sitting here in the shade and you're gonna be bent over under that hot sun with tobacco juice up your arms and you won't be asking me any more of them stupid questions."

Lilly ignored this. "What do you like best?"

"The crickets at night outside our window."

"What do you not like best?"

"The booge-wazie," said Morning Glory. She paused. "Okay," she went, "that's enough. Look at our poor Panni Mooi. I'm good, but she's all done in."

Liza May lifted Panni Mooi from the chair, cradled her in her arms, and stroked her painted tears. "No more stabbings," said Liza May, although she knew it wasn't up to her. The puppets did whatever was called for.

7.

Puri Dai feels Zelda's hand slide into her back, pulling the strings that lead to her eyes, eyelids, lips, lungs, heart. Here's that jasmine-heavy scent again. It goes down her throat.

Dik, says Puri Dai. Dik over there. She turns her head. Do you see?

Zelda looks. From the white wall at the far end of the building over to the edge of the forest, a drift of white. The flowers appear lit from within.

Night-flowering tobacco, says Puri Dai. Nightshade, she says. It's brimming all around us. Soon the hawk moths will come.

That pretty white devil has got her hooks into Zelda, and Zelda doesn't know. But Puri Dai knows Zelda's secret. Zelda wants to be like night-blooming tobacco. She wants to be white as these flowers glowing for the kauli ratti, white as a sheet drying in the sun, white as the bottle of White Shoulders perfume given by the parni beng. Zelda wants the high heels and the sky-blue car and no foot on the brakes. Breathe white, sleep white. White says: White isn't just white, it's a life.

8.

"You're lucky," my mother said from time to time. "You look like them. Being a didikai and all." Me, the didikai, the posh-rat, the half-blood. Not standing here, not standing there, not standing anywhere. Buddy Watmore's tattoo. *Love* on one hand, *hate* on the other. Love hate, hate love. My green eyes, white skin—even though not white. Mam said that all the gorjos needed to know was that we were ordinary hard-working tobacco pickers with a little family of puppets. She said if you're like the gorjos you never have to dwell on it, but if you're like us, being Romany and always the other, it burns inside you. We thought about it, being the other. We talked about it. It. It. Bigger than itself. It hid itself behind every word. We tried to shrink it, and the smaller it burned, the hotter it got. The fire that could spread across fields and forests, compressed into an ember, carried in our tissues and blood.

My mother didn't talk much about the doctor, only the bare bones: After she stopped travelling for a while, back in England, she was his housekeeper for eighteen months. He dared bring her, a Romany Gypsy girl, into his house, as no other person would have done, and she was both puzzled and grateful. She washed the dishes and floors and windows, polished his bookcases and chairs, served at his table. He trusted her with the silverware, with his wife's rings and necklaces, with the coins that lay on a tray in his library. He trusted her with silence.

In my mother's narrow bed, the doctor's hands pulled me, their daughter, into the world. He told my mother she would relinquish the baby. That he and his wife would keep me. My mother would be shown the door; he'd give her money and send her away.

He must have been rich, that doctor. He'd have had a big house. What would my life have been if he'd kept me? I thought of white linen sheets, twenty dresses, soft feet, short, perfectly curled hair. The gorjo part of me, whichever part that was, wanted to be there, wanted to run to meet the past, throw away the old signposts from the past and see the one ahead. *This way, girl. This way to Gorjoland.*

⋆

In the tobacco field they saw how hard we went at it, how we didn't stop till supper—or later, if we were told to keep working. Not that we had a chance to stop. We ate our sandwiches while we worked and used the hedgerow at the edge of the field as a bathroom.

One evening after work, I was sitting out front of our motel room with Puri Dai in my lap. Missus Tormentine showed up again, tearing around the corner, sky-blue car aiming for our parking lot, foot off the brakes till the last minute. She waved and stepped out in a cloud of dust. I tried not to let her see my heart lift.

"So," she said, "who's that you've got there?" She was looking at Puri Dai.

"Our puppet."

"Wow. She's nearly as big as you."

"Not quite," I said.

"Hi, old lady," went Missus Tormentine, bending down to Puri Dai. She put a pink box on Puri Dai's lap. "This is for Zelda," she said to Puri Dai. "Make sure she gets it." The box was covered with silver stars. "Can't stay," she said. She tapped the lid with a red fingernail.

I watched her leave. She ripped the car back around the corner toward wherever it was she'd come from. Inside the box, wrapped in tissue paper, lay a bra and a slip. They were the same colour as the box. I lifted them out. The label inside the slip was crumpled and I couldn't read anything except *100% Nylon*. The bra had a slight give at the back. I knew Missus Tormentine had worn these things; they'd pressed against her skin.

"What's that?" said Mam, coming out. I held the lid down tight.

"Nothing."

"It doesn't look like nothing to me."

"That Tormentine raklie showed up again," said Lilly. "Soon she'll be moving in."

"She's just being nice."

"You watch her," said my mother. "That raklie's up to something. You watch them gorjos."

"I'm tired of hearing about her," called Liza May from out back. "Tormentine this, Tormentine that. Just stop."

"Okay, okay," snapped Lilly, who always resented being told what to do.

Liza May went on talking, this time speaking quietly, as if to herself, and then she called again. "I need some help here, quick."

We rushed out to see her bent over a motionless sparrow lying on a rag.

"Liza May," said Lilly, "you do know it's dead, don't you?"

Liza May explained that she would restore the sparrow to life, and she told us to count for her. Lilly rolled her eyes. We stood around Liza May, counting slowly to five as she sent her breath into the sparrow's open beak. After each breath she stopped, waiting to see the tiny quick rise and fall of its breast. "Count again," she said, and we kept counting as she pressed a finger to the keel bone, giving ten quiet compressions. The bird lay limp and still, beak open to the sky.

"Thinks she can raise the dead," said Lilly, and Mam stepped on her foot.

"I can," said Liza May. "I can raise the dead." I was sad to see tears gathering in the corners of her eyes. "Again," she said, quiet and urgent. We counted. She breathed. She brought her finger to the sparrow's breast. "Please," she said to the sparrow. "Please." After a long pause, the tiny breast rose, then fell, and a breath came, then another. Liza May lifted her finger. The sparrow was breathing on its own. Liza May looked up. "I need a safe place for this little chiriklo. He needs a bed. A place to lay him down," she said, but we had no pail or basket or tray. "A floor is all. And four small walls."

"Zelda has that pink box," said Lilly.

"What pink box?"

Lilly looked at me. "The one from your Tormentine lady."

"She isn't my Tormentine lady. And I'm keeping my things in it."

Lilly didn't speak. Nobody did. They waited patiently. Their patience pushed me inside to my suitcase. I pulled out the pink box and lifted the starry lid. A faint lemony perfume met the air. I brought out the pink things folded inside. They were slippery and soft and slid through my fingers down into the suitcase.

Back outside, the sparrow gave a faded chirp. I was unhappy about the sacrifice of the box, especially with the holes Liza May was now making in the lid. She put the sparrow on its rag into the box and took it to a small shed she'd discovered in the trees. She fed the sparrow worms she'd pulled from the ground, and she fed it water, one drop at a time. She went out every fifteen minutes for the rest of the day. I heard her talking to the sparrow like a quiet cheerleader.

We got reports after each visit. I wanted to see the sparrow as it got stronger with Liza May's love, but I also did not want to see the state of Missus Tormentine's box. So I stayed away from the shed.

The next afternoon, the sparrow sat on Liza May's finger and flew away.

"Can I keep the box?" she asked. "Just in case."

I said yes, but I knew she could tell I was unhappy.

9.

You did right, my girl, Puri Dai says later. That lady of yours can get herself a new box. The chiriklo can't get a new life.

Puri Dai's watching Zelda. Zelda thinks Puri Dai doesn't understand. She tries to explain why she is angry and sad about having to give up the pink box.

Puri Dai says again: The bird can't get a new life.

She can see Zelda doesn't like this, because Zelda brings down Puri Dai's eyelids and carries her inside to the bed. Zelda doesn't want Puri Dai to see her shame. Zelda wouldn't call it shame, though. She doesn't yet know what it's called.

10.

We were out at dawn, and there was a wet chill in the air as the mist burned off the fields. I hated the haz-mat suits. They were too hot, but we had to wear them to keep off the dew and tar that would otherwise stick to our arms. Later in the morning, we got to take the suits off, and Musselwhite sent Mam and my aunties to work at the sewing tables under the shade. "Not you," he said to me with that flat smile. "You're gonna be priming, so you're staying put here in the field where we can keep an eye on you."

He kept me out under the sun. I followed the cart with my tobacco knife, slicing off the bottom leaves and heaving them into the baskets on the tobacco boat. At the end of a row, I had to take the baskets off the boat, which was the hardest part. *This is like the weight of a hundred bodies*, I thought. I was slippery with sweat. It was as if the sun had magnified and heated up each drop of my sweat to its boiling point, so that the drops burned like small flames as they slid down my forehead and into my eyes.

Sometimes when I straightened myself up, one hand pressing the base of my spine, I'd see Musselwhite and one or two other mushes talking and smoking over at the barn. They laughed from time to time, looking my way. I guess I wasn't invisible, being the only girl in the field, because whenever I reached the end of a row, Musselwhite would call, "How ya holding up there, Green Eyes?" And he'd give a laugh. I thought he must be waiting for me to pass out.

The work kept me going till four o'clock, and then the tractor broke down. At least the kiln was full and we could finally leave. Musselwhite tried a joke, but I kept walking past him. I fell asleep in the truck on the way back to the motel, and when we arrived I went out to the back and fell into a chair. For a split second I woke when Lilly brought out the puppets to air, leaning them against the trees. Behind my closed eyelids, I saw the tobacco plants again, the rows and rows meeting the sky. There was tar stuck to my arms. I felt my barbed-wire spine, hands bruised and scorched, the lines of dirt scraped into my skin.

A soft voice said, "Hello" so I half said a hello back. I felt a cool hand on my arm and opened my eyes. Missus Tormentine was looking down at me. I was ashamed to have her see me like this, so dirty and tired. "I just decided to come round the back," she said, "because I called out and you didn't answer." She lifted a rag from the back of the chair beside me, wiped the seat, and sat down. "I was just driving by," she said, "and I was wondering how you liked that cute bra. And the slip." She said she was sure we were the same size and wanted me to know there were lots more where those came from. And dresses too. I'd love her dresses.

I heard my mother inside, clicking her tongue to Lilly. "Dik at that tikni parni beng," she started. "Marching in like this when we're asleep on our feet and our girl can hardly keep her eyes open."

"What are they saying?" asked Missus Tormentine. I didn't tell her that Mam was calling her a little white devil, saying who does she think she is, swanning in here like she owns the place.

Lilly said: "She does own the place."

"They're saying how it's too hot out to even lift a finger," I told Missus Tormentine. "The heat is supposed to break next week."

"Let's hope so," said Missus Tormentine. "I don't know how you girls do it, working your hearts out under this crazy sun." She glowed, but it wasn't from heat, for there was no sweat on her skin. "A glass of water would be lovely. Oh," she said, "you stay put. I'll get it." And she went through the back door and right into our room.

I heard my mother say, "I'll just run the water nice and cold for you."

Missus Tormentine brought out her glass of water and sat down. She started talking too fast; my eyes kept closing and I had trouble keeping up with her. Then she zeroed in on the puppets. "Wow," she went. "I thought you had just the one. And now there's a whole family. What's all this about?"

She went over to kneel beside them and said they were like nothing she'd ever seen. "I like the blue one with the tears on her face," she said, "but the old lady's my favourite. May I?" Without waiting for my answer, she lifted Puri Dai to her lap. She cradled her in her arms and buried her face in Puri Dai's hair, rocking her back and forth, humming a tuneless song. Her whole body rocked, and she started whispering into Puri Dai's ear.

"Does the old lady have a name?"

"Yes."

"What's she called?" she asked, looking up.

"Puri Dai."

I shouldn't have said that.

"Puri Dai? What's that?"

It was exhausting, and even more exhausting in this heat, to remember the things we weren't supposed to tell. And now, here I was, telling. I told because I was half asleep and feeling sorry for her cradling Puri Dai, because Missus Tormentine was looking so sad, and because of her halo of rich gold dust. I told because you don't say no to the owners, the owners who can send you packing with no reason at all. I told her our private name, instead of the name we shared with everyone else. "Puri Dai. It means grandmother."

"She's touching Puri Dai," Mam said from the window.

"Get her away," said Lilly.

"No," said Mam, "we can't tell them what to do."

"Them," spat Lilly. *"Them."*

"Now what are they saying?" asked Missus Tormentine.

"They're talking about whose turn it is to wash the dishes and whose turn it is to dry." I sat up straight, because I needed to stay awake for Missus Tormentine. She talked about the puppets, about the new language coming from our room. How when she came here, she was walking into a strange, wonderful world, and she wished she could stay to soak it all in. *Soak what in? The walls blooming with mould, the endless thin meals of fried tomatoes and eggs and bread, the hands scrubbed raw from endless work?*

"My life and I are so boring," Missus Tormentine said. I found myself beginning to feel sorry for her. She looked lonely. Then she brightened and asked what language Mam and my aunties were speaking. She had a way of making me tell her things without even thinking—I lost track of myself, and I told her that too. *I told her.*

Missus Tormentine widened her eyes. She came to sit beside me again. She moved an inch away from my face. Her blouse was crisp and white. Her eyes went *wow*. "So it's true," she said. "You're real Gypsies." She reached out to touch my arm as if it belonged to a strange new being who had only five minutes ago been an ordinary girl.

She stood up. "Thank you," she said. "I mean it. Thank you." The makeup above her eye was cracking. "Well," she said. Her lemony perfume fell over me. Her hair glowed. She said again, "Thank you," as if I'd given her something. Maybe I had, by accident. My mother called me in for supper. "Oh my goodness," said Missus Tormentine. "Look at the time."

★

Working in the heat was like swimming through flames. My body was on fire, and I had to keep pulling my sleeve across my forehead to stop the sweat from dripping into my burning eyes. I heard Mam and my aunties talking back and forth at the sewing table. Their voices made fluting sounds, and I couldn't tell who was saying what. My hands were bruised, and my swollen fingers were stuck together with tar.

My tobacco knife dropped to the ground. I couldn't pick it up because I felt as if the bones were softening in my hands. I looked at my hands, stained, hanging there. Missus Tormentine came into my head. Where was she? What was she doing? I saw her in a blue-and-white-striped dress, sitting on a green lawn, drinking a glass of iced tea. Turning to me, holding out another glass with cool beads of water slipping down the sides.

Come, she said. *Drink*. I heard the ice cubes sliding around like the crackling of river ice in winter. I called her, but she didn't answer. She kept drinking and drinking. I thought, *She's here*, but she wasn't. She was gone. It wasn't real, I told myself, it was only the heat. *Only*. The heat wrapped itself around me, squeezed my innards. Soon they'd turn to soup.

At the edge of the field behind the leafy bushes of the hedgerow, I pulled down my jeans and squatted, and hardly anything came out. I was dehydrated, dried up like a fish on the Lake Erie shore. Something deep in my head was melting.

Through the leaves I saw a few of the mushes standing around at the far end of the field. You never knew with them. I should have been more careful. There were stories about things that happened, especially with people like Musselwhite. One of the mushes looked like him, and I thought he saw me coming out of the hedgerow as I was doing up my jeans. I tried to stand straighter but my body was sliding. The sun lashed my back. "Mam," I yelled. Her voice came at me from somewhere off the field. Maybe from the sky. Why was the field turning upside down? The sun was so white it turned black. Everything turned black.

★

Mister Tormentine and my mother were standing over me. I was stretched across a bench in the hiring shed. It was dark and hot, and an electric fan sent sips of cool air ribboning around the room. I couldn't stop shivering. My mother brought a cold cloth to my forehead.

"This happens," said Mister Tormentine. "It happens all the time."

"I have to get her home," said Mam.

Mister Tormentine lifted me in his arms and carried me to the truck. "I'm a jellyfish," I said, my arms around his neck, and started to laugh. My laughter turned to shrieks until I could no longer breathe. I stopped, and in that moment of stillness I felt a lick of heat like smoke coming from his body. I think I said, "Put me down," but I clung to him even as he slid me into the truck.

Mam drove me home to the motel and carried me out to the trees behind our room, where she laid me on a sheet under the towering grandmother oak. "I'm a jellyfish," I sang while she took off my clothes and draped a wet towel over my body.

She lifted my head and made me drink. I blew bubbles and she told me to stop. "It's the sun got you," she said. "The sun and the heat." I turned and vomited on the grass.

It was dark when I woke. No sound from our room. The lights were out. They must have all gone to sleep. The scent of night-flowering tobacco filled the air.

I saw Puri Dai in a chair next to me, the air ruffling around her. I saw moths as wide as my hand settle on her wrists, her hair, the backs of her hands, all over her body. I wanted to ask her, "Why are you covered with moths?" but my tongue lay in my mouth like a stone. The tobacco flowers were glowing. The moths rose in the air. They were dark, coarse, heavy. They left Puri Dai and fluttered to the tobacco flowers. Threadlike tongues emerged from their mouths and entered the flowers, then delicately withdrew. Puri Dai and I, we sat and watched.

Tucked under the trees, I rolled to one side, folded my head and knees to my chest, curling up as the foxes do, and slept. I woke before sunrise, and in that moment I knew my collapse in yesterday's heat was about to change everything.

II.

Puri Dai wants to fly to the river beyond the tobacco fields. She wants to gather it in her wooden arms, bring it to the yard, and lay her girl in its cool waters. The beast Musselwhite had no business sending her out into them fields, such a delicate thing she is, and the heat! The punishing heat. And now she sleeps like the dead, curled in on herself like a caterpillar.

Let the hawk moths come, let them fan her with their wings. Let the white-blooming nightshade send its perfume into her dreams.

But even in her tenderness, Puri Dai has a bone to pick with Zelda. My girl, Puri Dai goes on, yesterday you gave away my name to that farmer's brassy little devil. You told her about your mother's fowki. You gave us away, and you had no right. No right to expose us. Our names are our own.

Word always gets around, says Puri Dai. Oh, that family, the gorjos say, did you hear? You know what they are, that gang of sisters with that girl, them witches, them thieves? And out come the names, the accusations and threats: You'll steal our babies, you'll chor them from the cradle, you'll chor our money and the shirts off our backs, you'll chor the tobacco knives and the leaves from the curing barns. Anything that isn't nailed down you'll stick in your pocket or hide under the tarp in the back of your truck. You'll put love spells on our men and a curse on the women. But we gorjos, we can give as good as we get. We'll trash your stuff and cut off your hair. Run you out of town.

Once we're known, says Puri Dai, there goes everything.

Any week now will begin the fall into darkness. Each thing will unwind itself. Her girl will see the tracks of the devil-man himself along the tobacco rows, or worse, she'll feel his breath at her ear.

Puri Dai sees Zelda tossing and turning in her sleep under the tree. Her girl won't yet know that what is about to unfold will be like a stone thrown into a pond, and the ripples will reach us all.

★

It must have been two days and nights that I lay under the cooling branches of the grandmother oak. I saw two separate moons and two separate suns, each marking its own night and its own day. I opened my eyes in late afternoon to watch the birds gather over the seeds at Liza May's feeder.

Liza May had returned from the fields and was bandaging an injured red-winged blackbird. I looked over and saw Missus Tormentine's box, no longer pink but grey, on the far edge of the picnic table.

"You're awake, then." Liza May placed the bird in the box and went inside. I heard her comfortable clattering in the kitchen. "You got it bad," she said, bringing out a glass of lemonade, helping me to sit up.

At supper, Lilly told us that Mister Tormentine said I didn't have to return to the tobacco fields, and instead I would start tomorrow at his egg barn.

"Thank goodness," said Mam. "It's thoughtful of him, isn't it. Finding a better job for you."

"I wouldn't call it thoughtful," Lilly said. "He just hates the idea of Zelda sitting around on her arse in this dump. Especially on his dime."

"Can't you just stop?" said Liza May, and nothing more was said.

In the morning on their way to work, Mam drove me to the barn, and I was happy to walk into a cool cavern with a high roof and a breeze, and the clean smell of concrete and straw. The raklies were wives and daughters from the smaller farms, and they welcomed me, showing me what to do. I sank into my work. It wasn't hard. I went through the eggs by size and colour, white ones here, brown ones there, and watched for cracks in the shells. Cracks meant you had to throw them away. I slid an egg carton down beside my feet to collect the cracked eggs, and when it was full I hid it in a corner behind the sorting belt.

At lunch break the other egg sorters saw my sandwich of nightshade jam.

"You'll turn into a toothpick, little miss starveling," they said, and they gave me celery sticks, a slice of meat loaf, and two spoonfuls of apple crisp with Velveeta cheese. They told knock-knock jokes and stories about Musselwhite's brother showing up drunk at the wrong church for his wedding, and about Willard Crowshank, the butcher, who put his finger on the scale to drive up prices. They all had something to say about Missus Tormentine. They talked about the shortness of her dresses and the value of her gold bracelets.

"I could feed my family for a year," said Diane DeVrees, the head egg sorter.

"How crazy can you be to wear high heels on a farm?" said Rita Slack, who was one notch down in the pecking order.

What can you expect, the women asked, when she comes from that family up in Hamilton, her grandfather in real estate. Him owning the company and a good chunk of Hamilton Mountain, said the egg sorters. What is she even doing down here, they'd like to know.

"It's that husband of hers," said Rita. "That's why she's here. I'd follow that man anywhere. I'd set my shoes under his bed any night of the week."

"Shoes?" went Coral Peplinskie. "I'd be running barefoot into his bedroom."

They all said Mister Tormentine was too handsome for his own good.

At the end of the day I got out to Mam's truck quickly, the carton of cracked eggs tight against my body. I lifted my apron to show her, and she stroked my face, not because of the eggs, for which she was grateful, but because she was glad to see me on my feet and working again.

The next morning the raklies laughed, seeing me try to hide the eggs. They said they all did it. They stashed them behind the straw in one of the old stalls and took them home when the cartons were full. At lunchtime they fed me again, this time with Crowshank's summer sausage and Rita's mustard between two slices of her rye bread. They told more jokes and offered to fix me up with a younger brother, a cousin, a son. Then things turned again to Missus Tormentine and the talk became dark.

"Her grandfather's housekeeper was murdered on Hamilton Mountain."

"The last girl she hired killed herself."

"Wasn't that the kid from somewhere near Mattawa? Roxanne Pettifer. Such a tragedy."

"Her brother visits and she does it with him. It. Yeah. You know what I mean."

"This morning she drove her car into the ditch."

"That would be on purpose."

"Did she really do that?" I nearly dropped an egg.

"Yes, and she ended up in hospital."

"Did she really do it on purpose?" I asked.

"Who knows?" said Diane DeVrees.

"I'd say yes," went Coral Peplinskie. "She's up to something."

"Faking it," Rita said, "like she does with everything."

I saw Missus Tormentine's sky-blue car upside down, one wheel spinning, and her body flattened in the ditch, arms out, legs twisted at a sickening angle, head yanked back, one high heel over in the field and the other jammed under the brake pedal. Blood coming out of everything, her red mouth open in a scream—or slack like the fish on the Lake Erie shore. I didn't fill enough boxes to make my quota. I dropped too many eggs and they had to be swept away.

"Did you know Missus Tormentine was in an accident?" I asked at supper. "She ended up in the ditch."

"Oh, the poor raklie," said Liza May.

"She had it coming," said Lilly. "Or she's faking it. I wouldn't put it past her."

My mother put down her fork and cleared her throat. "Mister Tormentine dropped by the sewing table today," she said. "He needs somebody up at the house. To look after Missus Tormentine for a few weeks. He says she can't walk. They've asked for you, Zelda." Her lips came together. "I don't know what to think about this."

"The nerve," said Lilly.

"The thing is," said Mam, "he's offering twice what she makes at the egg barn." She shook her head. "We can't afford to say no." Because it was too far out of her way to drive me, she said Mister Tormentine himself would pick me up and bring me home in the afternoon every day till Missus Tormentine was back on her feet and could get permanent help. He'd come for me the next morning at seven. "Zelda, remember. You'll do what's expected of you and nothing more," Mam said to me. "Missus Tormentine is not your friend."

"What your Mam means, Zelda, is don't let her get her hooks into you."

Mam glared. "Thank you, Lilly."

After they'd gone to bed, I sat outside and looked at the trees. I heard night birds, first a whippoorwill close to the ground and then a distant owl. Later, far back in the forest, the coyotes started yipping. I didn't like what the egg sorters—and Lilly—had said about Missus Tormentine. I didn't believe she was faking. "I'll do anything for you," I whispered.

Puri Dai must have heard me. *You're walking into dangerous waters, my shey*, she said. *She's a tikni beng, that nasty little devil, and don't say I didn't warn you.*

You're just going along with the crowd, Puri Dai, I thought silently, certain she wouldn't hear.

See for yourself, she said, *and then tell me what's true.* I felt her shake her head in sorrow, but that was her and this was me. I went inside and climbed into my bed and lay without sleeping, tossing and turning and listening to the crickets for most of the night.

At seven the next morning, I was at the front window when Mister Tormentine's truck crushed the blue chicory flowers growing through the cracks in the parking lot. He did his wide-legged man-walk up to the door. He didn't say hi. He didn't say anything, only grunted.

We took off down the road and he stopped for a minute at the hiring shed to speak to Musselwhite. Musselwhite was out front smoking with a few of the mushes.

"Nice balls," said one of the mushes, circling Mister Tormentine's truck.

"Custom-made," said Mister Tormentine. "Road trip to Nevada."

The men laughed. I wanted to bury my face in my knees. At least I was forgotten when he got out of his truck to talk to Musselwhite, but the second they were done, Musselwhite turned to me. "Heat got ya, did it?" He angled his head back and looked sideways at the other mushes and they laughed. "That summer heat gets you every time," he sang. Then he winked at Mister Tormentine.

Mister Tormentine climbed back into the truck. I tried to keep my voice from shaking as I asked if Missus Tormentine was okay, and he put on the radio instead of answering. Somebody was talking about milk quotas, and then a song came on: "Another One Bites the Dust." He turned it up really loud.

After a while, he shouted over the music. "Idiot. If she'd've finished her driving lessons like I told her to, she'd be able to drive that damn car properly and she wouldn't've ended up in the ditch with a busted knee." He started gearing down. "Thinks she doesn't need brakes." He looked at me sideways and curled his lip and said, "Do you need brakes?" He stopped in front of a driveway. "You're here," he said.

As he pulled away, I noticed a pair of balls hanging off the truck's trailer hitch. They were dark pink and swung back and forth.

12.

She didn't look like Missus Tormentine, but instead like a grey rag doll left outside in the rain. Her leg was a dark blue, and she held it folded under her body, like a heron. "It's not broken," she said. "It just looks that way." I asked what happened and she laughed and said, "Who knows?" I thought about the egg sorters, their take on everything. I wished they could have seen her leg. That would set them straight. "My Jack thinks I should have finished with my driving lessons. What a bore," she said. "I never told him what I did when I was sixteen to get my driver's licence in the first place. Come on in," she said.

Missus Tormentine's house scared me with its beauty. It resembled something from the movies, the old ones, when they had girls in white aprons to open the doors. A grandfather clock loomed in the front hall. I could hear the quiet click of its gears and was startled by its sudden chiming. The ceilings were so high, and I felt dwarfed by them. There were too many rooms, sunlight flooding the silent polished floors.

You could walk down the curved staircase in a trailing gown, with all the guests looking up at you in admiration.

"Jack wants to knock the place down and build a split-level," said Missus Tormentine, hopping into the kitchen, holding on to furniture as she moved. "Don't you think that's a crime?"

I felt it would be dangerous to take a side here. Instead, I said, "I think you need a doctor."

She laughed. "No," she said, "I need breakfast." She told me what to make and how to make it, and she invited me to sit at the table with her. I watched her eat half and leave the rest. She offered me a glass of water. "But you'll have to get it yourself."

She leaned over to put her plate on the floor and called out. An old dog, a slobbering puro jukel, came running, its nails clattering over the hall's gleaming floorboards, tail swinging back and forth like a windshield wiper. "This is Charlie," she said. "Charlie, meet my friend Zelda." My friend. *My friend.*

Charlie's front paws landed on her knees and she winced. He dropped to the plate and ate everything in one bite, then finished by licking the plate till no crumb was left. I knew Missus Tormentine expected me to pick up this plate—defiled by a dog's tongue—and she expected me to take it to the sink and wash it. Instead, she pointed to a dishwasher; the dog plate went in with the other dishes. I washed and washed my hands. Charlie sat at her feet, lifted his leg, and licked. I could hear Lily: *What kind of people would see a dog lick its arse or eat a dead rat and then let it lick your plate and think it's okay.* I told myself that Missus Tormentine couldn't help it. She didn't know better. They have their gorjo ways, we have ours.

She pointed to a cupboard and told me to bring out the vacuum cleaner. She told me to vacuum all the floors. It took a long time because there were so many rooms. I had to vacuum around the legs of the many chairs and sofas, and the legs of the dining table, which was nearly as long as our room at the motel. Then I had to dust. I didn't see dust on anything, and I said so, but she told me to dust anyway.

We went upstairs, me dragging the vacuum cleaner and Missus Tormentine hanging on to the banister. She took me into a room off the landing, which she called the master bedroom. My mother and my aunties and me and all our puppets would be able to fit on the bed with room to spare. "Nobody else has a king-size around here," Missus Tormentine said.

She had a closet you could walk into, like an extra room. She showed me her dresses. "Why don't you pick one? I've got far too much stuff." I had never touched a rich woman's dress, let alone been offered one. "Go ahead. Help yourself." She stood back and watched me as I went through them. I'd only seen such dresses in magazines, or in the windows of stores in the wealthier parts of cities.

When I was eleven, my mother took me shopping at a Richmond Hill thrift shop, and I remember being enchanted by the three mannequins in the window. They wore long dresses in bright patterns with flounces around the hem, and stood on one foot with the other foot raised behind them, arms wide, as if ready to take flight. It was around Mother's Day and there was a sale. We were getting me a dress for a school concert. I saw one that I thought a rich girl or movie star would wear; movie stars had started to be a big thing in my life. They were all that the girls at school talked about. The dress I found was white and made of something my mother called Swiss cotton, with tiny raised dots. My mother bought me the dress. It cost four dollars. "Are we rich?" I asked.

"Yes," said Mam. "We're rich." She hugged me. She didn't know that when I went to bed that night I put on the new dress, and as I fell asleep my small dark room glowed as if lit by unseen lights.

At the school concert, my class got up onto the stage and sang two songs. Because the teachers said I was gifted with the best singing voice, I had a solo. I was too young to understand invisibility or the protection it offered me, so I sang standing out in front of everyone else. Me, a rich girl in a rich dress. My voice soared. Mam and my aunties sat in the front row, and I saw Mam's eyes shine with tears. When we finished, after the audience stopped clapping, I heard a girl behind me whisper, "See that dress she's got on? It used to be Jackie Henderson's." I didn't understand, until years later, the meaning of what she'd said: there was shame in having to buy your clothes second-hand.

Along the row of dresses in Missus Tormentine's closet I saw a slice of green. My hand stopped. "Well?" said Missus Tormentine. "What do you think?" The dress under my fingers had a fitted bodice of emerald-green taffeta with a flared skirt that stuck straight out, papery and stiff like the leaves of a basswood tree. "Try it on."

Standing in front of the mirror, in the green dress, I was unable to move, not from nerves but from enchantment. "Dance," said Missus Tormentine, "like this." She took me in her arms.

"No, Missus Tormentine," I said, "your leg."

"Shhh," she said, and swept me across the room to the door and back.

How, suddenly, was she able to dance? Was it sheer determination, mind over matter? Or something darker? Rita's words came back to me. Was Missus Tormentine faking it? No, I decided, she was incapable of such deception. She was leaning against me. Her breath was on my hair. In front of the mirror again, I made myself stand like the mannequins in the Richmond Hill thrift store, arms raised, ready for flight. That was how I felt. Almost airborne.

"It's yours," said Missus Tormentine, clapping her hands.

I took off the dress, knowing I couldn't bring it with me back to our room. My mother and my aunties would find it. They'd sit me down to talk about the dress. Mam would say, "What did we tell you about doing your work and nothing more?" Lilly would say it was a bribe. "Like I said. She's trying to get her hooks into you." I'd have to give back the dress and maybe never see Missus Tormentine again.

I took a plainer dress, one I'd never wear. Missus Tormentine looked disappointed. "You'll never go to a dance in that thing," she said. Then she told me to shut the door when I started cleaning because she hated the sound of the vacuum; she found it annoying. I had to help her get downstairs. Her leg seemed to be worse.

Back upstairs, I shut the closet door so I wouldn't have to see the emerald-green dress, and I ran the vacuum cleaner from side to side and into the corners, making patterns. The floor was wall-to-wall beige carpet, good for making patterns, and I thought of the mountains I'd made when washing the floor for the first time in our room—the high meadows lush with wild-coloured flowers.

After the master bedroom there were eight more rooms, but Missus Tormentine said I was to clean only four. I kept thinking of the dress. The four rooms ran along one side of the hall. Each was exactly like the others: empty and painted the same dark blue as Missus Tormentine's bruised leg. Each contained a closet door of polished wood, a brass handle. I opened the doors. The closets were the kind that would turn into dark narrow tunnels in a dream.

I went back to stand at the door of the room next to Missus Tormentine's bedroom. Somebody had painted stars on the ceiling. I wouldn't want to lie here at night with those stars watching me. There was a softness to the floor, as if it might melt under my feet. Ghosts were here. Ghosts that hadn't yet been born.

Moving to the window, I looked down over a curved garden with flagstone paths and banks of ferns, and many flowers and leaves I didn't recognize. A pattern of light and shade worked its way across the plants so that some receded into darkness while others came forward. I was puzzled by a length of meandering cedars off to one side. Beyond the cedars and through the hanging branches of a willow, I saw a pond. The dark room and the bright garden seemed to be at odds with each other, and I wondered if they had been dreamed up by a single mind or by two opposing ones. As I finished cleaning, I shut the door behind me and closed my eyes, trying to place the vivid brightness of the garden over the darkness of the house.

After vacuuming all four rooms—although I didn't think it was necessary—I brought the vacuum cleaner back downstairs, careful not to let it touch the polished baseboards, and put it into its cupboard. Missus Tormentine told me to make egg salad sandwiches. "You can have one too." I stood eating at the sink, avoiding a plate. "You can sit down, you know."

After swallowing the last of my sandwich, I perched on the edge of the chair across from her. She sat Charlie on her lap and fed him bites from her sandwich. Then she brought the plate to his mouth and he started to lick the crumbs. His pink tongue curved and flattened itself against the plate and then pulled into his mouth and ran over his lips, and he turned to look at Missus Tormentine. She held his head between her hands and kissed the end of his nose. I could never tell my mother and my aunties that I'd sat at a table with a jukel who ate from a plate and was kissed by Missus Tormentine. And if the plate went through the dishwasher and I ended up eating from it, what then?

What if this wasn't a job I should have, being in this mokkadi gorjo house that would never be pure or clean, no matter how much I scrubbed or washed or dusted? But then there was Missus Tormentine herself, calling me her friend, taking me in her arms to dance, the skirt of that emerald-green dress floating around me.

⋆

Later, Missus Tormentine took me outside, hopping on her good leg and holding my arm, moaning from time to time. I almost couldn't believe the change in her.

"Missus Tormentine," I said, "You're clearly in pain. I'm supposed to be looking after you."

"Oh, shush," she said. "You're here. That's what matters. Don't you be worrying about me, I'm fine," and she yanked on my arm. "Come. I want you to see the garden."

She led me under tall bushes whose branches were covered with white ruffled blooms leaning over our heads. Everywhere I looked, the leaves were a deep green, the flowers all white: some like frilled crepe paper, some like small bursting stars, others were hanging trumpets that sent out a ripe, intoxicating scent. Missus Tormentine named them: rhododendron, peony, hellebore, hydrangea, night-scented stock, and datura, which she said she particularly loved because of its perfume. "Very poisonous," she said, "deadly, even, and a nightshade. But you already know what that is, right?" We were enveloped in a pale hush. "It's what's called a white garden," she explained. "At night," she said, "everything glows."

I could hear Puri Dai's voice: she'd have something unkind to say about this. *Where's the colour? What's with the white? Isn't there enough white already in this world?*

We came to an opening in the wall of cedars and I saw many paths. Missus Tormentine pushed me down a trampled dirt walk that turned in on itself, and I began to panic. With the trees closing in over me, I found myself struggling to breathe. After many twists and turns, the path finally opened at the pond, which narrowed and then almost disappeared behind a far stand of willows. Crowded fronds of the willows moved in the breeze and skimmed the water. A yellow scum floated on the surface.

"Missus Tormentine. You need to sit down." She let me lower her onto a bench. She was breathing heavily.

Out of the blue, she said, "Did you not wash the windows?" I'd never thought of the windows. "That's part of your job, you know," she said. "To wash the windows." She looked up at the house. "I can see the dirt from here. On those four bedroom windows, look. The kids' rooms." I hadn't seen any children, or any clothes or toys that might belong to a child. "Well, we don't have them. Not yet," she said. "Mister Tormentine wants four boys." Her hands went to her stomach. She told me all the things she and Mister Tormentine were doing to be able to have a baby, and I went *lalalalala* in my head. "This is my fifth try," she said. "I keep losing them."

She got up and lurched forward, hanging on to my arm, propelling me further along the shore. "I want to show you the swans," she said. "They're my temporary children till the real ones come along." She stopped. "Wait," she said, leaning hard against me.

"Missus Tormentine. You shouldn't be walking around like this."

She took her hand from my shoulder. "I can walk any way I want," she said, and I felt as if I were the mother and she the child. "The swans are away from their nest right now and we have to get there before they come back." She yanked my arm. "Do you have any idea what those birds can do to a person?"

With Missus Tormentine leaning, hopping, sometimes putting her bad foot to the ground, we went around the side of the pond and approached a huge mound of criss-crossed reeds and twigs. Inside, in a scooped-out hollow, lay five eggs. She reached in. Her fingernails were a dark red against the white shells. "They're weeks late this year," she said, stroking the eggs, "but I'm told they could be hatching any day now." She pulled my arm. "Let's go."

"Can we stay a little longer?"

"They're just eggs," said Missus Tormentine, "so no, we aren't staying. There's nothing else to look at right now." She sounded annoyed. As we started up to the house, I turned back to see five swans gliding through the yellow scum.

We reached the kitchen door just as Mister Tormentine pulled up and honked the horn. I helped Missus Tormentine sit down at the table, then pulled out another chair to support her bad leg. "Thank you," she said, looking up at me with soft, clouded eyes. "I really mean it. Thank you for looking after me." I hadn't looked after her. I'd let her dance me around and then I'd been made to go with her through the maze and down to the nest by the pond. I would take better care of her tomorrow. I got ice from the fridge and wrapped it in a towel and laid it over her leg.

"She okay?" said Mister Tormentine, coming into the room, nodding at his wife.

★

Back at the motel, they asked me how it went. I said, "Hard," and I didn't know what kind of hard I was talking about. Hard to know if Missus Tormentine was faking it? To know that I was negligent because I hadn't stopped her from dancing and taking me to the garden? To see her kiss her dog, a dog who licked a plate she'd put on the floor? Hard to come home to this? I think they were satisfied with my one-word answer.

"What's the dress?" said Lilly. She looked up from the book she was reading to crane her neck at Missus Tormentine's plain cotton dress draped over my arm.

"Just an old one that Missus Tormentine was giving away," I said.

"It doesn't look old."

"It was in a pile for the thrift store."

"Let's see the label," said Lilly.

"There's no label," I said, crumpling the dress and going over to my bed, sliding the dress under my pillow. I did not like the dress. It had a loose shape and an indistinct pattern that felt unrelated to Missus Tormentine.

After dinner I washed the dishes instead of going outside with the others to watch the night come. I lay in bed. I thought of Missus Tormentine's dog and the plates and the four empty rooms. Little darknesses that I was certain were only a glitch. I thought of the garden, the pond, her bedroom. Dancing in the green dress, the staircase, the polished floors, the perfumed air. I layered the beautiful moments over everything until I was overwhelmed. I had stepped across the lines drawn around our lives and into the lives of others. I'd approached a cliff with my arms raised like a thrift-store mannequin.

After my day with Missus Tormentine, I was even more fed up with our room, with all the rooms we'd lived in from one end of the province to the other. I didn't want my mother's tidy, imaginary house. I wanted Missus Tormentine's palace. I wished I could tell this to Mam and my aunties, but they'd think I was unfairly comparing them to Missus Tormentine—which, in a way, I was. They wouldn't like it. Mam especially would be ashamed. Shame was such a blurry thing, a web that weaves itself tighter the more you try to escape its hold. It wasn't sharp, like envy: it was heavy and dull.

I was thirteen when I first felt shame about our poverty. We had moved to Elijahtown, where there were more rich people than poor. They probably weren't all that rich, but at the time it seemed to me they were. We lived outside town, just beyond the spot where the paved road ended and the dirt road began. There were few houses along our road and they were far apart, separated by abandoned pastures filled with alders and scrub bush. The houses were mostly rented, and almost all had bare yards or patches of grass here and there, cars on cinder blocks, dogs tied up outside. Our house was not brick like the houses in town. It had peeling green wood siding and worn linoleum floors.

Mam and my aunties worked packing eggs at a big farm on the next concession road. Most of the mothers in town didn't work. They played cards and went swimming at the rec centre. The fathers owned businesses like the garage, the car dealership, the pharmacy, the law office, the grocery store. One father was a doctor. We were known as hippies because we were different and they couldn't place us.

Some of the town girls kept diaries with locks on them. They brought their diaries to school, gathered together, and opened the diaries to show their friends what they'd written. I was never invited to join them, and sometimes when they were turning the pages, whispering their stories, they'd glance at me, or at other girls who were either unpopular or poor. The town girls plucked their eyebrows, and their hair was arranged in wave-like sweeps or in gleaming oversized curls. At school those girls spent time in the washroom putting on blue eyeshadow and spraying each other's hair. They whispered when an unpopular girl or a farm girl came in.

And then I was invited to a party. I'd just turned fourteen. My dress was the wrong colour, last year's style, with a skirt that was too full and from the Salvation Army thrift store. I stood outside the party looking at the backyard, a grass rectangle with a thin border of begonias. Down in the rec room, there was music and dancing, and one of the boys had brought beer. I didn't know what I was doing there. The following Monday, a girl called Patricia Frobisher told me I was invited because they felt sorry for me, and because they wanted to talk about me after I left. I heard they gave a chocolate-flavoured laxative to an unpopular boy from Lithuania. His name was Petras Zukauskas.

More than anything, I'd wanted a pair of platform open-toe shoes like the ones the town girls wore. If I had those shoes, I would get invited to parties for the right reasons. I worked on my mother for two weeks until Lilly told me to stop. She told me to show respect. But I had no idea what Lilly meant by respect.

One day after school, my mother said, "We're going shopping." We drove to the next town over, and she bought me a pair of platform shoes.

I showed my shoes to Puri Dai and she responded with *I understand your need. And I understand that's two weeks of your Mam's wages.*

For the year we lived there, we gave only one puppet show. It was in town at the local library, on a Saturday morning, and mothers brought their children. After that, we were no longer called hippies. We were officially weird. At least they hadn't called us Gypsies, but that was only because they didn't know the truth. We kept that to ourselves.

At Halloween, Patricia Frobisher dressed up in a Gypsy costume. She put on black eye makeup and extra mascara and borrowed her mother's lipstick. She wore a long red skirt, an off-the-shoulder white blouse, and fake gold necklaces and earrings. She shook a tambourine borrowed from music class and didn't wear shoes or brush her hair. Of the two Grade 6 classes, she won first prize for the best costume.

Even though I wore my new platform shoes whenever I could, their magic didn't work. I wasn't invited to any more parties. The next year, when my breasts grew, the boys in my class whistled at me and called me Marilyn Monroe. And then we moved again—we went wherever the work was.

I hated my mother for her plain clothes and pulled-back hair and cracked hands and bare nails. I hated her for working. I hated her for our poverty. When we moved, I threw out the platform shoes. I felt guilty over the expense, but they hadn't walked me into a charmed life.

I thought about Missus Tormentine and her own charmed life. I thought about the swans. When I closed my eyes I could see them, swimming through the yellow scum.

13.

The sisters are nodding off. Where's Zelda? Why is she not here? Puri Dai waits for her to walk through the back door, throw herself onto a chair, sit with the others to mark the day as it ends. But she doesn't come outside. In bed, maybe? So early? Puri Dai saw her face when she came in after work, head down, eyes averted. That's not like our girl, she thinks. My girl, she says. What's going on?

Now the sisters yawn and stretch. They stand up. It's moonrise, and Puri Dai sees how exhausted and heavy the women's bodies are. Heavy to the bone.

Let's get you inside, says Lilly, lifting Puri Dai from the chair.

Please, goes Puri Dai, let me stay out a little bit longer, but Lilly doesn't hear. Maybe Zelda will still come to sit in her chair and they can share their wordless words. As Lilly carries her inside, Puri Dai looks back at the white-flowering tobacco. It's growing brighter as the dark draws down. Soon the hawk moths will be out, fluttering from one bloom to the next, sending their tongues into the narrow throats of the flowers.

14.

Aside from the time I danced in the emerald dress, most days with Missus Tormentine were ordinary. But certain others stood out. One morning I started out scrambling eggs for her breakfast, and then I washed the inside windows of the four rooms. "Forget the laundry and the vacuuming," she said when I came back downstairs. "I need you to do some work outside." She said the gardener was stuck at home caring for his mother, who'd had a stroke, and he wouldn't be back for weeks. "Just my luck," she said.

I was to trim the branches of the maze. Its unruly growth annoyed her when she looked out the back windows. I had never trimmed or cut back any tree or bush before and feared I'd ruin everything and get fired. "I've never done this kind of thing," I told her.

"There's nothing to it," said Missus Tormentine. "You just take the clippers and go snip snip snip wherever something looks out of place. You'll need a ladder too." She told me where to find the hedge clippers and the ladder. "It's a piece of cake," she said. "Our guy does it in half a day. You can see from the looks of the branches that they're taking over the path and we don't want that. Let's get out there and I'll show you what's what."

"I think you should sit down," I said, "with your leg up."

"Stop hovering," she said.

"I'm supposed to be looking after you."

"You are. You're looking after me very well," she said. "You have no idea."

She told me to forget about the clippers for the moment and said we'd walk through the maze slowly so I could get a feel for the place and see which branches needed cutting. I thought I'd be familiar with it, having already been through, but today I found the maze even more confusing. There were so many different directions to go. I tried to remember which path we'd followed my first time through.

Shortly after we entered the maze, Missus Tormentine disappeared, somehow getting ahead of me. Every turn of the path took me to a new corner. I heard, "I'm here." I tried to follow her voice.

"Come," she said, "come on," sounding as clear and close, as if she was only around the corner. But she wasn't. I tried right, left, straight ahead. "Can you see the ends that need trimming? They're everywhere." Her voice kept moving. I couldn't see an end. "Can you see them?"

"Yes," I lied. I had gotten myself turned around, and I looked up, hoping to see the house, a corner of its roof or wall, but the cedars were tall and all I saw was a thin strip of sky. At first, I laughed. "Missus Tormentine!"

"Yes, I'm right here."

"I can't find you."

"Follow my voice."

"That's what I'm trying to do."

She laughed and I made myself laugh again in return.

Missus Tormentine kept saying, "Come here." Her voice got soft and distant, "Come," and she kept saying, "Come," till her voice was coming at me from so many different places. The paths turned me away or ended up going nowhere, until finally a white hand pushed itself through the cedars. Her fingers waved at me. Her hand pulled back and disappeared, and I heard her laugh again. "Keep going, turn right," she said. But there was no turning right. There was no turning anywhere, except backward.

Backward was different now. I smelled the hot filigreed leaves of the cedars and the dirt of the path. My lungs burned. The dust had gotten into my shoes. My hands were cold, even in the heat, and my fingers stuck together. I crashed into the sharp branches I hadn't yet trimmed.

Then the maze was behind me. I was at the edge of the pond. The swans on the shore twisted their heads around, their beaks working the feathers on their backs. Missus Tormentine was waiting for me. Her smile was wide and bright. She told me she was starving and it was time for lunch. She wouldn't let me help her walk back up to the house.

My hands shook as I buttered the bread for our sandwiches. She said, "I see that you didn't like being lost, but you'll get over it." Behind the gaseous blue of her eyes, something flashed. "Fear is an important part of any new experience," she said. "I'm glad I could help you learn this."

My hands froze. *Is that why I'm here? To be afraid?* Before I could figure out what these words of hers really meant, they broke apart and dispersed. The butter knife fell from my hands and dropped to the floor.

"Zelda," she said, snapping her fingers. "What's got into you?"

Yet I didn't know how to be angry. Not with Missus Tormentine. I wanted a safe anger, like the anger I'd felt before for my mother. I'd never lose my mother, but I could lose Missus Tormentine. I'd already decided that such a loss would be irreplaceable.

That night, I stood in the front door of our motel room and looked out over the tobacco fields. A vague shadow shimmered, then dissipated. I knew it was only the effect of the darkness on my eyes. *Only. Only the darkness.*

Before I fell asleep, the swans appeared in a watery dance around my bed, their five eggs floating up at the ceiling.

★

My job for the rest of the week was to finish trimming the maze. I hated it, both the maze and the work. I never knew where I'd end up or if I'd get out. I'd rather clean the house and make Missus Tormentine's breakfast and lunch, the work I thought I'd be doing. I told my mother I was vacuuming and washing floors and doing the laundry, even though no such work got done. Dust and dishes piled up, but Missus Tormentine only said, "I need this maze finished." I couldn't understand why. I asked myself why she'd decided to make me do it rather than wait for her gardener, but I couldn't ask her because you don't ask your boss such a question. I thought that if I was finally able to untangle the maze, I would have a path into Missus Tormentine herself. I would move past her dazzling, blurred borders to a central core. I would begin to learn who she was. What I did understand was that the maze and its manicured well-being were important to her, and that what mattered to Missus Tormentine trickled down to the rest of us sooner or later.

After lunch, she sat in the kitchen, coffee cup half full, dog at her feet. I went outside and saw her watching me from the window. She nodded at me, waved her hand. *Go on in*, her hand said. *Go on in.* If she were here with me, I thought she'd be saying something like "What are you waiting for? It's not going to bite you." But who would guide me out?

I took the clippers and started at one edge, moving carefully, step by step, studying the bend of each separate branch, the shape of each filigreed leaf; for no two branches, no two leaves, were alike.

I had to lean the ladder against the trees to reach the upper branches. The ladder, old and made of wood, swayed from side to side on the uneven ground. More than once I had to climb to the top rung, and even then, branches remained out of reach. I feared I'd be forced to leave the topmost layer untrimmed and Missus Tormentine would notice. What if she got angry? What if I cut the branches badly? Would I get fired? I didn't want to disappoint her. I wanted her to see I could be trusted, no matter how risky things got. I stood on my toes. I needed both hands to use the clippers, and cedar leaves dropped around me. The ladder lurched dangerously, then righted itself, and I climbed down.

As I rounded the fourth corner, or maybe it was the fifth, my heart beat a little faster. I clipped any branch that grazed my shoulder as I walked. I went the other way, turning back. I looked at the dirt path and saw my footprints from just minutes ago. Now I had to watch the path as well as the branches and the leaves.

Where was the air? My lungs were tight. I stopped to try to breathe. A branch caught my hair. I couldn't get loose. I pulled and my hair came away tangled with leaves, and I smelled the sharp crush of cedar.

I had to lean back to see the upper branches of the trees, the sky a thin ribbon of blue between them. One branch was sticking out, and the ladder tilted as I climbed to the top rung. I had to brace myself against a lower branch to reach the one I wanted, but that branch gave way and the ladder skidded out from under my feet, and I fell. Missus Tormentine must have heard me, because I heard her calling, "You okay out there?" I couldn't answer because something was crushed. One side of my body was on fire, each breath a knife at my ribs. I couldn't let her know I'd been hurt. I wondered for a minute what I'd been sent into, and why. The disorienting path through the trees felt like something more: a dark test, a dangerous passage.

I lay there drawing careful shallow breaths, and I was nine years old again. My mother had bought me a bike from a thrift store, and I rode it for the first time on the road to my neighbour Mary Lou's house—she said her friend Dahlia had a surprise for me. I told my mother I was walking to Dahlia's.

In the outbuilding behind Dahlia's dad's rabbit coop, Mary Lou told me to "stand still" and pulled a cloth over my eyes. Dahlia tied it behind my head.

"It's too tight," I said.

"It has to be tight so you can't see," said Dahlia. "Or it'll spoil the surprise."

Dahlia gave me a little push. "Come on, come on." The floorboards creaked, and there was a smell of mice.

"Are we at the surprise yet?"

"Not yet," said Mary Lou.

"Not yet," said Dahlia.

"Keep going," said Mary Lou.

Then Dahlia took my shoulders and said, "You have to climb down now."

"Where?"

"Through the floor," said Mary Lou. "The surprise is down there."

"It's my new cat," said Dahlia. "Her name's Cherry."

They wrapped my hands around a wooden ladder. "Only five steps down," they said. "It isn't very far."

It was hard reaching for the rungs. Slowly I counted them, one, two, three, four, five, and then the trap door dropped overhead. I took off the blindfold and moved along the dirt floor, which went on and on. "Cherry Cherry Cherry," I called. My hands didn't find Cherry. Only earth. There was earth on my knees, palms, in my face. I pressed my fingers into my eyelids and saw patterns. Later, my hands found the ladder and I climbed up the five rungs. It was hard lifting the door by myself.

A skinned rabbit lay on a table in Dahlia's yard. Her dad held a knife. He told Dahlia to bring a basin from the kitchen, called her "you bugger." They didn't see me dart behind the bushes. They didn't see me take my bike from the side of the house.

I was crying and riding fast through the bright day. The pedals rose and fell under my feet. Plastic streamers fluttered from my handlebars. Mary Lou was at the corner of our road. "Hi," she said in a surprised voice. "Do you want to go to Halliday's for ice cream?"

"Okay," I said. The sun shone across the fields and we rode our bikes to Halliday's gas station.

Mary Lou paid for both our cones. "Do you want a waffle cone or plain?"

"Waffle," I said.

"Waffle costs extra," said Mary Lou, but she got me a waffle cone anyway, and had Missus Halliday put three scoops on mine, vanilla, strawberry, and chocolate. We sat on the bench outside to eat our ice cream. When I got back home, my mother asked me if I'd had a good time.

"Yes," I said. "We played with Dahlia's new kitten."

Get up. A knife ran through my body. Dust in my mouth, branches of the maze above me. *Get up*. I thought I heard Puri Dai's voice. *It isn't the trees or the maze that's the problem*, she went. *You don't yet know who or what the problem is, but in good time you'll find out*. I imagined her lifting me from the ground and digging her wooden hand in my back, pushing me beyond the last tree. My lungs opened. My heart slowed. I saw the swans in the pond, swimming through their scum. I made my way up to the house.

"Did you fall or something?" asked Missus Tormentine. She was still at the kitchen table, blowing on her freshly polished nails. "That was an awful racket out there."

"No," I said, "I just dropped the ladder."

When I got home, Lilly asked, "Why are you walking like that?"

"Like what?"

"Like you hurt yourself."

"I didn't hurt myself."

"What's going on with that job of yours?"

"Nothing," I said. "Nothing's going on."

★

The next day, after I'd cleared away her lunch dishes, Missus Tormentine brought out a parcel wrapped in tissue paper. "Here's your reward for being so brave." I detected something in her voice. "So open it," she said. Folded inside the tissue paper lay the emerald-green dress. The dress of my dreams, beautiful as the forest. "For you." She took my hand and ran my fingers across the taffeta. "So stiff," she said. "Isn't it gorgeous?"

What would I do with this dress? I wanted so badly to wear it, but where? I couldn't let my mother or my aunties see it. Lilly would say, "That raklie's got her hooks into you, like I said she would."

When I left, I tried to put the dress back inside its parcel, but the tissue paper was torn and couldn't conceal anything. I ended up stuffing the dress into a plastic bag; even so, the skirt couldn't be restrained, and the hem spilled from its confines.

Mister Tormentine noticed it as soon as I got into the truck. "Whatcha got there, then?" he said. I tried to cover the ends of the skirt with my hands, but it was too late.

"Missus Tormentine gave it to me."

He sent me a sideways look, reached across my lap, and tugged on the hem, and the skirt broke free. "Who you gonna wear it for?" he said.

I felt my face burn. "Nobody."

"Well, that's a crying shame."

He must have seen the burning of my face. He must have seen me wanting to hide. I tried stuffing the skirt back into the plastic bag, but my hands were shaking too hard. We drove back to the motel in silence. He dropped me off in the parking lot, and I avoided our room. Instead, I crept around the side and out to the back. The dress was half out of its bag and I kept trying to stuff it back in. Puri Dai was there in the yard, propped up in one of the chairs. She frowned at the dress. I imagined I heard her say, *What are you doing with that thing?* Or maybe: *What did you have to do to get that thing?*

Shame was already upon me with this dress. I hung it from the branch of a tree deep in the forest, where I hoped the camouflage of green would protect it from the prying eyes of my family.

Every night now, our room filled with swans. They swam through the window and down from the ceiling. The lift and fall of their wings ruffled the air above me.

15.

Puri Dai listens to Zelda's words with her eyes, her ears, the pores of her painted skin. A shady reward, and at such a cost. Imagine. That Tormentine woman sending her Zelda up a rickety ladder. Puri Dai sees the bruises on her girl's hip and shoulder, another on her arm. But why hadn't Puri Dai gone to her, saved her from the fall?

What's a cast-off dress compared to those bruises? she asks Zelda.

Zelda shrugs her shoulders. All she can say is, I'm okay, but her body says otherwise. Puri Dai wants to see Rhodie's arms and the arms of the aunties around Zelda, but they've been pushed aside. Two smooth white arms have taken their place. Puri Dai watches Zelda carry the dress into the forest and hang it from the branch of a tree.

16.

I left the laundry in the basket and brought the tea down to the pond. Balancing the tray, trying to keep the cups from rattling or the biscuits from falling off the plate, I picked my way over the flagstones. A man was sitting at a table under the tree across from Missus Tormentine. He appeared boneless—only his white linen suit gave any shape or volume to his body. He looked as if he'd never walked anywhere.

I set down the tray. The man lifted his head to study me. He and Missus Tormentine had almost the same look—wide-eyed, alluring—but his was also watchful and sly. "What's this?" He waved a hand in my direction. "Is this the one you told me about?" One long finger flashed a gold ring with a ruby the size of my fingernail. "I see you like my ring," he said to me. "Just don't go stealing it in the dead of night." He laughed, and so did Missus Tormentine.

"Leland," she exclaimed in a cross voice, while to me she said, "Ignore the brat." A satisfied smile spread across Leland's face. "This is my brother, Mister Leatherby," said Missus Tormentine. "Brother, this is Zelda."

"Oh my goodness," said Mister Leatherby. "Zelda as in Zelda Fitzgerald?"

I didn't know what he was talking about.

"I don't expect Zelda has time for novels or writers," said Missus Tormentine. "She's too busy working. Aren't you, Zelda?"

"I need to get back up and hang the laundry," I said. I tried to ignore the way they were talking about me in laughing tones, but their voices kept breaking through.

"No," said Missus Tormentine, "the laundry can wait." I gave up, and she told me that she and Leland Leatherby were twins. She told me how on Sundays when everybody slept in, Leland would come down to the dining room to eat his breakfast as well as his sister's. For this, he paid her a dollar. As they got older, they learned to blame each other for small crimes like stealing money from their grandmother's purse, putting salt in the sugar bowl, getting into the birthday cake before a party.

"Join us," said Mister Leatherby. He was looking at me from a dark place behind his eyes. Appraising me. I was reminded of Musselwhite. "We're playing blackjack," he said.

"But shouldn't I get back to work? I'm supposed to hang the laundry."

"Zelda needs to forget the laundry," he said. "This is much more fun, isn't that so, Trixie?"

Missus Tormentine sighed. "Will you just sit, Zelda," she said. "He's right, it's a fun game, and it won't take long."

"Okay," I said, and sat. I didn't want to be there and kept myself at the edge of the chair, trying to concentrate on Mister Leatherby's instructions, even though I hated his light and careless voice and how he told me several times to pay attention.

Mister Leatherby explained that blackjack was a betting game and told me he once bet three of his grandfather's houses. His name was on the deed for some reason I couldn't follow, and he lost. The houses were in bad shape anyway, he said, and they barely brought in a decent rent, so it was no loss, really, in the grand scheme of things. I wanted to ask what happened to the people who lived in those houses. Lilly would say, "Go ahead, ask the bastard devil, ask the baro beng," and my mother would say, "Don't ask, hold your tongue."

"Grandpa didn't speak to me for six months," said Mister Leatherby. He went on to tell me about the time years ago when Missus Tormentine lost a racehorse and her great-aunt's lace shawl in a poker game, but then she went and won the shawl back.

"But we're all grown up now," said Missus Tormentine. "We're on the straight and narrow."

"Aren't we just," said Mister Leatherby. He turned to me. "Now she's married to a rich, beer-swilling tobacco farmer, although for the life of me I can't figure out why," he said, "except that she's always liked them rough."

"Leland," said Missus Tormentine again, "speak for yourself."

"Oh, we don't go there," he said with a light laugh.

I hadn't known people led these kinds of lives, and I didn't know why they would want to talk about them, especially private things. I concentrated on the cards. Mister Leatherby went over the rules again: "Are you following?" I understood that if I got a score of twenty-one, I could win. But if I got more than twenty-one, or the dealer got exactly twenty-one, I would lose. "Remember," said Mister Leatherby, "Zelda's not playing against Trixie, like in regular cards. Zelda's playing against the dealer. Who is me."

He showed me a complicated series of taps and hand gestures to use instead of speaking. He said we'd be betting quarters, and he emptied his pockets, dropping a handful of coins on the table. "We don't want to bankrupt you, Zelda. Not yet."

We started. I won three rounds out of five.

"I like Zelda," said Mister Leatherby. "She knows what she's doing."

I went up to the house and hung out the laundry. Winning the three rounds of blackjack was satisfying. I thought of Mister Leatherby and Missus Tormentine, and wondered if I could become one of them if I was able to master their game. Later, after I got home, I left my mother and my aunties sitting at the front of the motel, slipped out to the trees behind, and put on my secret green dress and danced.

17.

Where have you gone? Where have you gone, my girl? Puri Dai sends her sorrow out into the air. We're at a big river and you're sliding close to the current. I feel your warm hand in my wooden one, I'm holding as tight as I can, but it's getting tough to hang on.

Puri Dai knows what's happening, although Zelda has told her nothing. Her girl has been given away for money. Puri Dai understands the need. She feels for Zelda's poor Mam, who has a foot on one cliff and the other stretching across a river to a cliff on the other side. But Zelda's being taken over by a tikni beng, and Zelda's desire is bigger than any strength Puri Dai can summon right now. She thinks, I'll have to loosen my grip, release Zelda into the current. That's the only thing I can do.

She hears Morning Glory and the other puppets rustling. As usual, painted tears fall down Panni Mooi's face.

18.

I woke from a dream more real than a dream: I was down at the pond, sitting at the card table with Missus Tormentine, her brother, and the swans. Missus Tormentine was dealing. There was to be only one round, and we were playing for the highest of stakes. We placed our bets: the swans bet their five eggs, Missus Tormentine bet her house, her brother bet his ruby ring. I bet all our jars of nightshade jam.

When Missus Tormentine turned to look at me, her eyes filled with tears. There was no rich red smile for me. In the dream I knew what she wanted. She wanted Puri Dai. Missus Tormentine looked at the ten jars of jam and said to me in a voice I could hardly hear: "Only this jam? I thought we were friends."

"Okay," I said. "Okay." I heard my voice, coming not from me but from another place.

Our lives were on the table. Puri Dai for Missus Tormentine's house. Missus Tormentine dealt the cards. I didn't get face cards, only an eight of hearts and a nine of clubs. She dealt me a three of diamonds. I ended up with twenty. The swans lost their eggs. Leland Leatherby won them and laughed.

"Watch this," he said to the swans, as he cracked their eggs into a floating electric frying pan. He lost his ring to Missus Tormentine, and I suspected she'd give it back because he was her brother, but you never know.

I was last to play. I needed only one more card. "It will be an ace," I said. I could see the ace before me. Only one ace had already been revealed. Three left. With my ace I'd have twenty-one, and I'd win the house with its polished wooden floors and the curved staircase. I'd win the perfumed air; I'd win the closet of dresses and shoes. I'd paint the blue rooms white. I'd sit at the window and watch slanted sheets of sunlight brighten every floor. I'd cut down the terrifying maze. The swans would lay new eggs. The new housekeeper would bring her vacuum cleaner to the shore to suck the yellow scum from the pond.

Missus Tormentine dealt the card—my winning card—but on the table in front of me lay not an ace but a king. Missus Tormentine turned up her second card. Now came the slow red smile. She had an ace and a queen. Twenty-one.

Puri Dai clung to me. I struggled to unwrap her arms, but her hands were locked behind my back. "Puri Dai," I said, "you have to let go." Her tears flooded my neck and ate away my skin. I handed Puri Dai to Missus Tormentine and walked away.

19.

Puri Dai soars over an unsettling dream. From the sky she sees the dispersal of the puppets. They scatter like ripples from a stone thrown into the river. The dream ends when Zelda lifts her down from the bunk and carries her outside. Zelda is crying. She stands, rocking back and forth, Puri Dai in her arms. Puri Dai tells Zelda that it's a good thing to cry, but you must know when to stop. Your cries will wake the dead, she says. Each thing will unwind itself. That's how it always goes, she says. The wheel never ends.

Over Zelda's shoulder Puri Dai sees the hawk moths approach through the dark. They're on their way to the night-flowering tobacco, the fragrant white nightshade, but before they reach their target, they see Puri Dai and hesitate. Get them away, says Zelda. The moths flutter around Puri Dai in droves, and a few land.

Get them off you, Zelda says again.

But Puri Dai tells her: They always come toward the light, even if they have to travel through the darkest veil.

20.

It wasn't Mister Tormentine picking me up today but Musselwhite. He was wearing a dark suit, and he was crying. "It's my uncle George," he said. "Killed by his own combine harvester."

"Sorry." I wasn't sorry. Sorry for Uncle George, maybe, but not for Musselwhite. He was up to something. I remembered his smile when I'd passed out at the edge of the field.

"You can call me Manny," he said through his tears.

After a while he stopped his crying sounds and turned to me. "You don't look so good yourself, Green Eyes." His hand dropped to my knee. "Have you been crying too?"

I looked at his hand. Those tobacco-stained fingers. "No. It's poison ivy." He inched his hand up toward my thigh.

"Poison ivy? Oh, I don't think so," he said. His voice was quiet and sneaky now, calculated to draw me out. "Something's troubling you. I have an eye for sorrow." He wanted me open and vulnerable. He wanted me on his side.

I removed his hand. "No, Mister Musselwhite, that's not the problem."

"Manny."

"I'm not lying." I was. It came so easily to me in that moment. "It's everywhere. The poison ivy is. Really. I got it in the woods behind where we're staying." I sensed he knew I was lying, and he tried again for my knee.

"I'll bring you over to my place after work," he said. He was wearing an earnest expression now, trying for a helpful tone. "I have a good remedy for poison ivy."

I bet you do. And go to your place? Really? With your hand on my leg for starters? I didn't answer. I stared straight ahead till we got to Missus Tormentine's and he let me out.

All she wanted for breakfast was toast and coffee. She wouldn't have lunch because she was waiting for her brother to pick her up at eleven. They were driving to the botanical gardens up in Hamilton. She told me what I needed to do after she left, and we spent the rest of the morning watching the swans.

Later she came downstairs in a pink suit with oversized gold buttons and black trim around the edges. Her hair was up and she wore sunglasses.

"What do you think of this?" she asked, turning herself around in front of the hall mirror. I didn't think she really wanted my opinion, because she began right away reciting a list of the things she was wearing. The pink suit had been her mother's, and when Missus Tormentine was fourteen, she nagged till she got to wear it for Halloween. She went to a party as a movie star in disguise. She started asking to wear it again, and her mother told her to stop. Then one day she told Missus Tormentine, "Oh, just go ahead and take it." That's how her mother talked to her, she said. "Oh, just go ahead and whatever." Missus Tormentine stopped. "She didn't really care what I did. I was invisible to her. But I'm not invisible anymore, right, Zelda?"

She said the way she met Mister Tormentine was when her car got a flat tire on the road out of Grimsby six years ago, and he'd pulled over and changed it for her. She told me about their courtship. He came to the house for dinner and didn't know which fork was which. "They hated him," she said with a huge laugh. He called Grandpa "Pops" instead of Mister Leatherby, and said "youse" and "I seen." I didn't tell her that was how we talked, because she might have thought less of me. But what saved her Jack Tormentine, she said, was the fact that he had money: loads of it. Grandpa had a deep, unwavering respect for money. When he learned about Mister Tormentine and his operation, about the number of acres, the number of plants per acre, the high quality of his tobacco and the price he got for it, her grandfather's scorn for bad grammar fell away. "A man who owns property and fills his coffers is a real man in my books," he said.

By the time her brother picked her up, Missus Tormentine was still laughing. She said, "Don't do anything I wouldn't do," and went out the door.

I got everything finished in just over an hour. It was much faster doing my chores without her interruptions. Then I sat in the kitchen, quiet, my hands folded on the table and warmed by the sun. Her jar of nail polish sat on the windowsill, and I wondered how my hands would look with red fingernails. I thought of Leland Leatherby and how I disliked him. What would my mother say about me learning to play blackjack and his joke about me stealing his ring? She'd say, right off the bat, "Watch out for any mush who wears a white linen suit and calls you a thief. Even as a joke."

I knew what Lilly would say: "That Tormentine raklie should've stood up for you. She should've, but she didn't want to. She doesn't care." But not everyone stands up for things. Maybe they care in other ways: the emerald dress was to make up for her carelessness toward me, any unpleasantness or oversight.

The clock in the hall struck twelve thirty, which meant it was time for lunch. I stood at the refrigerator door and ate three slices of leftover pork roast and a piece of lemon meringue pie, and then I threw a piece of ham on the floor for the dog. In my socks, I skated along the polished floor of the front hall, then lay down and rolled across its dull gleam. I went into the living room and lay down again, this time on the carpet, close to its woven birds, vines, its tangled shapes and patterns. The patterns I'd made washing the floor of our room felt distant, as if in another world.

I listened to the deep rich silence of the house. "My house," I said to the room. "For the rest of the afternoon you're my house."

★

The last place we lived before we moved to this part of the province was on another dirt road, near Holland Marsh. That was three years ago. We picked potatoes and onions alongside the Yorks, a family from Rama First Nation near Orillia. We got along with them a lot better than we did with any gorjo family. They invited us back to their house one weekend. I shared a bed with their daughter, Leona. We were both fifteen, our birthdays only two weeks apart. Mam slept in a room with a wall of shelves. The bottom shelf held old *TV Guides*, and the rest of the shelves were filled with mason jars of medicines from meadows and forests and shorelines. Mam and Mrs. York talked into the night about what was in each jar and the ailments they treated. I had never seen my mother happier.

You could have fit five houses like theirs into this one. I didn't want to remember the medicine talk, the venison stew, Mrs. York's photograph album, Leona and me trying not to laugh out loud all night. The Yorks stood up for Liza May when two gorjo ladies, cousins of the boss, accused her of stealing onions, and Liza May ran crying to the edge of the onion field. "You'll be okay," said Mrs. York. "That stuff happens to us all the time." It was like the Yorks knew us down to our bones. Mrs. York told us stories from her life that made us cry. Leona put her arms around me. I'd never had a best friend before, and when we moved away at the end of the harvest, I cried for days. There was a lot of crying during that time.

After what happened at Holland Marsh, Liza May steered clear of people. She would talk only to my mother and Lilly and me and the puppets. She'd sit Panni Mooi on her lap and they would sing to each other and tell stories.

My mother would tell me not to cry if she thought I was going to start, but Puri Dai always said, *Crying is not a bad thing. Think of all the times your fowki had to cry over the hundreds of years, and you're still here. You think a cup of tears is going to make any difference? But you have to know when to stop. You have to be able to get on with things*. I looked at myself in Missus Tormentine's mirror and thought of all the sadnesses. Mine and my family's. At that moment I ached, missing Leona. I wondered where she was and what she was doing. How could we have lost touch? There was so much to miss—but Puri Dai was right. I looked at myself and saw there was nothing to cry for right now. I had to get on with things.

I looked in every mirror in the house. There were twelve, all with gold frames. The same girl, the same shey as the one in our motel room, looked back at me, blurry in the room's dim afternoon light. I sat in every chair. I let myself fall onto the sofa. The ceiling loomed above me, high as the maze's cedars.

I climbed the stairs, my fingertips stroking the banister. I counted each step. The master bedroom door was open. The walls and ceiling were the colour of pale sunlight, and the light flooding through the window was barely distinct from the room itself. I lay down on sheets soft as water and spread my arms wide. I rolled from one side of the bed to the other. My eyes closed, and the swans found me. They drifted across the ceiling in slow flight, braiding themselves together, neck around neck. I woke to Puri Dai's voice in my ear. *Watch the path you're walking on,* she said. *Watch each encounter, each moment, each obstacle as it rises to meet you. You will learn its true nature along the way; the threads will unwind one at a time.*

My mouth was dry. The closet waited. Here were the dresses, jackets, blouses, the shelves of high heels, the fur stoles. Here was the lace shawl Missus Tormentine had won back in the poker game. I didn't know which dress to try. Velvet, polished cotton, shot silk, taffeta under the slight pressure of my fingers. It took a long time zipping up, going out to appraise myself in the mirror, then hanging each dress carefully back on its hanger, all dresses in the right order. One dress at the back of the closet was painted silk that felt like a waterfall on my skin. It was the kind of dress that asked, *Shall I cling here or there, drape there or over here? I'm the water. You're the riverbed. I'm the current. You're the shore grasses. Move in me however you want. Don't forget shoes. I wasn't made for bare feet.*

I moved closer to the mirror and turned this way and that. For a second it was as if two reflected Zeldas were looking out at me—the gorjo doctor's daughter, Rhodie's daughter—two halves, each a part of the other, the dress clinging to both, joining us, making us complete. *That's what being rich does,* I thought. *It makes you whole.* I remembered Puri Dai's words: *Each thing will unwind itself.* Standing here before the mirror, I told myself, *This moment will unwind me into riches.* I put on a pair of shoes. Blue ones, dyed to match the river. *How does she walk in these?* I wondered.

I heard a sound. Was it the dog coming up the stairs? There was no clattering of nails, no panting from the steep climb. A shadow moved across the dressing table's mirror. Mister Tormentine came through the bedroom door and pulled off his T-shirt. He saw me. His eyes—cave-dark eyes. He stopped. His mouth curved into a slow smile. "I oughta tell Missus Tormentine," he said. "But I don't think I'm gonna."

II
Each thing will unwind itself

21.

The sheet under Puri Dai is twisted and damp. Such a hot night. Such dreams. Please don't send me more dreams, says Puri Dai, I can't deal with the ones I've got. Such a backlog of dreams. What the old fowki must think of this life. Puro Dad, the old grandfather, a man of blood and bone, would not know what to make of it. Back there over the bari panni, the great waters of the ocean, he carved and painted wooden horses for carousels. His girls were such a delight, scampering around the yog, handing him the brushes, mixing the paint. And then the girls growing, not only mixing paint but brushing it onto the horses when his eyes failed him. What a broken heart he had when his eldest, his darling Rhodie, battered by love, left the open air and the road to serve a gorjo doctor. A gorjo doctor in a city, in a house with no painted horses and no yog by a vardo. No open glittering sky at night, no rabbits or birds in the hedgerows.

And now, our own girl, our Zelda. Where's she gone? We all know the answer. To think what Puro Dad would have made of this. Each thing will unwind itself and spiral down into the empty dark.

22.

I got out of bed and went to the front door, thinking of a walk through the tobacco field. I didn't tell Puri Dai: I knew she would once more warn me against the devil-man with the cloven hoof. My mother and aunties would say going out into the fields, especially at night, was a crazy thing, dangerous even. They didn't know that the true crazy thing was the faint crack needling its way into my didikai self. I was a girl who'd dipped her foot into the shallows of the gorjo river—and then thrilled to wade out to the heavy current that raced down the middle. *Don't let her get her hooks into you*—Lilly's warning about Missus Tormentine echoed. My new self, the secret self, wanted to be in the current, to let it pull me down the river and through the rapids.

Liza May stood leaning against the door frame, looking across the road. "My favourite time, the night is," she said. She always said that. There were none of those other people she'd have to talk to, the scary ones, the ones who weren't us. They'd be asleep with their dreams, the air around her untainted.

We stood together, listening to the crickets. Off in the woods, a few concessions over, the coyotes yipped and then went silent. The tobacco leaves shone silver under the moon. "Nightshade," she said, as if speaking to herself. The whole field was silver. We stood caught in the silence. A shooting star's path divided the sky as the current divides the river. "I never figured out why they called it that," she said. "The night's already got enough shade." The kushti kauli ratti. The beautiful black night. Breathing, shifting, the overturned bowl of night with its glittering stars around us.

The night's got enough shade.

She made us tea and we brought the cups outside to the motel stoop. Then, from the back bunk, she carried out Panni Mooi, beloved little water face, and braided her river-green hair. As we sat together, she stroked the painted tears falling from Panni Mooi's eyes. The tears looked fuller and wetter than usual.

"What's she crying for?"

"Tonight?" said Liza May. "You tell me."

I didn't want to see Panni Mooi's tears.

I looked at the stars and the field. We drank our tea.

"Let's turn in," Liza May said when the tea was gone. "We have to be up with the birds." She carried Panni Mooi, I carried the tea things, and we went inside to bed.

23.

Missus Tormentine sent me upstairs to gather the dirty clothes from the bedroom floor and put them in the laundry basket. Aside from watching the dog lick her plates, this was the worst part of the job. The Tormentines left their clothes all over their room. Why couldn't they put them in the basket themselves? I wondered about Mam, if she'd had to do these things when she worked at the doctor's house. Maybe there was another servant whose job it was to wash the clothes. What did they do back then? Wash everything by hand? I couldn't imagine having to put my hands in water with their dirty clothes, especially Mister Tormentine's. Some of Missus Tormentine's things had to go to the cleaners, others were to be washed: whites in warm water, colours in cold.

Today there were more scattered clothes than usual, a lot of them Mister Tormentine's, thrown on the floor by his side of the bed. I looked away when I picked up his underpants. But as I was putting one of his T-shirts into the basket, I stopped. Oh, the smell that rose from it. My nostrils opened themselves wide, and I did something very wrong: I brought his T-shirt closer to my face and sat there on the bed with it. I was so close to that terrible man with his shock of black hair and the scar sweeping up his cheekbone. As if I were standing against his body with his musk and salt and sweat washing over me.

Missus Tormentine called from the kitchen. "Don't take all day up there," she said.

I went down with the basket full, the dangerous T-shirt on top, and put the coloured laundry into the washing machine. I became even more confused than usual by all the dials and the numbers around them. For lunch, she asked for lobster sandwiches, which I'd never heard of, but there was lobster in a tin on the kitchen counter, so I made sandwiches for her and the dog. I had brought a sandwich of nightshade jam for my own lunch, and I ate standing up at the counter, as usual.

"Very good," said Missus Tormentine. "You're turning into a real pro." As she left the kitchen to head upstairs, she called, "Get that laundry out on the line. And don't wake me."

While I was hanging out the washing, a man came around the side of the house. He introduced himself as Mister Tormentine's brother, Laird, and said he'd come to pick up a power drill that Mister Tormentine had borrowed and not returned. He was nothing like Mister Tormentine. He had a wide face and smiled easily. "Call me Laird," he said.

"Hi, Laird." It was strange calling the boss's brother by his first name.

"And you are…?"

"Zelda."

"Good to meet you, Zelda." Laird shook my hand. "You must be Trixie's new helper."

"Yes, I work here."

"How is it?"

"Okay."

"Can I give you a hand?" Laird asked. He bent down to the laundry basket. I'd never met a man who offered to help with a task meant for a woman. He handed me one thing at a time, starting with the sheets. As we worked, he told me about his garage, Laird's Automotive, and his diner next door, Laird's Lunch. "Drop in for a burger sometime," he said. "On the house." Laird told me he liked detective stories and horror stories and thrillers, and got all his books two towns up, at a place called Annie's. "Annie and me had a thing going for a while," he said, "but it didn't work out, but we ended up being good friends. That's better, don't you think?"

I wouldn't know. I didn't answer him. Why was he telling me private things about his life? To avoid answering his question, I asked him instead what it was like being Mister Tormentine's brother.

He paused. "Not sure how to answer that one," he said.

After that, we carried on in silence. Before he left, he said, "Maybe with him being my brother and all I shouldn't be saying this, but I'd watch my back if I was you."

"Oh, they're okay. Missus Tormentine is nice."

"Just letting you know."

24.

She's left. Our girl has left the bright space empty. What happens to this space? Does it fall in on itself? Does it wait for her to come back? She no longer sits out with the others to watch the night fold in around us. She doesn't see the night-flowering tobacco or smell the flood of its perfume in the air. She's been taken over by the swans. They come into our room late at night with their long slow wings and gather on the ceiling over her bed.

Our girl asks why Panni Mooi cries. I bet Liza May could tell her. I could tell her too, but she'd just put her fingers in her ears and go lalalalalala like she always does when she doesn't want to hear. I could tell her Panni Mooi cries for the thread that's breaking, the thread that binds us.

25.

A bus pulled into the motel's parking lot and about ten raklies piled out, sleep-drunk and dazed. My mother looked up from the nightshade vines. "Dik," she said, "we have neighbours." I could tell from the way she looked at them that she wanted to make them tea, help them unpack, help them clean. "Them raklies are gonna get treated different from us because they've been brought from away," she said. "That Missus Tormentine isn't going to be giving them their meals like the other farm wives do. They'll be stuck here except for going out to the fields."

The raklies saw us looking, and they looked back, squinting their eyes against the half-dark. Maybe they thought we were the moving shadows of branches in the breeze. They disappeared into the motel's rooms, dragging backpacks and suitcases behind them. I heard their faint voices for a while and then the empty sound of sleep.

Mam and my aunties brought out the puppets, and I hid, not only from Puri Dai, but now from Panni Mooi and her tears. They went outside to be with the last of the light, and their voices came through the window.

"Look at the flowers, how white," said Liza May. "They're almost glowing."

"And moths!" said Lilly. "Here come the moths."

"I hate the moths," said Liza May. I heard her make a quiet shuddering sound.

"Oh, for goodness' sake, Liza May," Lilly said. "They're getting pollen from them flowers. The flowers need them."

"They're ugly," said Liza May. "Every part of a moth is ugly. Look at their bodies. All that fur."

"They're beautiful," snapped Lilly, "and they're necessary."

Liza May went silent.

I lay in my bed and waited for the swans. They appeared later, drifting down from the cracks in the ceiling, as if they'd been waiting for me.

★

The next night I visited the emerald dress. Its stiff skirt was frayed in places, and the bodice streaked and faded slightly from the sun and rain. I lamented this, but didn't know where else to keep the dress hidden from my family.

When I went back to the motel, I heard new voices in our room. Five of the neighbour raklies were at our table with Mam and Lilly. They were all talking at once. They didn't understand each other's words—the raklies were speaking Spanish—but it didn't seem to matter. My mother was nodding and saying, "Nightshade," slowly, pointing at two new jars of nightshade jam on the counter by the stove.

"Nightshade." The raklies repeated this in their own way,

even more slowly. Then they laughed, and Mam and Lilly laughed with them.

Mam pointed at me. "Zelda," she said, and the raklies together said in careful voices, "Zelda."

Mam called for Liza May to come out from hiding and pulled her into the little group.

"Liza May," said Mam, and the raklies said, "Liza May." Liza May looked at the raklies, who were standing there so warm and friendly, and she took a step forward. One of them came to her and hugged her, and Liza May hugged the stranger back.

The raklies went outside and returned with handfuls of leaves picked from the nightshade vines. They put them in the large bowl on the table. They began to bruise and crush them, making a greenish paste, and through elaborate gestures they showed my mother and aunties that the nightshade leaves could be crushed to relieve pain.

"Ah," said Liza May. "Pain."

"Pain," said the women.

One of the raklies held up a small book she'd been carrying: a dictionary with words in Spanish and English. The pages were creased, some torn at the edges. The cover was half off and taped together. She went through the pages and stopped. "Pain," she said. "Dolor." Together, we said, "Dolor."

Then the raklies started laughing. They pointed to the smallest girl. "Dolores." They made us understand that her name was Dolores.

Lilly frowned over the dictionary. "Pain?" she said. "She's in pain?" The raklies shook their heads and laughed even more.

They made complicated gestures and crowded around the dictionary. "Sorrows," one said. Dolores meant sorrows.

I would not want to have such a name, but Dolores just laughed along.

★

We saw each other come and go during the week. Mam said some of the raklies were sewing leaves at the tobacco table, some had been sent to the egg barn, and three were in the fields. We learned their names. On Sundays we cooked together, all of us crowded into our room, and then we took our supper out back. We made stew of a rabbit caught in the forest, and onions and carrots and potatoes stored in the kitchen. We made good fires—nice yogs—and put sharpened sticks into the butcher's sausages to cook over the flames. They taught us their cooking, we taught them ours. They sang us their songs. Through the dictionary, Mam asked the eldest, Mercedes, where they were from. "Guatemala," she said. Mam told Mercedes that we were from here, although we came from England a long while back. She tried to explain that we were now really more from here than there. I saw she didn't want to talk about England. It brought too much sadness, she said.

"Dolor," she said, and Mercedes took her hand.

"Dolor," said Mercedes.

★

Another kushti yog was going, a nice hot fire that burned down to the embers. My mother and the raklies set a chicken over the grill. They sent a spit through the chicken and turned it so that the fat dripped and crackled in the flames. Then they laid new carrots and onions under the chicken. We ate sitting around the fire. My mother put out a pitcher of water. The crickets sang from the edge of the forest as we ate.

"Good," said Alma, the quietest of the raklies. She looked around. "This is good."

Mam taught her our word. "Kushti," she said. "It means good."

"Kushti," said Alma.

We washed our hands and faces in a basin that Lilly had brought out. I leaned against a tree. Dolores came to sit beside me. "Friends," she said. "We can be friends."

Nobody went in to fetch Puri Dai. I didn't want to see her. I didn't want to see any of the puppets, but from their back bunks inside the room, they reached for me. Their not being here made them more vivid. If I couldn't see them, it wasn't supposed to matter, but it did. *I'm here*, Puri Dai said. Her voice was faint. *I'm always here*.

Mercedes brought out a guitar, and the raklies started singing. They tried to teach us the words, and we sang along brokenly, although we didn't understand what they meant. But the music still slid into our feelings; a couple of the raklies started to cry.

26.

How kushti to see these new raklies bringing their light and kindness to my fowki, Puri Dai thinks. So cleanly they have folded themselves into each other's lives.

This will be especially good for her girl, who needs such women right now: not family women, but new, outside women who are fresh and wise. There is a younger one Puri Dai has her eye on. Dolores. She wonders what's behind this name of hers. Sorrows. Dolores looks as if she carries many sorrows, and too much wisdom for one so young. She'll fill Zelda's life in a new way. Puri Dai sees this.

She's sorry to have been left inside and not brought out to join them around the fire, but she knows Zelda has her reasons. Puri Dai is patient. She waits.

27.

Missus Tormentine took me upstairs to sit on a low bench that somebody had brought into the dark blue bedroom next to hers. "I like to sit here sometimes," she said. The window was open and the slight breeze had blown dust across the floor. From here we could see over the maze and down to the pond, where the swans were preening themselves in the scum; its froth seemed to be more densely gathered today and was greenish in places. Missus Tormentine turned her head away, and I heard what I thought was muffled crying, so quiet it was hard to tell. I said useless things that seemed to comfort her. "Thank you," she said. She didn't tell me what had made her cry, but she did take my hand in hers and clench it.

★

The next day I brought her a stolen jar of nightshade jam. We spread the jam on slices of bread and ate outside in the garden.

Charlie lay beside us in the grass, and Missus Tormentine fed him little pieces of the bread.

Down at the swans' nest, the eggs had hatched. The fresh grey cygnets tumbled against each other inside their shelter of twigs and reeds, and made soft wittering sounds. Missus Tormentine asked me if this was a sign. Maybe she thought there was a connection between herself and the hatching of the eggs. She repeated, "Do you think this is a sign?" I had no idea, but I thought she wanted me to say yes, so I said that yes, I thought it was a sign.

She didn't know about the day I'd preened in front of the bedroom mirror in her long silk dress. She didn't know about her husband and the silent agreement that knotted us together.

He hadn't touched me. I'd scooped up my things and ran from the bedroom and downstairs into the library, praying, *Please don't follow me,* as I struggled out of the dress and into my clothes. I threw the dress over the banister of the staircase and bolted outside to the end of the driveway to wait for Musselwhite. I'd looked back to see if Mister Tormentine was watching me, but the windows and doors had been empty. It was ugly to have shared that encounter with him, the two of us against his wife. It put me on his side, a place I didn't want to be. In Musselwhite's truck, I sat looking straight ahead, and he didn't even start talking. But I know he saw my hair in a mess, saw my blouse with the buttons done up wrong.

Back outside our room, under the grandmother oak, I'd taken a pail of water and poured it over my body, but even after that, I still felt unclean.

★

Musselwhite continued to bring me to work. When I got into his truck, he didn't speak, just glared at the road ahead. I guessed he was angry about my refusal to go with him back to his house. His bad mood made him hit the brakes hard, and he took the corners fast. He slammed on the brakes again in front of Missus Tormentine's driveway and then slammed his foot on the gas when I was barely out of the truck. *Slam slam slam.*

It was as if Mister Tormentine had vanished into thin air. I spotted him once during a stop at the hiring shed, but when he saw me through the window of Musselwhite's truck, he turned his back. I knew we each felt the weight of the secret between us; of this I was certain. His truck was parked next to Musselwhite's and the pink balls hanging from his trailer hitch were heavy and sagged as if filled with rocks. I watched him get into the truck and drive away, the balls slapping from side to side as if getting ready for a fight.

★

Missus Tormentine was walking well and back driving again. She got a new car, dark blue, like the walls of the second-floor bedrooms. In a way, I wished her recovery could have been slower, because I wasn't ready to leave her. I felt we'd only just started getting to know each other.

She jangled her keys at me. "We're going for a spin," she said.

What if Mam or my aunties saw me? They'd think I was up to no good, driving around the township instead of vacuuming her floors and washing her windows. I crouched down in my seat as we went past the tobacco fields, and this made her laugh.

"It's my mother," I told her.

"Your mother?" she went. "I thought you people were free as birds."

"My mother loves me."

"What's that got to do with it?"

"I don't want her to see me."

"So we won't tell her," said Missus Tormentine.

We drove in silence. The dew was still burning off the leaves across the fields.

"At the very least, you have a mother who loves you," she said. "All of you together in that kitchen, with all your family stuff going on, all that cooking and making jam. I never did anything like that."

"You didn't?"

"No, the housekeeper made our jam. Well, actually, she didn't. She went out and bought the jam."

"You never cooked with your family?" I worried I may have crossed a line, and I stole a look at her, but she didn't seem bothered.

Then she laughed. "When I was little, I sometimes went into the kitchen, and she'd let me stir the pudding. Or help her roll out a pie crust."

"Your mother?"

"No," said Missus Tormentine. Now she seemed bothered. "The housekeeper."

It sounded lonely. I felt bad for her and didn't say anything further, not wanting to make it worse. We drove in silence. I thought of my mother. How lonely it must have been in the doctor's kitchen, cooking and sweeping and washing without her own fowki beside her or their language in her ears.

"The reason I came over to your place those couple of times was the commotion and all the talking," said Missus Tormentine. "It felt nice. I hate how my house is quiet. Sometimes it feels like a grave. That'll change when the babies start coming. Fingers crossed." She looked over at me and I crossed my fingers for her. It seemed the nicest thing to do, and I sensed it was a gesture she needed. "My lucky charm," she said. "You're my lucky charm."

The fields and trees unrolled around us. I caught sight of water from time to time. "Another thing I have to say about you people is that you do things together so nobody's left alone," she said, "and you never stop talking or working. And you keep a spotless house. I don't know how you do it."

She slowed down. "Look," she said. "We're at the Tobacco River. I've been wanting to bring you here." She pulled off the road down a narrow track, stopping beside a river, and she brightened. "My Jack and I like to visit this place. We've dared each other to swim out into the current, although I have to say that a mother and her three kids in a van drowned last year during spring runoff, and confidentially, it was no accident." She gave me a dark look. "Everybody said her husband fiddled with the brakes, but the investigation went nowhere. Anyway," she said, taking off her sandals, "it's August now. Look. Smooth as glass." She put one foot in the water and waded out. "Come on," she said. "A bit cold, but nothing to be afraid of. But just to be careful, we have to keep to this part of the river, because further down it widens out and gets deep and fast, and if you end up in there, you're done."

Between this shore and the other, in the middle of the river, the water flowed differently. It was lighter, higher. It was in a hurry. "That's the current," she said. The sunlight shot like tiny needles off the water. What you had to do, she explained, was get as close to the current as you could. "Before your feet get yanked out from under you, you have to pull back. And don't let it drag you downstream to the deeper water." She took my hand.

I felt the movement of the river against my calves. "What about our clothes?" I asked.

"Clothes will dry," she said. We moved into the water. I went slowly, up to my waist, where I felt a slight pull. She tugged at my hand. "Keep going," she said. The water rose and gathered under my arms, and I kept going till it reached my shoulders. My feet lifted. I was weightless. My body slipped forward at the edge of the current and my head went under for a second. "Now," she yelled, and pulled me back to the shore. My feet searched for—and found—the riverbed. I was weighed down. My feet dragged behind me. "Keep coming," she said. She was breathing hard ahead of me. Weeds flowed sideways like Panni Mooi's blue-green hair. Missus Tormentine yanked me hard and we fell onto the grass. "Wow," she said.

I shut my eyes, then opened them. The sky, the grass, the trees shuddered. The air shimmered, and I felt like a moth or butterfly splitting open its cocoon. Was it like this when the preachers dunked people in the water so they came up fresh and reborn? I wanted to go in the river again, but Missus Tormentine said no, that it was enough for one day.

"I was here three weeks ago with Jack," she said. "In this very spot." She sat up and turned to me. "I hardly even knew you back then," she said, "and you hardly knew me. How quickly things change." We lay back and let the sun dry our skin and clothes. We listened to the droning of the cicadas and the rush of the river.

"You know how all this makes me feel, right now?" she said in an intimate voice, sounding more like a girlfriend than an employer. "It makes me want my husband. There is nothing so good as lying under a rough, sweating man in the heat of the afternoon, in the heat of the night, by a river. How does it make you feel?" I didn't answer. Those thoughts were outside my life. "I brought you here to show you this place. So you'd know me better. Jack and I've done it many times here. We've even rolled off the shore into the water by accident and had to swim for dear life." I imagined Mister Tormentine's heavy-lidded eyes, Mister Tormentine pulling off his T-shirt as he had done that afternoon in the bedroom, when we'd looked at each other in the mirror. "Someday," Missus Tormentine was saying, "we'll bring my brother here for a picnic. Would you like that?"

"I guess."

The sun beat down on us. A shadow crossed the water. "A city man doesn't understand," she said. "He wants it tidy, on top of the sheets. He needs somebody wild to shake him up. To make a child with a man like my Jack is the best thing there is." She looked at me with those piercing blue eyes. "Remember," she said, "there are three of us in this together. My husband, me, and you, my lucky charm." *Three. There are three of us.* Me, Zelda, standing between them, turning first to one, then to the other, our hands loosely laced. Missus Tormentine and I got up and went to her car, the backs of our dresses still soaked.

After the river, we drove to a place where it widened out, and then we headed down to Lake Erie, to a beach with many rocks. Missus Tormentine decided the rocks would look nice in a garden beside the pond, and she showed me the ones she wanted. They were big and heavy and hard to carry. A man saw us and came over. "What do you think you're doing with them rocks?" He spoke to me, not to Missus Tormentine, who was leaning against the car. "Those are the people's rocks," he said. "They're not yours. They're not private property."

"Ignore him," said Missus Tormentine.

Lilly would have said, *Just leave the rocks. That guy, he's right. Those are not her rocks*. I didn't know what to do. I looked over at Missus Tormentine, but now she was fiddling with the trunk's latch. I went over to rocks that were further away, but the man followed me, so I went back to Missus Tormentine.

"What should I do?"

"For goodness' sake, Zelda," she said, "just get the rocks."

I went back to the further rocks. I kept picking them up and taking them over to the trunk of her car. The man started to wave his arms. "You're stealing those rocks," he shouted. He said he would call the police. Missus Tormentine didn't have to worry about the police because they would be on her side, but if they saw me carrying them, I'd be in trouble. Worse, I'd be in trouble with my mother.

I watched the way Missus Tormentine looked at the man, as if he wasn't to be taken seriously. I called to her: "He says he's going to call the police."

"He doesn't know what he's talking about. Get the rocks. Period. Just get the damn rocks." I returned to the rocks, and she moved to the other side of the car where I couldn't see her.

The man came over to me. He was so close I could feel his breath. He tried to get the rock away from me, and we each pulled in a different direction. I called Missus Tormentine, but now she was down at the water, had taken off her shoes, and was walking away from me along the shore.

The man, who was bigger and stronger than me, pulled his edge of the rock so hard it came out of my hands. He fell backward onto the sand. The rock glanced off his ribs and landed on the ground. If he hadn't been on his back, I think he'd have tried to hit me. "I'm sorry," I said. "I'm so sorry."

"Who do you think you are?" said the man, and I heard a sound in his voice that hadn't been there when he was shouting. His breath was going in and out with noise.

"I work for that lady," I said, pointing to Missus Tormentine. "She told me to get the rocks for her garden."

"And you do everything she tells you?" he said.

"I have to," I said. The man was getting himself up into a sitting position. "Can I help you up?" I asked, and held out my arm.

"Just get out of my way," said the man. "Leave me alone."

I left the rock on the ground where it had landed and went down along the beach. Missus Tormentine was coming back now, wading through the water. She looked in the trunk. "Good for you," she said. "I think we have enough." I looked back at the man as we left.

"He's hurt," I said. He was still sitting in the same spot, head bowed over his knees.

"It's his own fault," said Missus Tormentine.

I had to unload the rocks and carry them down to the pond's shoreline. "We'll do a rock garden," she said, "first thing in the morning."

28.

Missus Tormentine seemed to have forgotten about the rocks. After I made her toast and coffee, she said, "Let's dress up and go to town." She took me upstairs and put me into what she called the perfect dress for eating lunch, with a design of black and white zigzags and shoulder pads wide as a football player's. The pattern on the dress made me feel as if I were standing on a slanted floor and about to lose my balance. She stacked her gold bracelets up my arm, handed me a pair of giant earrings, then brought out her lipstick and lined my lips in red. From a box, she produced a blond wig. She took me over to the mirror. It was hard to see that it was me, Zelda, reflected there. The hair's golden gleam washed over my face and body. I was a new Zelda who would pass Rhodie and her sisters on the street, and they wouldn't know who I was.

Missus Tormentine parked in front of the supermarket. She gave me a pair of sunglasses and some money. "Are you excited?"

"I guess." I was too excited. I was that shining girl, and I was going to step out of a car, one long leg at a time. Gold hair. Gold bracelets. Rhinestone sunglasses, zigzag dress.

"Congratulations on your first day as a blonde," she said. "Get some hair dye and make it permanent. Go to town in there. Get anything." Inside, I saw two of the raklies from the egg barn, Coral Peplinskie and Diane DeVrees. They walked past me, not knowing who I was. A man gave a low whistle and said, "Babe." Another man made a kissing noise. I didn't like them noticing me in that way, and I briefly thought of taking off the wig, but other people stared at me with wide eyes, and I knew then what it was like to be Missus Tormentine. I didn't know if it was intoxicating or ugly. The kissing sounds made me want to run back outside, but I couldn't disappoint Missus Tormentine. I went up and down the aisles without seeing any hair dye, and I tried to figure out what would be a good substitute. I finally settled on oranges. A woman behind me at the checkout tapped me on the shoulder and said, "Trixie?" I turned around, and she said, "Oh, sorry. I thought you were Trixie Tormentine." She kept looking. "I could have sworn."

"Somebody thought I was you," I told Missus Tormentine as I climbed into the car beside her.

"We could fool everybody," she said. "We could pass as sisters."

Everything was heightened: her smile as she turned toward me, her eyes that said we were both more beautiful than the sky. Beauty lit everything. The fields and scattered clouds were beautiful; the dust and the potholes on the county road were beautiful; the cracked pavement of the construction zone was beautiful, as was the weedy teenage boy who lowered his sign and waved us through. I've never been drunk, but I was certain this was how it must feel. We drove up into Hamilton, past run-down houses, parking lots, stores with newspaper taped to the insides of the windows, people lying on sidewalks or swaying outside taverns.

She took me to eat lunch in a French restaurant. The man at the host stand said, "Mrs. Tormentine, so good to see you again."

She announced, "This is Yvette Lavigne, the young film star visiting from Paris." The thin corners of the man's lips turned up, and he inclined his body toward me in a half bow. Other women with sculpted hair and gold chains turned to look at us. We followed the man to a table beside the front window, where I chewed and swallowed new and strange foods, although I wouldn't eat the snails. I didn't know what to do with all the forks, but I was glowing, and that was the important part. I understood what it was to be visible in the right place with the right people, and to stand out like a stoplight at a crossroads.

29.

Lilly brought Morning Glory and our other puppets to meet the raklies. Young Chavo was shy around them, bent his head and lowered his eyes, and tried to stay in the background. The old man Mr. Yesterday was flirtatious, a scrapper, rough around the edges, and started an argument with Morning Glory. She put him in his place. He laughed. "That's me told," he said, winking, and made a low bow, not to Morning Glory but to his audience.

Morning Glory was in a questioning mood. "How's it going?" she said to the raklies. "How's the work?"

The women talked among themselves. "Hard," they said.

"What's the hardest?"

They had different answers.

"And what about the boss? Have you met the boss?"

The women consulted.

"Mussel. White," said Mercedes.

"He wants to touch us," said Dolores.

The raklies shook their heads against Musselwhite. They looked at the dictionary.

Alma spoke. "He comes close. He tells us, 'I like white meat but I like other meat more.'" She asked, "What does he mean?"

Lilly flipped through the dictionary. She told them, and I saw them react. They told us Musselwhite had made Dolores go with him behind the kiln, but she got away. The next day he told them to stop slacking and work faster or they were out. They asked us what this meant.

Mr. Yesterday started up, flexing his muscles. He was getting ready to challenge Musselwhite. Morning Glory bridled. "Relax," she said. "We'll handle Musselwhite." She went on about the richest of the tobacco farmers, and the raklies looked confused.

Mam told Lilly that the women didn't understand everything Morning Glory said, and maybe it was better for them to have a good time tonight. "Let them hear something nice."

Through Lilly, Morning Glory sighed. "What do you like best?"

"Cooking together."

"Fire out here."

"Songs."

"You. All of you."

★

We held a flurry of shows. Willard Crowshank hired us to perform at the opening of his new shop two towns over and paid us well in cash and sausages and three stewing hens. One weekend, we did four separate garden parties. We performed from Port Dover up to Ancaster, each story tailored to each place and its people. The puppets made their audiences laugh themselves sick, cry with sorrow, melt in love, and teeter at the edge of terror. Sometimes people came up to us afterward to tell us how our shows had changed them; we saw the change in their eyes. But we never strayed from what mattered to us: vanquishing cruelty and restoring justice.

At the end of each weekend my mother counted the money. One day she said, "We're nearly there." We would have our house, with a bedroom for each of us. The puppets would share a room. We would have a big kitchen with a harvest table and a living room with a case for Lilly's books. We'd have many windows—in every room we'd have light. Even so, I knew there wouldn't be enough light for me. Not in that house.

⋆

Dolores and I came to know each other through the dictionary. She was twenty, two years older than me. I'd thought she was much younger, with her dragonfly lightness, her small chin and gentle girl's hands. I wondered how she ended up here. She told me she had to help support her mother and three younger sisters. Her father, a car mechanic, had died three years earlier. His bones were riddled with cancer, and then it gnawed its way through the rest of his body until everything was gone. She said they'd loved him, although he was not a nice man. We turned the pages of the dictionary to find *although* and *nice*. We looked for more words, but many of the pages were brittle, the corners bent or broken so that there was no paper where the word should be. Dolores explained that she'd learned some English in school, but spoke only Spanish at home, so it would take time for her to become comfortable with English. Last summer, though, while she was picking grapes in Niagara, she said she'd become a little more fluent.

I learned she wasn't as fragile as I'd thought. Two summers ago, she'd worked in a greenhouse picking tomatoes and cucumbers. Her mother was sick a lot and relied on Dolores to supplement the small family income. Except for her second sister, Lucy, they all wished Dolores could come back home to them, but because of the support they needed, it wasn't possible.

At home in Guatemala, they kept a garden to grow what they needed: corn, three kinds of beans, onions, peppers, squash, and other vegetables with names I couldn't pronounce. They also had a few coffee trees and roasted the beans in a pan over the fire. The corn and potatoes would be ready for harvest in three or four weeks. She was sorry she wouldn't be back in time to help, because the garden was her paradise. It was she who collected and dried and saved the seeds, and then when it was time, she planted them with her sisters. She and Lucy didn't get along. They each had their own ideas about the garden—and about much else. They liked each other when they lived in separate countries. Dolores said she thought it was good that they were far apart for at least some of the year. She wasn't like the gorjos we knew. None of the raklies were.

Every day after work, the forest was waiting for me, sending its cool green breath into our little yard. The fluttering of the birds, the singing, Liza May's trays of seeds. Sometimes small creatures like voles or mice would come into the yard and I'd hear their rustling sounds under the leaves. At night we often heard a bird's small cry from further away, off in the forest. Liza May said it was a saw-whet owl, a tiny owl that lived near farms. She said it was her dream to see a saw-whet owl someday.

★

One hot Saturday I said, "I know a place we can go." We got into the truck with a few of the raklies and drove to Tobacco River. I didn't tell my mother I'd visited the river with Missus Tormentine.

The sun sparked off the waves in glittering points of light, as if stars had fallen to the water. The afternoon was dizzying in its brightness. "You have to watch out for the current," I said, as we pulled up our skirts and waded out to our knees. I didn't tell them Missus Tormentine's story about the drowned mother and her children.

"It's cold," my mother said.

"It's perfect," said Lilly.

The raklies didn't want to go any further. I tried to coax them, waving toward the middle of the river, saying, "Just a little deeper." I borrowed Missus Tormentine's rich nonchalance. I wanted the raklies to feel the air tingling and luminous as I'd done when she pulled me from the river that day.

"Let's go," I said to the raklies. The water was blue, reflecting the sky, and it was smooth and flowing. I thought of the pull that lay underneath. I was more with Missus Tormentine than with anyone else in that moment. "There's nothing to be afraid of," I said. Mercedes, hesitant at first, lifted her skirt and sent her legs out into the water. I could see the motion of each slow step. She turned back to me, uncertain.

"You just have to watch for the current," I said, and it never occurred to me that she didn't understand.

I waded out to join her and took her hand. As we went deeper, I felt as if stones were tied around my ankles. "We're okay," I said. I led her now, fighting the water toward the middle, and then came the lift of my feet—I was weightless.

"Come back," called my mother. Our skirts floated around us like petals. Mercedes must have felt the current, because her hand tightened around mine. Then her body shot out into the torrent like a hooked fish on a line and was swept away.

30.

Puri Dai wakes up to shouting. Rhodie and the aunts are shouting at Zelda, and she's crying and saying she's sorry. There's the sound of running feet, and Puri Dai bets it's Zelda trying to get away. The back door slams and Rhodie says, "Get back in here. You stay. You sit down right here and listen to me. You are not leaving this room."

Zelda is crying. She doesn't stop. Rhodie shouts Mercedes's name, saying that she nearly drowned. Rhodie says, "How could you take her into the middle of that river?"

Zelda says, "I didn't know about the current."

"Yes, you did," says Rhodie. "You told us when we got out of the truck and walked into the water. How did you know about the current? Who told you?"

"Nobody," says Zelda, around the crying. "Nobody."

Panni Mooi wakes up. Be quiet, she yells through her painted tears. Now all the puppets are awake and everybody's at it. Puri Dai waits for a slap or the crack of a dish against the wall. Everything sounds wet like the river. The tears, the crying, the yelling. Puri Dai imagines Rhodie's spit flying across the room with each shouted word. She makes a joke to herself, not a kind one: she says that if all this crying and spitting keeps on, it'll be deep enough for a pond, and at least the swans will have something to swim in when they come to visit Zelda at night.

Zelda stops her blubbering. Puri Dai wills: Let her hear me. No matter how loud it gets, or how far away, or how wet, even if we're drowning in rivers, tears, mistakes, betrayals, let her hear me.

★

My mother's whole body shook. "I don't know you," she shouted. "These women are our friends. What were you doing?"

"Mercedes said it wasn't my fault. She said it was hers, for going into the middle of the river without thinking."

"She's just saying that," Mam said after Mercedes had gone back to her room. "You led her out into that current. *You.*" Then she said, "I don't want to look at you right now," and left, slamming the door.

That night we ate our supper alone. "I'm ashamed," Mam said. "My own daughter." She stabbed her potatoes with her fork. "I can't look them raklies in the eye."

Lilly brought out Morning Glory, who clacked her jaws up and down and shook her head in despair. She reared herself up and raised her voice, saying I was playing fast and loose, treating people like them rich gorjos do. Like Missus Tormentine would do. I shouted at her that I was not Missus Tormentine, and Missus Tormentine would never do such a thing. Panni Mooi sat slumped on Liza May's lap, crying her painted tears.

As the dark came, not soft or beautiful or welcome, my mother took me further out into the backwoods, away from the others. She sat me down on a log and put my hands between hers. I didn't want to smell the night-blooming tobacco, but there it was. I didn't want to feel Puri Dai, who was far away and everywhere, waiting. I felt Puri Dai's sad breath on my hair.

Mam stroked my face and I pulled away. "We're on our own here, we four. We need each other. My brother and his family are back in England, only a few of us still left. And we've lost touch. We four are our own fowki in this place." Her hand stayed at the side of my face. "We have no others, murri shey, my daughter. We have no village, no town. We carry our village with us. We're our own village. Love it, hate it, that's the truth of our lives." I leaned into her hand. I started to cry.

"Them people out there," she said, "we aren't like them. We will never be like them. There's no magic that'll turn our blood into theirs." She asked about work, said how even though I was still her little girl, her tikni shey, I was becoming a woman. She asked if I was having problems. "Where are you?" she said. She asked how things were going at the Tormentine house; she hoped Missus Tormentine respected me and was keeping her distance. She asked me to wait because soon we'd have a house of our own, and we would be happy at last. Every answer I gave was a lie.

*

I didn't know why my mother had never returned to her fowki, or why they didn't come here. She wouldn't talk about it. Nor would Lilly. It was Liza May who eventually told me it was because my mother went to visit her family after my birth, with me, her own child, who was half one and half the other. Their dai folded me into her arms and buried her head in my neck.

Liza May remembered her words. "My beauty, my own beauty," she'd said. "We'll keep you safe. We'll give you a good life." Their father and brother, however, were angry. They didn't want a poshrat, a half-blood, in the family.

"What do you mean, you had a baby with that doctor of yours?" my grandfather shouted. "Who is this man? He isn't one of us. He isn't ours. This baby will bring his stain into our lives."

My mother's dai said to her, "Take no notice. He'll get over it."

But he didn't. The sisters took my mother's side.

"This baby, she's your blood too," they told their daddus.

"My blood will never mix with theirs," he shouted.

"It's too late," said my aunties.

My grandfather told my mother that she'd have to give baby Zelda back to the doctor and then she could return to the family. They all fought into the night. They went at it for three days. On the morning of the fourth day, my mother said she would leave. She wrapped me up, and her sisters said, "We're coming with you."

They took the puppets as well. Panni Mooi, Morning Glory, Puri Dai, Young Chavo, and Mr. Yesterday were packed tightly together in a trunk. The puppets had been with them since childhood. They were like sisters and brothers and would protect my mother and her sisters in their new lives. When their daddus repeated his demand, the last time they saw their parents, my mother said: "This baby is my heart. I choose her."

In a rage, their father left. Their dai ran after them, crying, clinging to them, saying, "Don't go, don't go." She put her body between her daughters and the road, trying to prevent them from moving forward. They were all crying. Liza

May remembered her dai running after them till she couldn't take another step, her body bent over her knees, arms still out reaching for them, and her cries, "Don't go, don't go," following them down the road.

I looked over at Puri Dai slumped beside Liza May. Her eyes were shut; she seemed to be asleep, but I felt her listening.

"I was terrified to leave my parents," said Liza May. "But I couldn't let my sister go alone. What could happen to her in a world so far away and different from ours? It felt like I was being torn in two. We all felt it. I still have that awful fear."

They never stopped crying, my mother and my aunties. From Canada, Mam wrote to her parents, and my brother wrote back because their parents could not read or write. Liza May showed me the letter, which Mam kept in a small box. She didn't know Liza May had read it.

To my dear beautiful shey, Rhoda. We miss you like the sky and can't believe we may never see you again. Our hearts are broken. Your father fell on the ground when he came home to find you and your sisters gone. He cries all the time. We talked and decided that we'll save our money and next year we'll come and join you, and live together again. For we are not a family if we are broken into two halves, one half here and the other half over there.

Their plan to leave England was never fulfilled. My grandfather collapsed with a heart attack one day while they were out stripping the hop vines. He never recovered, and my grandmother had to look after him. Six months later, my grandmother died. Liza May said she died of a broken heart. Then my grandfather died after that, and there was nobody left but their brother and his family, and they never heard from him again. They believed he was still angry that they'd left.

"What your mother fears," said Liza May, "is that you'll do as she did. She's afraid she'll lose you as our parents lost us. That you'll walk away from her and never come back. And you'd be alone, with no sisters around you, but just you yourself."

31.

This is almost too much for Puri Dai to bear. It won't occur to Liza May that Puri Dai hears every word. How can she hear? She's made of wood. She's not human. That's what most people would say. Only Zelda can hear Puri Dai's wordless words in the quiet air of their small universe. Puri Dai senses Zelda searching her face for a shift.

Puri Dai remembers. It could have been yesterday: Rhodie lifting her from Puro Dad's arms. Carved and built by Puro Dad—the old grandfather who had birthed her, shaping her with his vision and his hands—Puri Dai was now to be taken from him and crammed into a trunk with the other puppets. Taken from him. Her body, her gears, her eyes, her hands, legs, all paralyzed with the deepest dread. Unable to move. Nobody heard her cries as the lid of the trunk was lowered over her body. The cries of a puppet don't reach the human ear. Except for Zelda now, who hears.

Puri Dai lay in terror, frozen, as the trunk was taken down a rough road and loaded into a place smelling of oil fumes and dust. As the trunk rocked and settled, she heard the sound of engines and men's voices around her. She heard the cries of the other puppets, whimper-

ing that they couldn't move, they couldn't breathe; their breath came from the wood and horsehair, the gears and strings and levers of their bodies, all of which were smothered in the box. She wanted to send her arms around Panni Mooi, around Morning Glory and Young Chavo and Mr. Yesterday, but in the suffocating space of the trunk she could not move and her arms stayed pinned against her sides. How she wanted to fly herself back to the old people. But then, torn, she also wanted to be with her young ones: Rhodie, Lilly, Liza May, and tikni Zelda.

32.

I had never heard the whole story. It stayed with me, and I was affected even more when Lilly came back from Annie's with another art book. It was called *The Works of Käthe Kollwitz*. "Take a look at this," she said, putting it into my hands. "She teaches us about loss. She understands the lives of women." The book had heavy pages of what looked like dark drawings with no light or hope. I didn't like them. If I was being honest, I hated them. They were unbearably sad, with mothers crying over dead children. The mothers made me think of my grandparents back in England, alone, without love or comfort. I turned the pages quickly.

"You don't like my book," said Lilly, laughing.

"No. It's sad. It's too sad."

"Well, that's that, then." She shrugged and slid Käthe Kollwitz into her book box, then took a pail out to the forest.

Much later she returned with oyster mushrooms and a rabbit she'd caught in the yard. We cooked it in a stew with the mushrooms, along with potatoes and onions that had been stored under the sink and were starting to sprout. My mother and I made two loaves of bread. The raklies had found wild apples in an abandoned orchard on the other side of the forest, and by the far wall of the motel, raspberry canes hung heavy with fruit. We feasted around the yog and played word games with words we didn't understand. We invented words that were part English, part Romany, and part Spanish, and strung them into questions and rants and stories that meant nothing and everything. Our made-up words would never be found in any dictionary. They were ours alone.

I still carried the shame of my negligence at the river. I looked through the dictionary for the words to properly apologize to Mercedes. The pages of the dictionary had been placed inside a plastic bag because they had detached themselves from the spine and it was impossible to keep them in any kind of order. With the pages in such disarray, it took a long time for me to find *I am* and *sorry*. I repeated these words over and over, and Mercedes, also going through the pages, found *mistake*, and *we love you*.

After licking the berry juice off her hands, she began to go through the pages again, shuffling until she found what she wanted. "Puppets," she said, and moved her arms as if holding marionette strings.

"Shall we bring out the puppets?" said Mam.

"Yes, please."

We crowded together in our little kitchen to wash the dishes, all of us singing. The sun would be going down soon.

My mother and Lilly and Liza May brought out the puppets, smoothing their clothes, dusting them off, fixing their hair. "We're making this up on the fly," Lilly announced. Everything unfolded as it should.

"First half," called Liza May, running out from the doorway of our room to flourish her arms and bow before the raklies. The early night sky was a flaming pink curtain behind her as she withdrew back through the door and then crept out to wait among the puppets.

"Once," said my mother from the middle of the parking lot, a sprig of nightshade in her hand, "there lived a river, along with the beings who swam and slithered and walked in and through and around this river." Panni Mooi became the river, rippling and billowing across the asphalt. She swelled herself up into the current, and the others began to wade in cautiously. Puri Dai at first held them back, reciting a long and frightening list of the dangers that awaited them, until she realized it was useless. She wrung her hands. She could not save them. At last, she saw the futility of her fear and called out, "You are all the river, carrying everything with you in your current: water plants, fish, branches, all the living, all the dead." The river-puppets swayed in the current. Panni Mooi's blue-green hair floated like the grasses. Young Chavo and Mr. Yesterday roared the roar of the water.

"Second half," announced Liza May, standing now in front of a sky that had turned from pink to blazing red.

"Near this river," said Mam, "there was a tobacco field. The tobacco plants didn't just grow there by themselves. They were planted from seeds in a greenhouse and carried by the tobacco workers to the earth when the time was right, and then over the weeks and months their leaves were harvested under the white-hot sun. And who," said Mam, "did the harvesting?"

The backs of the puppets were bent, furled like early ferns. They rose, holding imaginary leaves in their hands, and their backs straightened so that they were standing tall, and these movements seemed to be the only two known to them: bend, stand, bend, stand, bend. "Oh the sun," the puppets said to each other, "the white-hot sun." The sweat ran down their foreheads and burned their eyes. "The sun," they said again, and then came a whole chorus of their lament: "The sun, the sun."

Mr. Yesterday—as Musselwhite—came out shouting. "You don't work fast, we'll send you back," he said, marching up and down the rows. His orders turned into a chant. "Work fast or we send you back."

As night fell around them, the puppets lay down under the plants of the fields and slept. Then here came the sun again, rising too soon, white and hot, and the puppets stood up, stretched, and stooped to the plants. "Work fast or we send you back. Work fast or we send you back" filled the air around them. Again, the puppets worked till they dropped. They slept under the plants, and even as they dreamed, their hands reached for the tobacco leaves; they carried their work into their dreams. *Work fast flat on your back. Work, sleep, work, sleep. Work fast send you back work fast send you back.*

Morning Glory led the puppets to the river, for they were thirsty and needed to drink; they were up to their elbows in tobacco juice and needed to wash. And it was there, led by Morning Glory, that they hatched their plan. They became the river, carrying everything in its current: water plants, fish, branches, all the living, all the dead. They lured Work Fast Musselwhite down to the water and into a boat. They pushed the boat out into the river, and Work Fast disappeared under the rapids, pushed and jostled by the current.

The raklies clapped and cheered. The puppets bowed, silhouetted against the backdrop of the sky, which had now faded to a pale violet broken by pinkish threads. I'd have cheered too, before. I'd have been with the puppets in the middle of the parking lot, swimming in their river, standing in their field, Puri Dai in my arms. Puri Dai saw me behind the raklies. She saw me trying to hide from her. She nodded at me, and I didn't nod back.

My mother and Lilly and Liza May bowed. We turned then to see Mister Tormentine pull over in his pickup, getting out to watch from the side of the road, keeping a boss's distance from us.

Mister Tormentine came over to Lilly and Mam. He asked if we would put on a show at a party for his friends. "It's not free," said Lilly. I saw my mother's elbow at Lilly's ribs. "It'll cost you," said Lilly. "Half now up front, the other half after the show." She named her price. "We're looking at maybe three, four Saturdays from now," she said.

"No problem," said Mister Tormentine.

The pictures from Lilly's book visited me that night as I lay in bed. The haunted women, broken, all that death and despair. I fell asleep asking myself why she'd shown it to me, me turning and turning the pages, unable to look away.

33.

I see our girl hiding back there among the raklies. Not wanting to be seen by us, not wanting to see us. At least she isn't running back into the forest or down the road to avoid us completely. So there's that. But she doesn't know where she is, even though her feet are strong on this devil's asphalt. The green plants have pushed through and survived against all odds, and so will she. I know she sees in me the old things, the old people, the old places she's leaving. Running, running. Running from us all. Right now, she's running with nothing to hold on to, without anything or anyone holding her—without thinking there might be something she'd want to hold close as she runs. But I should understand this: Isn't this what her mother did? Running away, not holding on to the old language, not holding on to the old people, to our ways. But here she is now, trying to pull our Zelda back to the old ways in a new world.

Be thankful for her friend, the friend with the quiet voice. I can tell by the way Dolores holds herself, by her soft, strong voice, by her gestures, her gentleness, that she's been through a fire of the most terrible kind.

Here's her sweet bewildered Rhodie now, sitting down in the chair beside Puri Dai. Such sad eyes her Rhodie has. She turns to Puri Dai. "What do I need to do?" she asks.

Wait, says Puri Dai, even though she knows Rhodie can't hear her. What you need to do is wait.

34.

When I arrived for work, I saw Missus Tormentine's face in the door. She had it open before I could reach for the handle. She was still in her nightgown, her eyes inflamed, her lips clay-coloured, hair like the swans' nest. "Oh Zelda," she said. "I can't believe it."

"Are you all right?" I wondered if there had been another accident.

"No. Yes. Yes, I'm all right." She paced back and forth. "I'm pregnant, Zelda." She circled her hands around her stomach. She led me upstairs to the empty blue room. The sun coming through the windows cast a dark shadow. "I have to be patient," she said, standing in the doorway. "It won't be long, though. Near the end of March, fingers crossed. You're my beautiful lucky charm, and you're going to make it happen." She kissed me. "Aren't you?" She waved her arm to show where the crib would go, the dresser, the rug, rocking chair, the box of toys. "Do you think the blue's too dark?" she wondered. "Jack says this is a man's colour."

She walked around the room. "Will the baby like it? Will he feel loved? That's important, you know. That he's loved. You can be his godmother. Would you like that?" She was all over the place. She brought my hand to her stomach and I pulled away—Missus Tormentine's stomach was not a place for my hand.

"Jack doesn't know yet, but when he finds out, he'll love me even more," she said. She opened the window and shouted down to the pond, telling the swans they were going to have a little brother. She would give her husband a son, not only one son but four, all tall and beautiful and dark like their father.

The swans were in the short grasses of the shore, necks curved, beaks to the ground. They ate their way slowly along the water's edge, entered the water, and began to swim back in the direction of the nest. The willow fronds dipped in the breeze, and the yellow scum parted after the swans, leaving brief clear channels behind them, then the two sides came together again, rocked by the motion of the waves.

"I won't be like my mother. I won't be that kind of mother who says to her child, 'Just go ahead and whatever,'" whispered Missus Tormentine. She turned to me. She was crying.

★

I had to stay late to cook a special supper for the Tormentines. In the glow of candlelight, over glasses of sparkling water—whatever that was—she would make her announcement to her husband. A ham with roast potatoes crackled in the oven. She stood over me while I made a berry pie with a store-bought crust from the freezer. That went into the second oven. "He'll be here in an hour," she said, kneading her hands against her stomach. "You understand this all has to be perfect." I chopped the tomatoes and radishes and cucumbers. "Good, fine," she said, "we'll have a nice salad," and then she stopped and suddenly switched. "No," she went, "you're doing it wrong." She threw the vegetables in the garbage can. I started again. I sliced the side of my finger and got blood on the cutting board. "I don't want my husband eating your blood," she shouted, and made me throw everything out a second time. "For goodness' sake," she said, handing me a dish towel, "will you at least put this around your fingers." I picked up a tomato to start again and she stopped my hand. "No," she said, "we'll go without."

I looked at the kitchen clock. "Stop fretting about the time," she said, and clicked her tongue. "You're not done yet." I had to set the table in the dining room, and she showed me the tablecloth and candles and napkin rings, and the good linen napkins that lay folded in a drawer. The plates and knives and forks had to be one inch from the edge of the table. The dessert spoon and the cake fork went at the top, each facing a different direction. Is this what my mother would have had to do in the English doctor's house? I imagined him at the head of the table, standing to carve the roast, Mam handing round the potatoes and the gravy boat and then the vegetable dish, moving from the doctor to each of his guests, to his wife, Mam not speaking because she was only a piece of moving furniture and nothing more. How work shapes our bodies, I thought: every movement of her hand and arm hemmed in by those repetitive functions. Would I have been there then, a knot of little cells inside her? Had that thing happened yet in her bedroom, in her bed in the middle of the night? Or in his library, as she knelt to clean the ashes from his hearth?

"Well done," said Missus Tormentine. She was friendly again. "You'd think you've been setting tables like this all your life."

As I was taking off my apron and going to wash my hands, she said, "Don't mind me and my bad temper. It's hormones." Then she said in a careless way, "Oh, my brother's looking for someone to help out at one of his parties. I meant to ask you."

"Help out how?" I asked.

"Just serving canapés. He'd pay well." I didn't want to ask what a canapé was.

"I don't know."

"Well," said Missus Tormentine, "think about it."

"Okay."

Musselwhite drove me home before Mister Tormentine arrived. I'd hoped for Mister Tormentine. *No. No longer Mister Tormentine. Now he's Jack.* "Jack," I said under my breath. Jack with his shock of black hair, the scar across his cheekbone. If I touched the scar, would it melt under my fingers?

When I came in the door, my mother got up from the table and said, "Where were you?" They had almost finished eating. My plate of potatoes and bacon lay cold at my place.

"I had to cook supper," I said, "and set the table."

I went to bed, and no swans came to my ceiling that night.

35.

As we shared lemonade at the edge of the forest, Dolores and me, she brought out a gift she'd made: a small, embroidered pouch with flowers and birds of all colours, and a thread running through it to keep it closed so that whatever I kept inside wouldn't fall out. She ate supper with us. After we washed the dishes, and before the shadows grew long, we wandered into the forest. The emerald dress, hanging from its branch, was ripped at the inner hem. The way Dolores looked at the dress, I knew she wondered what it was doing there, and I just wanted to tell her. Instead, I said nothing except, "Who would hang a dress off a tree?" It was a question I was asking myself too: Who was I to do this? Who was I to have this dress, these secrets, in my life?

We went further into the forest than I'd gone before. The trees became more tangled and grew closer together, and miniature hills appeared. These were hard to climb; the earth kept shifting under our feet. Further along, we came across one hill with an opening, as if someone had taken a tobacco knife and sliced a wound in its side. I said it looked like bodies had been buried in the mounds. I meant it as a joke, but Dolores grew silent.

We followed more low hillocks and found another one gaping, so we pushed aside the twigs and leaves that covered it. Shampoo bottles, rotted diapers, a TV with a broken screen. We were in a dump. All these hills: little dumps. Flimsy graves for old jackets, coat hangers, empty paint cans. The resting place of things loved or used and now abandoned. Love and hate. The forest was a landscape of garbage. Further on, we found a chair with three legs and a plastic bag filled with shoes. A dress, ripped and crumpled. It looked as if it had once been pretty, pale yellow with a border of faded flowers. Almost as nice as a dress that Missus Tormentine would have worn. It lay without the shape of the person who must have inhabited it.

Behind one shallow mound, Dolores found a bike. She lifted it up excitedly and said, "Look." She said she would fix up the bicycle and we'd share it. We wheeled it out of the forest together. Before the trees gave way to the motel's yard, she stopped and turned to me. "Back there." Her voice was low and I had to lean in. "What you said wasn't funny." She brought the dictionary pages out of the plastic bag and laid them along a log. Through them, she told me what had happened in her village. Death squads came at night and killed people and threw their bodies into a well. I tried to understand how such a horror could have happened. The kind of people who would do such a thing—but I couldn't find the right words.

When night came, we sat on the stoop out front. The tobacco leaves were no longer silver because the moon had gone. I pointed to the North Star, then down to the Big Dipper. She knew these stars and more. She talked about her brother, Santiago, who'd studied stars. She looked through the dictionary. "Astronomer," she said. "My brother was an astronomer." She seemed lost for a moment. "Santiago," she said. "My Santiago."

"You're lucky. I don't have a brother."

"He's gone."

"Gone where?"

"Dead." She said they had found him at the bottom of a ravine. "The soldiers," she said. "The death squads." She waved her arm at the sky. The beautiful kauli ratti. She told me about the black holes behind the veil of stars. "They're hiding," she said. "We can't see them. Not even with the strongest telescope." Her brother had taught her about the black holes, and how they swallow everything around them. They swallow the light. He taught her the name of the largest: Sagittarius A*.

"But it isn't a star," said Dolores. "It's a hole. A giant mouth. Santiago dreamed about the day when scientists would not only see it but also record its voice."

"A black hole has a voice?"

"There are voices everywhere," she said. "We have to listen for them."

Seeing what couldn't be seen, hearing what couldn't be heard: Was that an astronomer's life? Could I too become an astronomer and continue the search for hidden things?

★

After we fixed the bicycle, we rode it across the parking lot and out to the road.

"You first," Dolores said. I was shaky, and the front wheel wobbled from side to side. When her turn came, she started out well but soon went flying into the ditch. The bike landed on top of her. Even as she lay under it, she couldn't stop laughing. She got up and tore off down the road and came back again, skidding the wheel to stop at my side. Later, we looked again at the sky and imagined the black holes out there. We talked about her brother.

I asked her, "How can you still laugh so much?"

She answered, "I have to."

36.

Puri Dai sends her arms around this dear raklie Dolores and imagines Dolores feeling her wooden embrace. Murri tikni raklie, she says, I'll hold you in your sorrows that are too much to bear. You've taught me that you too have the devil-man in your country, with his machetes and guns and hidden graves. And here you are now, laughing with my own girl, my own tikni shey, laughing like you're both as bright as the sunshine that comes through the morning leaves.

Puri Dai delights in the bicycle, although she's leery of the drivers and their big cars. She wants to tell the girls to be careful on the road. Ride on the side, not the middle. Don't ride in the dark. And then she thinks, Who am I to be giving warnings about bicycle riding?

37.

It was a Friday, and I was tidying things up for Missus Tormentine ahead of the weekend. I heard a sudden scream outside and tore out of the house. Missus Tormentine was at the end of her driveway bent over the dog. He made a high thin screeching sound, then his whole body twitched, then just one hind leg, and then nothing. He lay still, and the only sound was Missus Tormentine crying huge deep sobs and almost screaming, "Don't go!"

I got down beside her and she hung on to me as if she were being dragged away down the river, and I was the only thing she could reach. She kept saying to Charlie, "Don't go."

A truck was parked across the road. A man ran up to the driveway. "Oh Jesus, oh Jesus," he said. He was crying too. "Honest to God, that old guy just come out of nowhere," he said. "I couldn't even get out of the way, and I had no time to put on my brakes, honest to God." Missus Tormentine looked up from Charlie. She looked between the man and the dog, then back to the man. She didn't seem to know what they had to do with each other. A question clouded her face. Why was this stranger standing crying beside her and her dead dog? "I'll help you any way I can," the man said. "You look like you need some help right now and I'm here to do anything you need me to do."

Missus Tormentine only said, "Don't go," and I didn't know if she was talking to Charlie or the man. She gathered Charlie into her arms and held him tight, cradling him like a child, stroking his face. "I've never lost anybody before," she said, "anybody that I loved or who loved me." She rocked and rocked. The man's face was drained and helpless, and he looked around at the house and the trees as if they would tell him what to do next.

"Wrap him up," Missus Tormentine said. "Bring the nicest thing there is." I went to the house and found the tablecloth from last night's supper, still on the table. From the house I heard her calling, "Zelda, I want Zelda," over and over. She was like a picture from one of Lilly's art books: the virgin collapsed in terrible grief over her son. It seemed as if the air had pulled itself together into a dark cloud and gathered over her. I had never seen real death before; I had never seen anything so sad. "Here you are," she said when I knelt beside her. "Here you are." She looked up at the man. "This is my Zelda."

"Harry," said the man. He was young, with big arms and soft, hurting eyes of a startling green. He turned to me. "Hi, Zelda," said Harry. "Sorry," he said to nobody in particular.

They lifted Charlie together, and I slid the tablecloth under his body. He hadn't yet begun to stiffen. Blood had hardened in his ear and at the back of his head, but otherwise he looked unhurt. Missus Tormentine brought his eyelids down over his eyes, and it was then that I wanted to cry. I remembered that I was no longer closing Puri Dai's eyes at the end of the day and putting her to bed, and in that moment I missed her.

"Missus," said Harry, "what's his name?"

"Charlie," said Missus Tormentine, and she started crying all over again. We helped her stand up, Harry on one side and I on the other, Missus Tormentine slumped between us. Harry asked where he could find a shovel.

We went up around the side of the house. Missus Tormentine wanted to take Charlie through the maze. He loved the maze, she said. He could get through it in one minute flat, running around the corners like nothing you ever saw. I couldn't imagine Charlie running. I could imagine him waddling to the entrance of the maze, lying down, maybe lifting one leg to lick his arse, and going to sleep in the sun.

We went slowly, Missus Tormentine bearing Charlie's body. "This is where you hid your ball, here's where you caught a mouse." She stopped. "Oh, my baby," she said. "Remember when I first brought you in here, all those years ago, and you were so scared, until the day you stopped being scared and I put you on the ground and you started running and got to the end like a shot and barked your head off? Remember that? And remember that time I hid in the cedars and called and called you and you couldn't find me and then I jumped out at you and we raced to the end? And you won? Remember all those times? Times we'll never get back."

I didn't want to be watching this. Her feelings were raw, naked—so naked they shouldn't be witnessed—and it made me want to leave. It was like being in the room with somebody on the toilet. I started to laugh, and that was worse. To hide my laughter, I began crying over it. "See, Charlie?" said Missus Tormentine. "Zelda's missing you too." Her head was buried now in Charlie's fur. "My baby. Nobody loved you like I did." Then she was crying even harder and lost her balance, and she and Charlie keeled over and collapsed on the ground. "Nobody loved me like you." It sounded like lyrics from a song.

Harry and I stood there, not sure what we were supposed to do. I was shaken by terrible sadness. Missus Tormentine began rocking back and forth and the tablecloth came loose and started to unwind, and Charlie nearly fell out. Harry and I looked at each other over Missus Tormentine's heaving body. I wanted to tell her it was okay, but I knew the words were meaningless. What did *okay*, at this moment, even mean? Eventually, she got up. "I'm okay now," she said. We were right to stay quiet. She'd arrived at okay on her own. Her face was swollen and red and didn't look like Missus Tormentine's face at all.

At the end of the maze, unable to speak, she pointed at a place by the pond, and Harry began to dig. Harry and I laid Charlie in his grave. Missus Tormentine started sobbing again as Harry filled it in, one slow shovelful at a time. When the earth had filled the grave, she knelt on the tamped-down dirt and I came to sit beside her. "You're doing fine, Missus," said Harry. We waited. Missus Tormentine smoothed the grave, her hands moving from one side to the other.

As I sat with my arms around her, the smell of fresh earth rising around me, I remembered the one other burial I had attended. I was a child, and I'd felt nothing like the heaviness and despair I saw in Missus Tormentine. The burial was for a bird Mary Lou and I had found in her backyard. Mary Lou knew about burials. She had brought a shoebox and a paper napkin. As we folded the napkin around the bird, Mary Lou dared me to touch a small white worm that had emerged from the bird's body where some feathers had fallen away. "If you don't touch that worm, you'll have bad luck all your life," she said. I touched the worm, and then she said, "You have to eat the worm to make sure the bad luck is gone." She was a year older than me, and she knew more about such things.

I weighed the prospect of eating the worm against my mother's angry voice, which I could hear in my head. *Get that mokkadi thing out of your mouth. Are you dili, crazy, do you want to make yourself sick?* I decided to risk the bad luck and didn't eat the worm, and Mary Lou said I spoiled the funeral. We went ahead with it anyway and put the shoebox into a hole in her yard. She said you had to cry at a funeral. I remember her looking over at me. "Cry," she said, so I pretended to cry.

I watched Missus Tormentine rock back and forth on the dirt of Charlie's grave and wondered if she would touch or eat or do any repulsive thing to save a dog like Charlie. I thought about that girl who'd worked for her before me, the one who killed herself. Did Missus Tormentine go to her funeral? Did she cry then as she cried now for Charlie?

I excused myself and made my way back to the house, where I washed the floor, vacuumed the living room carpets, and gathered Charlie's toys and put them in his bed. Missus Tormentine came across the back deck and into the kitchen, helped by Harry. When she caught sight of her swollen face in the hall mirror, she said, "Don't look at me," and hid her face in her hands. "But stay, stay, don't move," she begged. "Don't go."

She ran upstairs and Harry looked over at me. "I guess I oughta stay," he said, shrugging his shoulders. When she came down a few minutes later, head covered by the lace shawl from the poker game, she looked like a ghost.

She was carrying an album, which she brought to the kitchen table. "Sit down, sit," she said. "I need you here." We sat. Harry shifted in his chair, looking around for the nearest escape route. All the pictures were of Charlie. Charlie was a rescue, she said, left in a ditch to die. "This is when I first found him," she said, and we saw a blurry picture of what could barely be called a dog, covered with scabs, skin hanging like a tent from every bone. She showed us Charlie six months later. His coat shone, and in the photograph he was leaping, caught in mid-air. Looking at Charlie as he had been, and then at the resurrected Charlie, I wanted to cry at the love Missus Tormentine had poured into him.

Harry stood up, finally, and said he had to go. I looked at his bent shoulders and thought the pictures must have made him feel worse. I walked him to the front door.

"I can't stay any longer. Sorry," he said.

"I understand." He gave me a look that said, *No you don't.*

"That lady," he said, "she's too much. She's a mess of shadows."

"Her dog just died."

"No," said Harry, "I'm not talking about the dog."

I watched him walk out to his truck and drive off. I didn't know what he meant. He sounded like Puri Dai.

I made lunch, but Missus Tormentine pushed away her plate. "All I can think of is Charlie beside me, licking up my leftovers. He was so happy doing that. I'll never have anybody to sit on my lap again like Charlie did when he licked my face," she said. "I loved him so much. He loved me more than anybody anywhere, even my family, has ever loved me." Her voice got quiet. I could hardly hear her. "Even Jack doesn't love me that much." After a minute she said: "I don't know what got into me, saying that."

I sat across from her and watched her pick at the salmon sandwich I'd made. I vacuumed upstairs, washed the windows of the dark blue rooms, and when I came down, she was asleep in the living room. When she woke up, she asked if I would stay with her for the night. I said no—I had to go back to my family. They would worry and wonder what had happened or where I was. And then Musselwhite called to say he couldn't pick me up.

"I don't know where Jack is," she said, "and I don't want to be alone here."

Harry returned a little later. I think he wasn't done apologizing for running over Charlie. He put a roast chicken and his mother's beet salad on the kitchen table. It was past time for me to go, and he offered me a ride home. He said "home" as if I had a house to live in, a place of my own.

"I can't leave her yet," I said. "I have to wait for Mister Tormentine." I took a glass of water to her. "Don't worry, Missus Tormentine. I'm not leaving you alone."

"Okay, okay," she said, and turned her back. "Let me sleep."

Harry and I sat at the kitchen table, waiting. "You don't need to stay," I said. "Mister Tormentine'll drive me home."

"No, no," said Harry. "I can take you."

We sat in silence till I heard Mister Tormentine pull up and stop the truck. He came into the kitchen, slamming the door, and stopped. "You still here?" he said. "I guess I gotta take you home now." Then he looked at Harry, and his eyes narrowed. "Who the hell's this?"

"It's okay," Harry said, "I'll take her."

"This is Harry," I explained.

"Whatever," said Mister Tormentine, and went into the living room, calling, "Trixie. Hey, Trixie."

As Harry and I drove through the darkening evening, I said, "We haven't got a real home. Not yet. We're in a motel. We work for that man. Her husband."

Harry looked over at me. "You're tobacco pickers? Oh, Zelda. Everybody needs a home." He stopped, as if he'd crossed a line. "You'll have a home," he said. "Someday." He gathered himself. "I'm the other side of Hagersville," he said. And then, "I'm really sorry about her dog."

He pulled into the parking lot and I got out. He didn't seem to be bothered about the scabby motel. "You were so nice with her," he said. "She's lucky to have you for a friend." I didn't tell him we weren't really friends, and that being friends would have meant we were on equal footing. Though at the moment of Charlie's death and burial, I had comforted her—I'd been like a mother to her, or an aunt, and she was the child. I wanted to ask Harry what he meant when he'd talked about the shadows. I didn't, though, because I was scared he'd sound even more like Puri Dai and start saying things I might not want to hear. "Good night," said Harry. For a gorjo man with big arms, he was soft and kind.

I opened the front door. "You're late again," they said. My supper was cold, congealing on a plate.

"Missus Tormentine's dog died," I said, and Lilly replied, "There is no end to that woman's bad luck."

They knew I was upset. I took my cold supper out back and ate it, feeling the cool air settle around me. I listened to their voices and the clattering as they washed up, and from out here I felt their embrace. Lilly brought me tea, and later, as I lay in bed, thinking of what I loved and didn't love about our life, thinking of Missus Tormentine and the push-pull of her anger and sadness and her bright shimmer, I felt my innards being yanked apart. It was like that old story—the four horses, one arm and one leg tied to each horse, and then the horses being made to gallop away, leaving you in pieces.

I dreamed about Charlie. In the dream, Mary Lou's prediction was real: to touch or eat a worm coming from a dead body would bring good luck. A question formed, and I heard Mary Lou's voice, or what sounded like her voice, ask: "Do you want Missus Tormentine to have good luck at any cost? If a worm had worked its way through Charlie's skin, would you tell Missus Tormentine to touch it? Eat it? Or would you be scared? Would you be scared you'd get fired?" Then Harry's voice broke in, talking about a mess of shadows. I woke up. I'd never been so confused by a dream.

38.

Puri Dai remembers how she sent herself out from her chair in the yard to that Tormentine woman's driveway, under the trees, as her dog lay dying. Death has a way of drawing Puri Dai to important places, pulling her like a night moth to the dark light, to the cracks between worlds. It's always been this way. She was there from the very moment the wheel of the truck passed over the dog to the drawing of its last breath. She saw the sorrow of the woman bent deep in grief over the dog she loved like a child. Even a devil can be overcome by loss.

Puri Dai heard the dog's cries grow weaker, heard its last quiet exhalation. But what shone was the softness and warmth of her girl as she comforted the woman. How Zelda's arms went around Missus Tormentine, how she held her, how she kept pace with her as they walked through the maze, as they emerged on the other side, as they lay the dog in its grave, as they watched it vanish under the last handful of earth, as they sat before returning to the house, the house now empty of its dog. The dog, one brief flash of life like a star shooting across the kauli ratti. Puri Dai did not enter the house. She left. Back in the motel's yard, with Liza May and the birds, the evening coming in, she reflects on her Zelda, whose kindness has never left her and will bring her back. Back to us.

The greater problem is, she thinks, our girl feels too much. There's never been a childhood lightness about her. She could be a thousand years old from the time her fowki were driven from their lands to follow hard roads through every country, and she's on one of those roads still.

39.

The following morning, Dolores and I were looking for a word in the dictionary, going back and forth, when the spine cracked and broke. The remaining pages came free and fell to the ground. We scooped them up and brought them inside to the table and started to tape them back into their proper places again, but the page numbers were small and hard to read, many faded and worn, others gone completely, ripped from the torn edges. I felt as if these endangered pages made our connection more urgent and at the same time more fragile, and I think Dolores felt it too, even though we were conversing almost always these days without the dictionary.

Lilly came in from sitting with Morning Glory and watched us for a while. We hadn't gotten very far. The pages were still all over the place. "I think you could use a new dictionary," she said. She offered to take us to Annie's bookstore a few towns north of here.

"Thank you, Lilly," said Dolores, a little formally, "you are very kind."

The bookstore was nearly halfway to Hamilton. On our way, we had to pass the treacherous Tobacco River. I didn't want to see it, in spite of it being as beautiful as I remembered, lined with willows and winding through fields and along the edges of forests. Dolores was looking at the road map Lilly had pulled from the glove compartment. "Tillsonburg, Delhi, Courtland, Hagersville," she read to me.

I was glad to be driving away from Charlie's death. I wondered about Missus Tormentine and her sadness. I knew how much she'd have wanted me to be there to sweep the floor around her while she cried, sit with her in her long silences, make sure she ate her sandwiches. I thought about the sun streaming across her kitchen floor. About how I hoped she'd remember to comfort herself and that almost-baby of hers. I thought about Harry and the mess of shadows, and how her darkness spoiled both her grief and her hope, even though she didn't know it.

The place Annie's bookstore was in could have once been a town but was now a collection of listing buildings on either side of a narrow road. Layered in dust and quiet neglect, this felt familiar, like so many of the half-abandoned villages we had lived in or travelled through. There was a comfort in the way the buildings leaned in to hold each other up, a recognition that without mutual support they might be in danger of collapsing into themselves. A few trees grew along the road, some lush, others dead or dying; green shoots pushed themselves through cracks in the sidewalks. A few houses, one or two boarded up, were scattered along a narrow side street. But the place appeared modestly cared for, in spite of its spirit of abandon.

Annie's bookstore was one of several storefronts in a short block, tucked between a hardware store and a thrift shop. I'd never been in a bookstore. When we entered and closed the door behind us, the smell of old paper washed over me, and I stood breathing the books into my lungs. It was a smell of safety, of home. The books made a cushion against the muted sounds of the outside world, mostly the few pickup trucks and cars driving along the road outside Annie's door. The voices coming from the back of the store were quiet, as if we were folded inside a quilt.

I looked at the packed floor-to-ceiling shelves and thought of Mrs. York from Rama, and her wall of medicines. I wondered how many millions of words these books held, who had thought up the words and written them down. And then I wondered how we'd ever find a dictionary—would we have to go along each shelf, book by book, from top to bottom, from the front of the store to the back? Then I noticed signs labelling the different kinds of books: History, Science, Romance, Religion. I found I liked this crammed bookstore more than Missus Tormentine's library of half-empty bookshelves, and I understood why: because this place is alive, and I'm scared that hers isn't.

Dolores came to get me. She'd found a rack with a sign that said *Sale 50% Off*, and at the end of the rack we found an astronomy book. In the centre of the book, a map named the stars that appear in the sky, so you could bring it outside at night and look up into the dark to see them. I found the price on the inside page: $5. I thought about the money I gave my mother each week, and that buying this book would leave us five dollars short, meaning five dollars less toward her house, the not-yet-real house. I calculated the importance of the house against the importance of the stars. I lifted the book from the rack and tucked it under my arm.

Lilly was calling to us from the back of the store. We found her in a ramshackle room with more books on the walls and a desk piled with papers. She introduced us to Annie, the owner. Annie invited us to sit down. She had to lift books off chairs and a bench to make room. This was the same Annie who knew Laird Tormentine, but this Annie didn't look like someone who'd ever had a thing with anybody. There was a dryness to her, a delicate pleating of the skin around her neck like worn crepe paper. Her upper arms were heavy, wing-like, and I tried to imagine them around Laird Tormentine's body, pressing him against her. *But who am I to think an old woman is no longer able to feel hot love?* She must at one time have been fleshy like the old paintings I'd seen of women in Lilly's books, but without their look of surrender. Her hair was unbrushed. Her glasses hung on a chain around her neck, and when she put them on, they listed to one side, and I could see they were heavily smudged.

Dolores brought out the plastic bag holding the dictionary's loose pages and the broken spine. Annie raised her eyebrows at the mess of pages, then went straight to a shelf halfway down the wall of books and brought back a Spanish–English dictionary. She put it into Dolores's hands. Then she started speaking to Dolores in Spanish. Dolores answered, and she must have spoken about having to leave her family to work here, and about her brother, because Annie sat very still and her eyes filled with tears.

Annie would take no money for the dictionary. "Not a cent," she said. "It's a gift."

As we left the bookstore, a truck pulled up behind ours. A man got out, and I saw that it was Harry. I think we were surprised to see each other.

"I know you," he said after a minute. "You're Zelda."

"Hi," I said. I didn't know what else to say. We looked at each other for a second too long, and then Harry went into the hardware store.

"Who's that?" asked Lilly.

"It's the man who ran over Missus Tormentine's dog."

"Look at them eyes. Kushti dikin mush," she said. "Pretty good-looking for a gorjo."

Dolores and I turned the pages of the books on the drive back. We drove by the river again, but it bothered me less—was less vivid. I opened the astronomy book to smell the pages, and it was like being in the bookstore again. Now Dolores and I had two books. One to understand each other's languages, one to understand the stars.

At supper we sat around the yog, roasting hot dogs in the flames, and passed the dictionary from hand to hand. It was almost new, and the words were bigger and easier to read. We read words aloud to each other, laughing at our pronunciation. The dark came, and the night-flowering tobacco glowed, even though there was no light from either the moon or the stars because clouds had settled over the fields. After a while, the moths appeared.

"The flowers smell beautiful," said Dolores. Her words were slow and clear. Before she left, she said we should harvest the seeds. I went to bed, remembering the days not long ago when I was overcome by the beauty of their perfume—then more recently wanting to avoid them because they made me think of Puri Dai. How was it that the scent of a flower could have such a hold over a person? Dolores had renewed their beauty for me, and I fell asleep with the jasmine air of the night-scented tobacco instead of the swans.

In the morning Dolores and I met by the flowers. She told me their scientific name. "It's Latin. They are *Nicotiana alata*," she said, "a nightshade. They're the sisters of the tobacco plants in the fields." There was no perfume coming from our flowers. "That's because it's daytime," she said. "Their scent comes only at night." She tipped a single bloom up with the ends of her fingers. The petals weren't white anymore, but wrinkled slightly, and were turning a shade of brown. Inside, she said, at the very back, were the seeds. Below the flower was a small green pod. "The seed pod," said Dolores. The nest: the cradle of seeds. In their pod, the seeds weren't yet ripe. She showed me a second pod, wrinkled and brown, and she brought my hand over to the pod. She opened it and tipped the seeds into my palm. "Those seeds," she said. "We want those seeds." They were tiny and black. I could barely see them. You could just let them drop wherever without thinking about them or what lush new life they contained.

Dolores told me we'd have to dry the seeds in a cool place for two days. Then they'd be ready to be stored and planted out in the spring. Maybe she'd be back next year, she said, in time for the flowers. Maybe we could sit here in the yard, or in another yard, wherever we were, nicotiana flowers blooming around us.

I hadn't thought that far ahead, but now her words were an ending looming over us, a wave waiting to break. I'd forgotten that Dolores would leave at the close of the season. She reminded me that she wanted more than anything to return to her family. She'd arrive home in time to harvest corn and potatoes and squash. Then she would make arrangements to return next year and work again in the fields.

What would life be like without her? I tried counting the months till she'd come back. It seemed too long. I'd never counted months nor waited for anything in the future, except for my mother's imagined house, and even that was in the realm of dreams and outside of traceable time.

"Pollination," Dolores was saying. The dictionary made everything move so fast: words, thoughts, time. She told me how the brown hawk moths went from flower to flower to flower, sending long thin threads from their mouths into the inner cave where the pollen lay. The moths travelled across fields and yards to all the gardens, pollinating each new flower as they went. These were the moths I saw around Puri Dai, the necessary moths that fluttered from her to the flowers at night.

40.

The seeds and the flowers! Zelda has returned to them through her beautiful friend! Under her sheet, Puri Dai is dancing. She sends a bloom-green blessing out to her Zelda and the dear raklie Dolores, although they don't necessarily recognize it as such. They know something's there, because Puri Dai sees them look at one another, sensing the threads of renewal. Like Puri Dai birthed from the wood of a tree, from the sheets of heavy paper and glue, from horsehair and paint and straw, the seeds will be brought to life.

These ones now have a name. Nicotiana, the small pale sister of the nightshades. The moths will lay their eggs on her leaves, and the offspring will spend their winter in loose cocoons sheltered in a protective chamber under the earth.

I've seen the hawk moths, says her Zelda.

Yes, says Dolores, wherever you plant the seeds, moths will come.

Puri Dai can only imagine where this new life will begin. If we feel all hope is lost, she thinks, we can still plant seeds.

41.

Missus Tormentine was lying on the sofa when I arrived. She was on her back with a cup of coffee balanced on her stomach, which was still flat: nothing yet was showing. "I'm keeping baby warm," she said. "How do I look? Any better?" Everything about her was rain-cloud grey, even her eyes. "Any parties I need to get to? Maybe I should do up my hair and put on lipstick?" She looked as if she'd had her teeth knocked out. She told me she'd had pain and spots of blood, and the doctor had warned her not to move but to lie flat with her feet up on the arm of the sofa. "It's Charlie's death that's done this. Half my heart is broken. At least the baby's in the other half," she said. "I might be okay." She didn't sound okay. "Off you go, then," she said, and waved me into the kitchen.

They'd left me a mess from the weekend. The floor was muddy around the door, apple cores and coffee grounds strewn across the kitchen counter, dirty glasses and dishes on every surface, crumpled paper and food wrappings around the garbage can. Mam would say you never know what to expect in a gorjo house. Lilly would say the rich can be as filthy as anyone else, except they don't clean up their own messes but pay other people to do it.

"Zelda," Missus Tormentine called from the living room, "do you think it's possible to be happy and sad at the same time?" It was a question a curious child might ask, and it surprised me coming from her. I tried to think of something she might want to hear, but she went on, not waiting for my answer. "Jack says it's not possible and I say it is." I turned on the vacuum cleaner so she'd think I hadn't heard. Over the din she yelled, "I'm sad about Charlie and thrilled because of the baby. You have to agree that I'm right about the happy–sad thing." Then she added, "Jack says feelings are for girls." She didn't say anything for a few minutes after that. I could feel her, unbalanced, closer now to sad than to happy, and sliding.

I vacuumed the dried mud and washed the floor and took the vacuum cleaner down the hall and into the front library, where the noise could drown out her voice. None of what she was saying mattered to me at that moment, and it was just as well I couldn't hear.

The shelves of Missus Tormentine's library reminded me of Annie's bookstore, and when I thought of the bookstore I thought of Dolores. I thought about Dolores and the other raklies, them leaving, and our family being alone again. That was what mattered. Every thread today led back to Dolores. Standing there, with these women in my thoughts, I had no idea of the ways in which they might soon be taken from us.

After she asked for and then refused a second cup of coffee, Missus Tormentine said, "I don't feel so wonderful." When she next returned from the bathroom, she told me there was blood. "No," she whimpered. "No." She shook her head and looked at me with those eyes. She grabbed me and cried into my neck. "No," she said. I walked her to the sofa and laid her down.

"I'm calling the doctor," I said.

"No," said Missus Tormentine, "I don't want the doctor. I don't like him." She tried to pull me to her. "Say a charm or a spell or something, or whatever it is you people do," she said. "That's what I need."

Say a charm. Say a spell. You people. I separated the words from one another, tangled them up in my mind, hoping to diminish or alter their meaning. It didn't work. *You people, you people, you people.*

"Do not call the doctor," she said again. I found the phone book and called the doctor, and he arrived twenty minutes later, an ancient white-haired gorjo marching through the door in fast-forward. He carried a black bag before him like a shield. His suit was dark and covered with white specks at the shoulders. He smelled of cigarette smoke and coffee and mouthwash.

"Missus Tormentine," he shouted, barging into the living room. He looked as if he didn't much like women. He sent me from the room while he poked around, and I heard him tell Missus Tormentine to stay in bed for a day or two. I came back into the living room as he was pulling down the hem of her nightgown. I didn't like his fingers—they looked like puff pastries and were stained with nicotine. "You'll be fine," he said in the direction of Missus Tormentine, then looked at his watch and aimed himself at the front door.

★

I escaped to the kitchen. A chicken was thawing on the counter and had to go into the oven. "At three," yelled Missus Tormentine. "My stomach isn't great and I want to eat early." The kitchen kept me going until five, when it was time for me to leave. Where was Musselwhite?

I brought her food in on a tray. She was looking worse. "The pain's back," she said. She wouldn't eat. She told me to take her dinner away and to make tea and two pieces of toast. When I took them in, she was asleep. I didn't know how to reach Musselwhite, so I sat in the living room across from Missus Tormentine. She looked like a child about to die. She must have felt me sitting there, because she opened her eyes and said, "Don't go. Please don't go."

I stayed; I didn't have a choice. I looked around, remembering the first time I walked into this house and it made me catch my breath. No house had seemed more beautiful. Now its gleam had dulled, no matter how much I polished. And now, above all, those words. *Say a spell. Or whatever it is you people do.* She didn't know how she'd cut me to the bone, and I was terrified to think she might not care.

She woke up again. "Clean the baby's bedroom," she whispered, before falling back asleep. Later she woke and said, "Where's that damn Musselwhite?" And then, "Where's my dinner?"

She ate her dinner lying down. She asked for her comb and lipstick. "My Jack. I have to be beautiful for him." Her voice was a cracked whisper. She could hardly get the words out. I brought her comb. It was the first time I'd touched her hair, and I remembered its shine from across the parking lot when she'd first driven up to the hiring shed. How her hair had looked like a halo.

A truck pulled up outside. Mister Tormentine came in the back door. "Jack," said Missus Tormentine, "take her home."

Jack. Jack. Take me home. Mister Tormentine looked irritated. He said something under his breath. I saw his fist close and open and then close.

"I'll be okay," she said, both hands laced over her stomach. "You go, Zelda." I could hardly hear her.

Mister Tormentine lifted his chin at me. "You coming or what?" He went back out the kitchen door.

I didn't know why, at that moment, I hated Mister Tormentine, or why I hated climbing into his truck. Was it the way he looked at me, as if I was a nuisance or an obstacle? I hated hearing him turn the key to start the engine. I hated sitting beside him. I looked from my shoulder to his. I looked down at the seat. At the space between us. I counted the inches between my body and his. Fifteen.

I moved so that the space between us was greater. When he stepped on the gas, I noticed certain muscles move under his jeans. Did he hate me the way I hated him? Or maybe it wasn't hate but something else. Love and hate, darker than the love and the hate simmering under Buddy Watmore's tattooed hands.

But still. I hated the way he slid his hand through his hair. Hated his hand on the steering wheel, the muscles and tendons under the skin. I hated the tilt of his hip when he put on the brakes—hard—because a rabbit had run into the road. I hated the smoking heat from his body. He smelled of salt and of meat. Of tobacco. Of smoke exhaled into the air. He reached past me—his arm went light as a moth's wing across my breast—and I tried to shrink back but couldn't. He reached into the glove compartment and pulled out a beer. He opened the bottle with his teeth and spat the bottle cap out the window. "Old trick," he said.

The heat from his arm stayed. I didn't know what to do with the unbearable congestion. Maybe I could be rescued by talking. "Missus Tormentine is excited about the baby" was all I could come up with. *Had he heard my voice shake?*

"Yup," said Mister Tormentine.

"Have you got a name picked out?"

"Yup," he said.

"What name?"

"She wants Leland."

"That's her brother's name."

"Yup."

I didn't know what else to say. Mister Tormentine drank his beer. *Not Mister Tormentine. Jack. Jack, drinking his beer.* He held it in the same hand that he steered with, because his other arm was angled out the window. He took his hand off the steering wheel and leaned his head back every time he took a sip. Out of the corner of my eye, I watched the working of his jaw. His exposed throat. He brought the fingers of his other hand to the wheel to keep the truck on the road instead of flying off into the ditch. Flying off. Flying. His fingers across the steering wheel light as the wings across my breast. The line of his throat. His mouth fastening around the bottle. *Don't look.*

He turned to me and held out the bottle. "Wanna drink?" I didn't want to taste beer. I started to say no. I didn't want to taste him. *I should say no.* I should say no. Our fingers touched when he handed me the bottle. I drank. He looked at me again. His face was a question mark. Then it was strangely angry, or something like angry. I couldn't name his expression. *Jack.* His jaw jutted forward. I saw the line of the scar across his cheek and had to keep my hand from moving to his face. After a while he slowed down to throw the bottle out the window and into the ditch. I was covered in his heat; it stuck to me like cobwebs and I couldn't get it off. It was greater than the red flames of the yog we all sat around each night.

He pulled into the motel parking lot and stopped.

"Thanks, Mister Tormentine," I said.

"Yup," he said, and drove off. The heat that had clung to me started to disperse, and I felt strangely relieved.

I didn't look at the balls swinging from his trailer hitch.

III
Sorrows

42.

Puri Dai sees how Zelda is torn now, torn four ways. She's stretched between her family, her beautiful friend Dolores, the tikni golden-haired beng, and the monstrous husband. That mush wasn't born yesterday. He knows what he's doing with our girl. The pull of his devil flesh makes her helpless. She sits and simmers beside him in his trap. Simmering? Is that all it is? It's more like a barn fire with a horse, a poor gry, frozen in terror as the door is bolted shut. Puri Dai has occasionally wished that she could at some time in her life have felt such a fire.

Her own fire comes from a different place. The tree she was born from sent out love and nourishment and warnings through its roots and leaves, and when it was felled, its mother-fire disappeared. But from that extinction Puri Dai was born, if you can call it that: a phoenix rising from the ashes, a new being sprouting from the dead, the spark of a new fire that gathered inside her. When Zelda, a babe in arms, was brought to see her mother's family, when Puri

Dai first set eyes upon her tikni shey, that spark ignited again into full-fledged love.

That is nothing like what's happening here in this dance between her Zelda and these four. Puri Dai knows. The only love that will ever be returned is the love of her family and her friend.

43.

In the backyard, we sat around a tiny saw-whet owl Liza May had found across the road in the ditch. I was trying to make myself pay attention. I had been taken over by Jack Tormentine and a hot bruise was blooming inside me; any relief I'd felt was cut short.

Maybe the owl had struck the windshield of a car or truck and dropped into the ditch. This was what Liza May thought might have happened. I saw Mister Tormentine tearing along the night roads, one hand on the steering wheel, the other around a bottle of beer, birds flying into his windshield and him not noticing. Not noticing because he'd be thinking of me. Driving over owls, blackbirds, sparrows, crows, their bodies piled on the road and in the ditches—he didn't see them because he'd be saying my name, either inside his head or out loud. Maybe he was singing some kind of made-up country song with my name in it. *O Zelda.* How his heart was torn in two and the only thing he had of me was my name. *O Zelda.* Running his hand along the seat I'd occupied, back and forth, feeling the heat I'd left there. And then he'd stop because he was home and had pulled into the driveway. He'd run a hand through his hair and go into the house and straight up to that giant bed, saying my name under his breath as he fell asleep.

"Hey!" said Lilly. I opened my eyes.

Liza May was holding the owl in front of me. "Look," she said. "She's so delicate."

Delicate, yes, the way he let the steering wheel slide under his fingertips. The way he lifted his hand to his hair like he had just roused himself from sleep, the delicate shift in his body I knew nobody else noticed.

"It'll be okay," Liza May said to the owl.

No. No. It won't be okay. I'm trapped inside his heat and I can't get out. Do I want to get out? No. I don't want to get out. I want to stay. Nothing else matters.

Liza May told us she couldn't find any broken bones. She held the owl in the palm of her hand, cradling it, trying to call the saw-whet owl call, but it was still. "The owl has to be kept warm," she said, bringing it close to her breast. "It has to eat." She took a small spoon and tipped water, one drop at a time, into the owl's mouth. We set many traps that night, and at dawn only two were empty.

Liza May held a mouse to the open beak of the owl and waited. She wanted to stay home—she didn't want to go to work. She wanted to stay with the owl. More than ever, she didn't want to see the tobacco men. She had started to complain, saying she was afraid of Musselwhite, who stared the women down as they worked at the sewing table, poring over each movement as they placed the slats over the tobacco leaves. She said he kept watching as they put the second layer of leaves over the slats, with a full, gluttonous gaze as they stitched the upper leaves and sent the slats up the escalator into the kiln. "It's like his eyes are eating us," she said.

That night, her mood seemed to improve after she successfully fed the owl a newborn mouse. The owl perked up, so she offered a second mouse, the owl perched on her finger. But the owl's appetite had been sated; it turned its head away. We all began to look forward to seeing the mousetraps filled with food for the owl. The owl gave us hope.

44.

The Tormentines bought a tree for Charlie's grave. I'd never seen such a tree: a flowering dogwood, which in coming years would be heavy with fleshy white petals. "Dogwood seemed appropriate," said Missus Tormentine. After the tree arrived, she sat in the kitchen and complained while I swept the floor around her. "Look," she said. "Would you call that a tree? It doesn't even reach my waist. I had such high hopes."

"But the flowers, Missus Tormentine," I said. "They'll be beautiful. The tree will grow, and someday it'll be covered with flowers." The dogwood had been placed on its side at the opening to the maze. I wanted to know why it was up here, but I didn't ask.

It turned out my job was to carry the tree through the maze. Why did Missus Tormentine think this was a good idea? The burlap-wrapped root ball was heavy, and the tree itself was awkward and kept getting caught in the cedar branches. If Missus Tormentine had been carrying it herself, I decided, she would have gone straight down to the grave. But no. She wouldn't carry anything, not in that dress. She wore black and had on all her sonnakai: rings, bracelets stacked up her arms, dangling earrings. She slid two of her bracelets onto my wrists, "to unite us in this moment," she said, and when we came through the far end of the maze, we went down to the pond, where Mister Tormentine had already dug a hole beside the grave, and where her brother was waiting.

A version of Missus Tormentine's red smile had returned, and in the sunlight her hair was as bright as it had been when I first saw her all those weeks ago. She went with Mister Leatherby up to the house, his arm around her. He turned to look back at me as they went inside. When I heard his car pull away, I let out my breath.

Musselwhite came to take me home while I was shaking out the kitchen rugs. He came up behind me, going on about something, his words running together into a rumbling noise. I thought about Liza May again, and about Musselwhite's cloying eyes. I said, "I'm busy."

He wouldn't leave me alone. I went down the stairs of the deck and he followed me. He kept talking. "Stop and listen to me," he said. I went into the maze and he followed me.

At first, he thought it was a game. "Well, I wasn't expecting this," he said, and he laughed. I turned a corner, a corner I knew well. Then I turned the next corner. I could hear his laughter getting further away. After a while he stopped laughing. "Where the hell are you?" he said. I kept going. I followed the path I knew in my body. The path I could have walked with my eyes shut. "Where the hell are you?" he said again.

I went out at the other end of the maze and down to the pond. The swans and their cygnets were there, nibbling at the short grasses of the shore. I went back up to the house, past the maze, and heard the crashing of branches. Musselwhite was yelling, "How the hell do I get out of here?"

I thought I'd save this for another puppet show. I'd tell Mam and my aunties when I got home. I went back inside the house, and while I waited for Musselwhite to reappear, I dusted the banister and the table and chairs and china cabinets in the dining room. I told Missus Tormentine what had happened, and she laughed. She said he deserved it. She was the boss, so she could say it aloud. I felt, then, that I had permission to laugh too. I liked us laughing together.

When Musselwhite made it back up to the house, he threw the door open so hard it hit the wall. His face was red as a stoplight. "You wanna laugh at me? No low-life laughs at me," he said. I moved back. He glared at me. "You haven't seen nothing yet." His finger came out and stabbed at the air. "Nothing."

I looked for Missus Tormentine, hoping for her to step between us, but she had left the room. "I'm going to bed," she called from upstairs. By this time Musselwhite was already out at his car, still raging, slamming the door and squealing the tires when he took off. Shaking, I walked to the crossroads and hitchhiked home. A stranger in a truck was safer than Musselwhite.

His threat stayed with me after I got back. We were used to his threats. It wasn't the first time I'd heard him say something like "You haven't seen nothing yet."

Before dark, Dolores and I went out on the bike. I pedalled and she sat on the handlebars, and then we switched places. Twice we ended up in the ditch, but it didn't matter, because we couldn't stop laughing. I found our laughter brought me a little relief after Charlie's death and Musselwhite and Jack Tormentine. *Jack. Oh, Jack.* I imagined us crashing into each other by accident in the maze and not being able to find our way out and it being okay because the trees closed around us.

⋆

Dolores lifted the seeds of the night-flowering tobacco between her fingers and then let them drop back into the tray. She said they were ready to be stored. I put them in the embroidered pouch she'd made for me, then drew the string so they wouldn't fall out. It amazed me to think that such beautiful flowers would grow from these tiny black pieces of grit.

At night, when it finally got dark enough, we brought out the astronomy book and looked up at the constellations, naming them in both English and Spanish. Dolores leaned against me as we turned the pages. We spotted swirls of light called spiral galaxies, and many stars: red dwarfs, white dwarfs, red giants, supergiants, all different sizes and luminosities.

Santiago had a telescope, she told me. This was part of being an astronomer: learning the stars and using the telescope to make them appear close. Dolores and Santiago would take the telescope up to the highest hill on a starry night and look at the Milky Way. I asked what the Milky Way was, and she pointed to the long narrow cloud of stars strewn across the sky, as if dividing the sky from itself. "Where is the black hole?" I asked Dolores. "Can we see it?"

She said that we can't, because people can't see a black hole with their eyes. "Someday," she said, "someday it will be seen."

It took some time for Dolores to translate all this, because her English wasn't quite strong enough for scientific explanations. "The black hole is at the border of two constellations, Sagittarius and Scorpius. It's close to the Butterfly Cluster," she said finally. "All you see is what happens to the things around it, like dust clouds or merging stars. You know the Sagittarius A Star is there only by seeing what it has done to them." She told me of a place called the event horizon. If you get tipped over the event horizon you have passed the line of no escape. The place of no return. The black hole swallows everything.

*

All the next day I couldn't stop thinking about the black hole. I too wanted to be an astronomer, with a telescope powerful enough to see into that endless hungry expanse. Could someone like me, who only had schooling to Grade 10, become an astronomer? I couldn't imagine finishing high school, going to university. My mother would object. She'd say, "What about our family? What will happen to us? We four, we're the only ones left." She'd say, "What about the puppets, or our fowki, we're too poor for that kind of thing," or "How will going to university and being an astronomer bring money into the family?" or even more drastic, "You'll leave us, and then what?" Even these thoughts felt like a betrayal. And yet all I wanted was to wait for the sun to set, stand out in the motel parking lot, and watch the stars appear in the darkening sky.

I wasn't yet ready to talk to Dolores about my new dream. We were out before dark, taking turns on the bike. We went a different way than usual, along a part of the road we hadn't been on before. The road divided the tobacco fields from the forest. I heard the call of a small saw-whet owl, and I wondered if it was the partner of the owl Liza May was now caring for, so I left the bike with Dolores and went to the edge of the forest. I wanted to see the owl so I could tell Liza May, but its call became increasingly faint, so I turned back to the road. Too late—I heard a truck and saw the headlights.

The truck was behind Dolores, and when it caught her in its lights, it sped up, then veered over for a near miss. Dolores flew off the bike and landed in the ditch.

I ran, and felt my feet dragging, as if I were running in a dream. "Dolores!" I called, as you'd do to wake a child from a nightmare. "Are you alive?" Dolores lay still as a sleeping puppet. "Wake up! Wake up!" Her eyes were shut. The truck drove off, but before it did, I caught sight of one of those gorjos, a man like Musselwhite or Mister Tormentine. I sickened. "Dolores, wake up!"

I started to shake her, and with my frantic hand on her shoulder, it felt to me like hours before she shifted to one side and opened her eyes. "What happened?" she said. I feared she would not be able to walk. She rolled to her other side, pushed herself to sit up, then slowly stood. With one hand I supported her and with the other I steered the bike. We walked back to the motel, both crying.

"Oh, Dolores! I'm sorry." I couldn't see her or the road through my tears. I felt her arm, clammy, shaking under my hand. "I'm sorry. I love you, Dolores." There were no other words for what I felt, and I kept telling her I loved her, as if that would undo the horror, spool time back to the moment she sped, laughing, at the edge of the road. If I hadn't left her with the bike, I'd have seen the truck approaching. "I love you," I said again. I said, "Please," and again, "Please," as if begging her for something I could not yet express. Across the fields, the saw-whet owl called. I heard the coyotes. We walked down the middle of the empty road, our road again, and back to the motel.

45.

The stars shift across the sky as the world keeps on its slow turn. Puri Dai feels the turning. In her dream, she hears the motel front door opening. Zelda half asleep, the moon high, Zelda sneaking outside to cross the night road and lie down in the tobacco field between the high-scented leaves. The black night drops its shade around her. A fright to fall asleep—what if the leaves, the thousands of leaves, fold her in and pull her down under the roots of Tormentine's field?

Puri Dai wakes and hears her girl crying. The walls, the floor, the ceiling, the windows are crying. The parking lot's crying. The backyard. The forest. All crying. Her girl cries all night.

46.

My mother wanted to take Dolores to the hospital. "No doctor," said Dolores. "Please." She did not want Musselwhite or Mister Tormentine to know she'd been injured, because they'd send her back home.

With the tips of her fingers, Mam touched Dolores here and there. "Where does it hurt? Here? What about here?" Wherever Dolores winced, Mam placed a poultice of crushed nightshade and plantain leaves, especially around her shoulder and ankle.

★

"We can't send her to work on the bus," said my mother. "She'll ride with us in the truck, and too bad if Musselwhite catches on." I watched Dolores put her weight on one leg, barely able to touch her right foot to the ground, her body leaning into Lilly as she readied herself for work. I thought of Missus Tormentine driving into the ditch. I thought of the differences in their lives. Of what an injury meant to each of them—and not just the injury, but the shadow behind it, the cost. Not money, but the real cost. I prayed that Musselwhite and Mister Tormentine wouldn't notice anything was wrong.

I was already home when Mam and my aunties brought Dolores back from work, carrying her from the truck and out to the yard, where they laid her down under the oak. An unbearable rage crawled across my skin, a rage against the man who had sent Dolores into the ditch; a rage against Mister Tormentine and his power over her life. But then, frighteningly, my rage started to burn for him. For his silence. His easy heat. I was flooded with shame. Was it possible to hold love and hate, or whatever these feelings were, at the same time? Buddy Watmore and his tattoos filled my mind.

"What can I do to help you?" I said to Dolores. My mother had prepared willow tea for her pain, and the raklies were feeding her and laying poultices across her body.

Dolores told me she wanted Puri Dai. She didn't know I was keeping myself away from Puri Dai, or why I was doing so. My shame about that piled onto my shame about Mister Tormentine, and in my despair I feared Puri Dai would somehow guess the truth. I'd never before thrown her away. My grandmother, my beloved. I'd never thrown anybody away. I'd never begged them back again. I knew Puri Dai had always held herself above such things; she waited, seeing what needed to be seen. Time was different for her, not being made of blood or bone or confined to the limits of life. She could wait forever. I felt her waiting. I could not hide from her gaze. I knew she heard me crying the other night. Dolores's need rose above my shame. I went inside to Puri Dai's bed and lifted the sheet.

Puri Dai, I started. Silently I told her, *I've been thoughtless with you. I nearly threw you away. Forgive me for not respecting you.* She responded, *There is nothing to forgive. These are the times we're in. You seem to be in the thoughtless time of your life right now. Others are not so lucky to have good fortune and love from somebody like me.* I thanked her—too many times, I didn't know how many. *Remember that I am your honoured elder*, she said sternly. *Sometimes I need to remind you to approach with humility and respect.* I kissed her hands. I lifted her down from the narrow bed and pinned up her hair and shook out her dress.

When I took her outside, Dolores opened her arms to us. We sat beside her and she stroked Puri Dai's hands. "My friend," she said. "My protector." She kissed Puri Dai's ancient face.

★

The next day after work, Lilly told me that Musselwhite had come to the sewing table. "Where's that girl?" he said, looking around.

"What girl?" said Lilly.

Musselwhite spoke between his teeth. "You know what girl."

"You mean Dolores?"

"Whatever," he said. Then: "Yes." Lilly said he could not seem to bring himself to say her name.

"Oh, right, Dolores," said Lilly. "Yes. She just stepped into the kiln." The kiln was being loaded with tobacco slats.

"What the hell's she doing in the kiln?" said Musselwhite. He stuck his head through the door, and Mam and my aunties heard him asking the kiln hanger, who said, "Ain't seen her." And then Musselwhite yelled, "Hey! Hey you! Dorothy or whatever the hell your name is, I know you're around here."

"Dolores," shouted Lilly. "Her name's Dolores."

Musselwhite went into the kiln and then came out again and was gone for a long while.

"Mush got himself lost," Lilly said, and the women laughed.

When he appeared again, he was mildly seething. "She's not anywhere."

"Relax," said Lilly. "She's probably over at the hedgerow now, doing her business, since you people haven't bothered to provide us with decent washrooms."

Musselwhite went over to the hedgerow and stormed back. "She isn't at the goddamn hedgerow."

"She'll be around here somewhere. I saw her just ten minutes ago."

They kept this up for another day. Then Dolores went back to work. She could barely pick up the slats at the sewing table. Mam and my aunties and the other raklies shielded her with their bodies and sometimes with clusters of tobacco leaves whenever Musselwhite or one of his mushes went by, so they wouldn't see how her arm hung like an injured wing.

★

We got out the puppets because we urgently needed to laugh. We didn't bother with the red curtains because it wasn't that kind of show. Mr. Yesterday was Musselwhite, flaring his eyes, baring his teeth, ready to throw punches. He curled his lip and flexed his arms, tore around the yard. The others disappeared into the forest. Musselwhite followed them on the path into the trees, yelling, "Hey! Hey you. Dolores, or whatever the hell your name is. I know you're in there." He tripped over rocks and branches. Mr. Yesterday got Musselwhite's voice exactly right. "Goddammit," he said, as he struggled to his feet and dusted himself off.

Panni Mooi clambered into the upper branches of a tree and hooted at him like the saw-whet owl. Musselwhite turned frantic circles trying to see her as she hid herself among the leaves. "Get out here," said Musselwhite. Young Chavo, disguised as a branch, tripped him as he charged into the green tangle. Morning Glory kept two steps behind, taunting him with whispers. As he got deeper into the forest, Musselwhite's voice became higher and more piercing till his question shifted from "Where the hell are you?" to "Where the hell am I?"

Morning Glory came to the middle of the yard for the finale, surrounded by the other exhausted puppets. She repeated Musselwhite's last words: "Where am I?" She carried on, waving an arm out to the night sky: "In the grand scheme of things, Musselwhite is low in the pecking order, allies himself with a big tobacco farmer, and yet is at his mercy. So his question 'Where am I?' is the right question to ask in these strange times. It is a question we may also ask ourselves." Morning Glory was met first with silence, then loud applause. She bowed deeply, and then the other puppets bowed and blew kisses. Morning Glory's speech took ages to translate for the raklies through the dictionary.

Later, as I lay in bed, the swans on the ceiling covered their cygnets with their wings and made muted muttering sounds, as if sensing an enemy.

★

There were more black nightshade berries on the vines. The raklies joined us at the chain-link fence, and we picked until we could feel the berries but no longer see our hands in the dark. The raklies gathered the leaves as well, crushing them into poultices that they laid on Dolores's shoulder and on her leg.

There were fifteen jars of nightshade jam now, so my mother began to branch out, making jam from pears, currants, grapes, and plums. We were running out of storage space. I imagined jam piled jar upon jar, towering up to the ceiling, leaving only narrow paths for us to make our way from the doors to our beds. Liza May found a length of wood behind her bird shed and washed it and brought it into our room. We put the finished jars in a row along the shelf.

I brought another jar of jam—currant this time—to Missus Tormentine. This was to stay on her safe side, because the air was now sometimes sharp between us. Mister Leatherby, in his pyjamas, was lying on a wicker sofa on the front porch when I arrived. "Be a love and bring me an ashtray," he said, blowing smoke rings into the air.

As I went inside and headed down the hall, another house dropped into this one, out of the blue. That house was large and grand, like this one, but it had been abandoned. Mary Lou and I rode our bikes to it one Saturday, even though we knew we weren't supposed to go that far from home. We thought of it as the haunted house. Somebody had tried to start a fire in one of the rooms, and the walls and ceiling were streaked with soot. People, teenagers probably, had written on the walls.

As we were leaving, the house attacked us. It sent a cupboard door sideways into the right side of my face. And then, in the front hall, three floorboards gave way under Mary Lou's feet, and one of her legs fell through, creating a gap into a cellar hollowed out of the dark earth.

For the few brief seconds that our childhood haunted house was overlaid on the Tormentine house, I was overcome with fear and sorrow for Missus Tormentine. I needed to keep believing her to be a good person; of course she was a good person, thoughtless at times, but still good. *She is at heart a good person*, I thought as the other house faded. I entered her kitchen.

Missus Tormentine wasn't alone. Beside her was a round woman with dyed black hair and Elizabeth Taylor eye makeup. She looked like a squat, brisk version of Cleopatra. This woman and Missus Tormentine were standing over the kitchen table, looking at a piece of dark blue fabric. I saw a pattern of lush tobacco leaves interspersed by men on horses riding through moonlit fields. Were those clouds of cigarette smoke trailing behind them? Or was it the morning mist burning off the fields? Was Puri Dai's devil-man embedded in there? She might have something to say about this, and I didn't want to tell her.

Missus Tormentine said she and Mister Tormentine had gone shopping in town, and he had chosen this for the curtains in the babies' rooms, both for the one in Missus Tormentine's belly and the three others not yet born. Now even less light would enter their rooms. The boys—"Jack swears I'll give him boys," she said—would live in a permanent twilight.

"What do you think?" she asked. She turned to me and frowned. There was a tension building inside her unrelated to the horse fabric.

"He'll love it," I said.

The woman beside Missus Tormentine, introduced to me as Myra Shuttleworth, was going to make the curtains. It turned out that she was Musselwhite's sister, "but we're not on speaking terms," she told me. She had a crushing voice that would be at home in a military parade. Her tone hinted that it was important for me to know her opinion of Musselwhite, and that I should take her side, which was not difficult to do. It was a decades-long feud, she said, although she couldn't remember how it'd started. "He's just generally an asshole," said Mrs. Shuttleworth. I was shocked to hear that word come from someone who otherwise appeared stern and proper.

After they'd rolled up the fabric, Missus Tormentine turned her attention to the currant jam. "What have we got here?" she asked. She opened the lid and dove in. "I could eat this whole jar in one sitting," she said. "You just try this, Myra." She sent a spoonful of jam into Mrs. Shuttleworth's mouth.

Mrs. Shuttleworth closed her eyes for a beat. She frowned and seemed to be considering something. Then she swallowed. She said the local fair was coming up soon. "I already told them," chimed in Missus Tormentine, "way back when," and Mrs. Shuttleworth carried on right over her, saying there would be a cash prize for the winners. She told me that my mother should enter the jam—she and her daughter Enid were two of five judges. Then she left, the horse fabric rolled up inside a plastic bag.

Missus Tormentine turned to me but was interrupted by Mister Leatherby, who barged in, muttering about getting his own ashtray. He rummaged around, then turned to her, empty-handed. "What are we doing today?"

"We are going to eat a late breakfast, prepared by Zelda, down at the pond," she said, "and we'll spend the morning with the swans."

"I like Zelda," said Mister Leatherby. "Even though she doesn't have my ashtray."

"Yes, Leland, whatever." Missus Tormentine sounded impatient. She turned again to face me. "I've been meaning to bring this up, Zelda," she said. "It does and doesn't concern you."

"Somebody's in trouble," sang Mister Leatherby.

"That girl who got hurt," said Missus Tormentine, ignoring him, "isn't she one of the ones from your building? I think you know her. Somebody said she got into some kind of accident."

"She did?"

"Mister Tormentine was really upset. He was so mad he was shaking."

All I said was "That's awful."

I thought about Dolores. I hatched a silent plan to hide her from Mister Tormentine and Musselwhite. I'd make her a bed on the other side of my curtain, or I'd clean out the bird shed, turn it into a simple room, and she could stay in there. I'd bring breakfast to her before I went to work and supper after I got home.

Then Jack slid into my plans. What would it be like sitting beside him in his truck while he was shaking mad? Would he press me against the back of the seat and say he should tell Missus Tormentine but he wasn't gonna?

"I knew you'd care about our situation," said Missus Tormentine. "All that money he paid to bring her up here. But it's okay, we can always get somebody else."

I made their breakfast and carried it down to the pond. I imagined not-accidentally spilling the coffee and watching it land on her lap, and was shocked by the thought that I could do such a thing.

Mister Leatherby spoke as if I wasn't there. "Does Zelda like nice dresses? Does she like picnics?" he said.

"Of course she does," said Missus Tormentine absently. She looked at me, and I knew she was still thinking about Dolores.

"That's settled, then," Mister Leatherby said, not taking his eyes off me.

★

That night I had a dream in which Missus Tormentine held a piece of paper to her face and lit it with her blue gas-jet eye. I threw the paper into her bedroom, where everything caught fire: the wall-to-wall broadloom, the bed, the mirror, and then the closet, with its dangerous blue silk river-dress, the French restaurant lunch dresses, evening gowns weighted down with beads and sequins and rhinestones, little black cocktail dresses, picnic dresses patterned with watermelons and sunflowers and cherries, Easter dresses with borders of egg-filled baskets, rabbits racing along the hem. Then a column of flame rose from my green taffeta dress. The flames reached the ceiling and began to feed on the walls. Out of Mister Leatherby's mouth came: "Poor little Zelda." He scooped the remains of my green dress into a picnic basket already filled with ashes. "Nothing to eat but her own rags." He tried to feed me the ashes, but I turned away. Missus Tormentine made a sad half-smile. They went downstairs, arm in arm, heads together, whispering, while the house burned around them.

47.

Puri Dai wakes to the calling of the coyotes. They're far away, maybe three concessions over. The pups have already left the den of their birth, venturing out to seek new territories, as do all young when the right time comes. She thinks of her girl, at this very moment holding Tormentine in one hand and young Dolores in the other. Soon one will get too heavy, and she'll have to let it drop. Her girl will learn that soon enough. Puri Dai prays that she'll make the right choice when the time comes: drop Tormentine into the flames of his special hell. There's much to hope for, especially when her girl, after so many lonely days, has started to come back. Puri Dai thanks Dolores for that. But her Zelda would have come eventually. This she knows.

There is also the question of Dolores herself. Puri Dai looks ahead a few days and sees a dark cloud. She sees that in the immediate future things will not end well and suspects Dolores already knows this. Then she looks ahead weeks, months, and the cloud disperses. It's not yet clear how or where or when the light will return. Everything will unfold as it should. She falls asleep to the voices of the coyotes as they sing along the hedgerows.

48.

Dolores was not getting better. She came home after work each day with barely enough strength to eat. We stood over her and encouraged her as she put spoonful after spoonful of soup in her mouth. "Just one more," said Mercedes. "Now a bite of bread." Then Dolores had to be helped to lie down. Mercedes and the raklies took turns massaging the healing poultice of nightshade leaves into her skin. Bruises had bloomed across her shoulder, her hip, the instep of her foot and her ankle, and now the length of her right arm. The bruise on her hip was a deep blue, the size of a small plate. She could not lie on the right side of her body. We offered her a quiet show of songs sung by the puppets, but she wanted only Puri Dai.

And then one night Mam and my aunties and the raklies came home furious. Around noon, Musselwhite and Tormentine had parked themselves in the doorway of the barn, with a good view of the sewing table. They stood there, leaning against the door frame, smoking their cigarettes, not taking their eyes off Dolores. They eventually left, but Musselwhite kept coming back. The women saw his pinched eyes watching her every move.

★

The fair opened on a Friday. My mother picked me up from Missus Tormentine's and we went to the fairground to deliver her entries: a jar of currant jam, one of nightshade, one of raspberry, and one of pear. "I'm scared," she said, clutching the steering wheel with both hands and not letting go.

"Mam. Don't be." I got out and went over to the driver's side and opened the door. I reached into the back and handed her the box of jam.

"I don't like this," she said. "I've never put myself forward before. I don't like the spotlight."

"Mother," I said, "it's just jam."

She looked down at the box in her arms. "You're right. It's just jam." I had to coax her through the door of the food barn, even as she was saying, "I'm not sure about this."

Mrs. Shuttleworth was fussing over the long tables, laying out plastic tablecloths and complaining about the thinness of the plastic. When she saw me, she dropped the tablecloths and narrowed her eyes at the box of jam. "Only four jars?" she said, frowning at my mother. "You're Zelda's mother who makes the jam?"

"Yes," said Mam. She made herself small. Her hands were shaking, and the jars in the box began to rattle. "I can bring more." She handed the box to Mrs. Shuttleworth.

Mrs. Shuttleworth looked irritated. She sighed. "It's too late now." She turned back to her tablecloths. "The judging is tomorrow," she said over her shoulder. "Eleven sharp."

"Do you think she's mad at me?" asked Mam when we were out at the truck. "I'll be lucky if I even get an honourable mention."

The following morning, Mercedes and Alma and Liza May stayed with Dolores, who was lying under the grandmother oak. She wasn't strong enough to come with us to the fair. Liza May brought out the saw-whet owl and fed her, which made Dolores happy. When we left, she was teaching Liza May to say owl in Spanish. "Búho," she said.

"Boo hoe," said Liza May.

"Yes," Dolores said, "very good."

★

The fairground was packed. We passed the Tillsonburg wrestling champion handing out autographs at a table that bristled with trophies. We passed the Eiffel Tower, the town post office, and a tobacco plant, all made from Popsicle sticks. We passed quilts that hadn't yet won prizes. We passed a St. John Ambulance demonstration, a competition for the biggest vegetables, hens that looked like feather dusters, and a school display with examples of handwriting from Grade 2 students, and drawings of tobacco workers done by eighth-grade students at the Tobacco Road school. One drawing struck both Mam and me: it showed two women bent over a sewing table and surrounded by tobacco leaves. We felt the heat, the blistered fingers, the drops of sweat running down their faces. One of the women could have been Liza May. My mother said she loved the drawing, intending to buy it to hang in her new house. "If I can afford it," she said.

"Yes, you can afford it," I said.

The woman at the table smiled. "It's a child's drawing," she said, "so it won't break the bank."

We had to fight our way to the food barn. The egg sorters, standing behind a table with their five entries of stolen eggs from Mister Tormentine's barn, greeted me like a lost sister. Rita Slack's eggs won first prize and Diane DeVrees got second. Coral Peplinskie came in third, and the rest received honourable mentions. "They're all the same eggs," they went, laughing. They pooled their prize money and said they'd be going out drinking after things shut down. We were invited to join them.

Willard Crowshank, two tables over, won first prize for his summer sausage. Rita Slack said he could enter a crayon drawing by his three-year-old grandson and he'd still come in first.

The warmth and noise of the fair washed over me. Babies squalling, men clapping each other's shoulders, twelve-year-old girls wearing lipstick and leaning, bored, against the walls. Children hid under tables and chased each other through the aisles. The judges wore bright aprons. The food barn was theirs: they used coded gestures and hand signals to do all the talking.

Jams and relishes were down at the back. Mrs. Shuttleworth and the other four judges stood guard behind the table, watching for thieves, because the Crowshank boys were known to help themselves to jam. There must have been at least fifty jars on the jam table. In the front row were three of Mam's, each with a gold ribbon. Currant jam, first prize; raspberry, second prize; pear, third. The nightshade jam was at the back with the others. "We didn't understand the nightshade jam," said Mrs. Shuttleworth. "It's not a taste we know." The nightshade jam did not get an honourable mention.

Mrs. Shuttleworth handed over an envelope, which Mam put straight into her pocket. "Well deserved," said Mrs. Shuttleworth. "I speak for each one of us when I say you've outdone us all." The other judges nodded agreeably. Mrs. Shuttleworth introduced us to them, and then to her daughter Enid. They looked alike, except for Enid's eyes, which were ringed in blue makeup.

"I've made a friend," my mother said. She couldn't stop smiling.

On our way out we stopped at the wrestling table, and the Tillsonburg wrestling champion, leaning over his trophies, flared his nostrils at Lilly and asked her out on a date. "Well, Mister Wrestling Champion," she said, "that's a nice big trophy you got there," and laughed, and he laughed too, but uncertainly, as if not knowing how to take this. Lilly, still laughing, blew him a kiss and slid back into the crowd. We were diverted to another aisle; we bought butter tarts to take to the raklies, and I bought a tiny piece of embroidery, a sprig of forget-me-nots, for Dolores. Lilly stayed on to go drinking with the egg sorters. She'd get a ride back later with Diane DeVrees.

Back at the motel, Dolores continued to decline. Mercedes told her she must not go to work on Monday. That we'd hide her here until she was better. "I have to try," said Dolores, but we knew from the look of her that it would be impossible.

49.

"You're due for a lunch break in half an hour," said Missus Tormentine. "Down at the pond. It'll be fun. He's packed sandwiches and a cold chicken."

"He?" I asked. "Who's he?"

"My brother. Leland."

"But I have work to do here."

"It's just a little picnic," said Missus Tormentine. "I can lend you my bracelets and whatnot, just for fun. I'm off to something in town so I won't be joining you, but you can save me some leftovers."

"I don't know if I want to go on a picnic," I said.

"Yes, you do." She prodded me upstairs. "You like all my jewellery, don't you?"

"I guess."

"You guess?" She gave me a sharp look. "What do you mean, you guess?"

The thought of Missus Tormentine's gold at this moment made me feel dark, heavy, weighed down with something I didn't understand. *Watch out.* I heard Puri Dai's voice in my head. *Watch out for that sly raklie. She's up to something.*

"You know you love my jewellery, and now's your chance to wear it again." Missus Tormentine switched to her girlfriend voice. "Remember the fun lunch we had in the French restaurant way back when? How glamorous was that?" It wasn't so long ago that I'd have given anything to wear all that sonnakai of hers. "And Leland's a fabulous cook," she said. "He roasted the chicken especially for you." I wondered why she was advertising her brother to me. I wondered why she had to leave. "Hold still," she said, loading my arms up with her gold bracelets and fastening two necklaces around my neck. "Now for the earrings," she said. She loosened my hair and backcombed it so that it stuck out like a bird's nest. "Take off your shoes," she said.

"I don't want to."

"Oh, Zelda, for goodness' sake, just do it."

I took off my shoes.

She put her hands on my shoulders and turned me to face the mirror. "It's the real you," she said. I looked like I was wearing Patricia Frobisher's Grade 6 Gypsy Halloween costume.

"I don't feel very well."

"Zelda, stop pretending. You look great, and you'll have a fun time. Now I have to get changed." She pulled a soft, faded dress from the back of her closet. "I hardly ever wear this," she said. The dress was the colour of butter and decorated with small bright birds. A sunny, innocent dress. "It reminds me of you," she said. "I'll give it to you one of these days, maybe for your mother or one of your aunties. Just feel the cloth." She pressed the skirt of the dress into my hand. "So soft," she said, "like the down on a new nestling."

"I don't feel well," I said again.

"Stop it, Zelda." She shot me a look I couldn't interpret. She undressed right there in front of me and pulled on the bird dress. "Zip me up," she said, and I did so. "What do you think? Am I showing yet?" She studied herself in front of the mirror, turning this way and that, hands on her stomach, and then propelled me back down the stairs. "I'm off now, but my brother will be here shortly." She kissed me. "You're a star," she said. "You'll be fine," and she left. I heard her drive away.

I went to the window. Clouds were gathering. I sat down on the landing. I wanted Puri Dai. I wanted her to tell me what to do. I wanted Lilly. I couldn't grasp what was about to happen. Lilly would tell me my feelings were real. I thought of the maze, of being snatched by its branches and held in there with no way out. Missus Tormentine's words that day in her kitchen were here, now, around me: *Fear. I'm glad I could help you learn this.*

I had started to take off her earrings when her brother walked in the front door. I heard the beginnings of rain at the window. "Oh, leave them on," he said, waving at the earrings. He carried a picnic basket.

Two men followed him inside. They were both different versions of Mister Leatherby, with white linen suits and cigarettes between their fingers.

"Wow," said the shorter one, "it's Carmen. Oh you beauty." He stopped dead. "I'm Alisdair, and you'll never guess how thrilled I am to finally meet you."

"I don't know who Carmen is," I said, "but I'm not her." The men looked at each other. They burst out laughing.

"What'd I tell you?" said Mister Leatherby, after they'd stopped laughing. "This is why I love Zelda."

"Oh, you thief," said the taller one, sneaking his eyes up and down my body, "you thief of hearts." He inclined his head. "Bond," he said, drawing on his cigarette and exhaling a hazy blue cloud. "Monty Bond."

Puri Dai, I thought. *Tell me what to do.*

Still another man came in, older, dressed like the others. White linen suits seemed to be their uniform.

"Ah," said Mister Leatherby, "here's Fraser." He turned to the one called Fraser. "Fraser," he said, "this is our Zelda."

Our Zelda. Our.

"Well. Here we all are," Monty Bond said, smiling. "Mad, bad, and dangerous to know."

"Who?" laughed Mister Leatherby. "Zelda? Or us?"

"I think it was about Lord Byron," said Monty Bond, "but come to think of it, it could very well be our Zelda here."

Again, our Zelda. Our houses. Our money, our properties, our cars, animals. Our playthings.

I wanted to tell them I wasn't theirs—I wasn't their anything—but my tongue froze. I had no idea what they were talking about. But that tone. Their sly, ugly tone. I took a step back, and Mister Leatherby held out the basket to me. His other hand, closed in a secretive fist, stayed at his side. I thought of Mister Tormentine's fist—his hands on the steering wheel. Mister Leatherby looked at the rain hitting the window. "What a shame," he said. "At least we can still do our picnic inside."

I looked at them. They were like four identical beings. I thought of Puri Dai and the devil-man. These men before me, they were devil-men. Real ones. Her voice was at my ear. *Get out.* Through her eyes, I saw their bodies poised to rip through the white linen suits. I saw the cloven hooves inside their shoes.

"There's a special treat in here," said Mister Leatherby, stepping forward, holding out his fist.

I picked up the thing that lay nearest me. It was the vacuum cleaner. I backed partway up the stairs and stood looking down on the men. I held the vacuum cleaner in front of me. "I'll throw it," I said. "I'll hit you with it."

"Come on, Zelda," said Mister Leatherby. "Alisdair here's brought a cheesecake. Come on down and try a bite." He held up the picnic basket. "Just a teensy bite. Just one." I raised the vacuum cleaner. "We don't want to hurt Alisdair's feelings," laughed Mister Leatherby, "do we." Alisdair made a pouting face. The vacuum cleaner was awkward and getting heavy. Mister Leatherby took another step forward and I raised it higher. We faced each other for what felt like forever.

Monty Bond rolled his eyes and shifted from side to side. "Quite the picnic," he said under his breath.

Mister Leatherby and I didn't move. "Come on, Zelda," he said in a whining drawl. "Give us a smile, at least."

Fraser looked at his watch and said something like "Forget it, let's go, boys, time is money," but I couldn't be sure.

Mister Leatherby took another step toward the landing. He opened his fist and in the middle of his palm I saw his wide gold ring, the ring from our blackjack game, its ruby flashing darkly. "Look," he said. "For you." He brought his hand closer. "It was my grandfather's, and now it's yours." My arms started to shake. "Go ahead. Take it," he said. "No strings attached." I didn't move. I looked from him to Alisdair to Monty Bond to Fraser. None of them moved.

Monty Bond sighed in a heavy, angry way. Did he say, "Are we doing this or not?" or did I imagine it? I could almost smell his exhalation.

I was trying to not drop the vacuum cleaner. It took all my strength.

Monty Bond whispered to Fraser. Fraser nodded. I watched a series of eye signals pass from one man to the next. Fraser coughed.

"Okay," said Mister Leatherby, closing his hand and jamming the ring into his pocket, "this isn't going anywhere." He backed away and dumped the picnic basket on the floor. A roast chicken slid out. Some of the sandwiches flew apart, landing on the hallway runner and across the floorboards. I saw what looked like mayonnaise making a wide smear from one side of the hall to the other. "It's all yours," Mister Leatherby said, grinding the sandwiches into the floor with the sole of his shoe. "To eat all on your lonesome. It was just going to be a picnic." *Just. Just a picnic.*

"Not very friendly," I heard, as the door slammed behind the men.

My immediate thought was to flush all Missus Tormentine's gold down the toilet, but I knew it would clog the pipes, and then she'd make me pay for a plumber. I piled the rescued sandwiches onto a plate and set it down on the kitchen table. Let her eat the dirt and polish and dust of her own floor. She wouldn't know the difference.

A fog settled around me. Why had she left me here alone? What had just happened? What could have happened? The sky grew darker and the rain was really starting to come down. When Missus Tormentine's car pulled in the driveway, I had not moved from my post at the kitchen table. I was still feeling the weight of the vacuum cleaner in my hands, still trying to understand what it was that had happened.

"Got rained out, did you?" she said, coming in the back door, handing me her umbrella. She took off her shoes and went over to the kitchen table. "Look," she said, "what's this? Leftovers?" She picked up a sandwich. While she was chewing, she said, "Now. I hate to keep revisiting this, but I'm going to have to ask you frankly, Zelda, and I want an honest answer." She swallowed and turned to look at me.

My stomach rose. "It was awful."

"Pardon?"

"Mister Leatherby," I said. "He—"

"Forget Mister Leatherby," she said. "This is important."

"No. He came with men. He wanted—" I couldn't say it.

"Will you just stop?" she said. She picked up another sandwich. "You listen to me." Her voice a knife. "Listen. It's been on my mind since yesterday. That girl they can't find."

What girl? Not the dead girl, the one who used to work for her? Roxanne Pettifer, the one the raklies from the egg barn talked about, the one who killed herself? Or was she talking about Dolores? Dolores. *It was Dolores.*

"Where is she?"

"I don't know."

"I think you do," said Missus Tormentine. Those blue gas-jet eyes of hers burned through me. "That girl. She isn't in her motel room; they've checked," she said.

Girl. That girl. Out of my mouth came: "What about the other girl?"

"There's another girl? This gets even worse."

"I mean the dead one." The words practically spoke themselves. "The girl before me, the one who killed herself."

Missus Tormentine's sandwich fell open and left mustard on her fingers and across the front of her dress—the butter-coloured bodice was now stained a harsh yellow. I couldn't stop staring at the streak across the pattern of small bright birds whose names I didn't know.

"I don't know any girl who killed herself," said Missus Tormentine. Her fingertips worked at the mustard on her dress. She brought her hand to her mouth.

"The girl that worked for you," I said. "Roxanne Pettifer. The one from Mattawa. The one who hanged herself." Would the dead girl have seen this friendly dress scattered with birds? Had Missus Tormentine worn this dress to minimize an ugly violation?

"Where are you getting this from?" said Missus Tormentine. There was also mustard at the corners of her mouth, and she licked it with her tongue.

"I need to tell you about Mister Leatherby," I said.

"Enough with Mister Leatherby," she nearly shouted. "Go vacuum the baby's bedroom. There are boxes in there to unpack. And you might try setting up the crib."

One of the upstairs bedroom windows was open and rain was coming in. When I went to close it, I saw the leak. Part of the wall was blistered and seeping, and the blister was raised and swollen like Missus Tormentine's car-crash leg. The rain rattled the windows. I came down without doing any of my chores. She hadn't moved from the kitchen table, and I saw the mustard was still smeared across the birds of her dress.

"It's one thing to have to leave work early now and then," she said, "and another to skip out altogether. Can you imagine the chaos if everybody did that? The farm would fall apart. My husband depends on his workers. He gives them a chance here. A chance to support their families." She sat back and folded her arms. "If that girl doesn't do the work she was brought here to do, she's taking advantage. She's going back on her word, and she needs to be sent back to where she came from." She watched me. "Don't you think?"

Missus Tormentine could fire me. I didn't care about that. I was finished anyway.

"Musselwhite's picking you up in half an hour," she said. "I want you to tell him where she is. Will you do that?"

I went to the front door instead of answering her. My first thought was to throw the bracelets and earrings and necklaces into the ditch, but she'd say I'd stolen them, and she'd like to be able to say that, so I left everything piled on the hall table.

It wasn't raining anymore, and the road was filled with puddles. I walked through them. I was calmed by the cool mud and the water splashing against my legs. I cried as I walked. I walked for what must have felt like an hour, and then I heard a truck coming down the road behind me, so I turned to face it and stuck out my thumb.

"It's okay, girlie," said the driver when he saw my red, streaked face. He asked me where I wanted to go. He had a comfortable silence about him, and I was grateful. He let me cry without asking me what was wrong. Even if he'd asked, I don't think I'd have been able to tell him. He dropped me off in front of the motel and said he hoped there was somebody in there to look after me.

"Yes," I said. "My mother. She'll look after me."

He waited till I was inside before he drove off.

★

"They're looking for you," I said to Dolores. We were sitting on my bed, the dictionary between us. "They want me to tell them where you are."

Dolores said she knew it would come to this.

"What should we do? I can hide you."

She shook her head, saying the risk would be too great. "Not only for me but for all of you. I have no choice."

In the kitchen, I heard only the chopping of knives. We ate our supper in silence. No songs. Dolores asked for my post office address and wrote it down in a small notebook. Before dark she asked me to go to her room to help her pack. She was distant, as if already gone. I understood, because in my family we also distanced ourselves, even from each other, when we were getting ready to leave wherever we'd been living.

50.

Our girl's friend, our Dolores, laments Puri Dai. How terrible and sad that is. The bosses could have taken her to a doctor, but they don't think their tobacco workers are human. They'd rather get rid of them.

She sees the sadness like a cloud covering her girl and her family and all the raklies. She hears the silence, everything becoming small, folding into itself.

And that other thing, she thinks, setting our girl up like that. I should have seen it from the start. Why did I not? It was so careful and simple, even from that first day. Just a little bit at a time. Maybe I did see, but not clearly enough. I was all about the big warnings and not enough about the small ones. That's how that Tormentine woman operates, one little giftie at a time. That sly white devil. That beng.

Puri Dai—arms around her girl, crying with her—can't find the words, but words are pointless at a moment like this anyway. The important thing is the holding, their arms around each other as the world falls around them. The waterfall of Zelda's tears pools on the ground.

She says to her Zelda: Watch the moon. Watch where the moon sends her light. Watch where she sends her shadow. Cover the win-

dows, shut the doors. The devils are not yet finished with us. The earth will open up under our feet, and we have to ensure that it's we who step aside so them cold-blooded ones drop like stones into the crevasse. Watch out. Dik. Dik. The devil-man's coming, coming through the fields.

51.

What a night of bright mist. The tobacco plants shimmered as if each one were shrouded inside its own private ghost. I went out into the forest and took the emerald-green dress from its branch. I wasn't ready to relinquish it, even after yesterday's ugliness, but believed I could give it a new life outside the taint of Missus Tormentine.

I stepped out of my nightgown and into the dress. It shimmered like a tobacco leaf, grey-green now in the mistlight. My bare feet made no sound on the leaves and twigs as I came around the side of the motel to the front door. Across the road, the field lay like a silent silver sea. No single tobacco leaf moved. The air was still. I heard the saw-whet owl calling in the forest and another owl answering.

Was Dolores awake? Or asleep, dreaming about how in a few days she'd be back with her family again? Should I knock on her door? Should I let her sleep? Back home, would she remember me? Tomorrow—here—nothing would change except for the empty space she'd have left. A space wide enough to fill the sky. The sun would rise over the fields, workers would sweat under the sun, tobacco leaves would be sewn, lunches and suppers would be eaten, the saw-whet owl would cry into the night, its mate would answer. The coyotes would yip from their dens. The fields would sleep again. Everything would repeat. Repeat without Dolores.

I danced from our door to hers, to the end of the building and back again, and stood on my toes to be closer to the sky. The emerald dress contained me. My hands felt the bodice stiff as a cocoon around a future moth. The petals of the skirt stood straight out from the waist, so the skirt appeared to be floating. I too was floating. In this dress I became a leaf-being, a forest-being, and I wanted never to have to take it off. I wanted to take up Lilly's needle and thread, let them melt in my hand, sew this dress into my skin.

The light shifted. I looked across the road and out to the field. The mist was beginning to disperse here and there. I looked up. The moon held itself over the field, a perfect silver sphere. Puri Dai often warned of the full moon, that it opened the path for the devil. I looked again out at the field. There was no drom. There was no beng. There was only the beauty of the night.

From somewhere back in the field, where tobacco met sky, came a distant wet sound like the intake of a breath. I had an audience: the tobacco field had seen me, and its breath was a gasp at my beauty in the dress. I danced for my audience, for the field of ten thousand tobacco plants, and they exhaled their praise.

Everything grew brighter and more alive. Something shifted. At the end of the field, a shadow. The one I'd seen before. It was among the plants. Had it moved, or had the moon-shadow dazed my eyes? Another slight shift. The shadow moved like a web shivering with internal commotion. I imagined it sticky with the juices of tobacco plants, gathering and rummaging itself into a shape, dark, blurred at the edges. The web solidified into a man.

I heard the moon's sharp voice like glass underfoot. *Watch out, watch out*, it sang, like a thousand ice cubes, like ice biting a river. It jangled and shone and sang.

The man glided through the tobacco leaves, and my body froze as if I'd dropped through ice. He was in the middle of the field now. He pressed forward under the moon's fanged light until he reached the near edge of the field. I could not tell who it was. The leaves parted as he advanced through them, but they were otherwise still. Like ghost leaves. My body, dipped in ice. The man stopped. His edges were less blurred, more distinct. A shift. He moved slightly and was now at the ditch. He moved as if floating.

I could see no face.

He was at the road. Then across the road. I could not move. The man. His face a dark smear. He was at the edge of the parking lot. I saw then that he did have a face, unclear, lost in shadow. The man brought his hand to his mouth. I saw the small red glow as he pulled on a cigarette. I saw his exhalation, a bright scattered fog. I smelled the smoke. The burning tar. He lowered his hand and the glow went away. He stared at me out of the mist. He was a blank, a zero waiting in its web. The moon too waited.

I turned my hands over and thought of Buddy Watmore's tattoos. Love on the left, hate on the right. Some good that would do me right now.

The man moved closer. He was halfway across the parking lot, his hand returned to his mouth, and then another red glow like a burning eye. With the sideways movement of his hand, the glow was gone. Heat came off him, and then a cold like a frozen river. My whole body frozen, I couldn't move. My hair rose and I wanted to call out, but I had no voice. The man had stopped my voice. I went inside and could not lock the door because we didn't have a key. He could enter our room. He could walk through the door, fly in the window, slither through a crack in the wall.

I ripped off the dress and stuffed it under my sheet, and lay in bed and waited. I tried to listen through the pounding of my heart. It was banging in my ears. Was listening any use? He had come here from another place, from other waves of sound. I dropped into a kind of sleep. When I woke up in the morning, my mother and my aunties had already gone. They'd be at the tobacco table, sorting and sewing the leaves and sending them along the belt into the barn. The mist would have burned off, the sun angled above the fields. I went outside. The sky was still the sky, the field was still the field, the road was still the road. I went to stand in the parking lot, in the place where the devil-man had stood. I thought of the cloven hoof. There was no trace of him on the asphalt. Would a devil even leave footprints? I crossed the road, and there were no prints on the gravel shoulder either. Everything looked ordinary. The way it always had been. On my way back to our room, in the middle of the parking lot, I found cigarette butts on the ground.

52.

It's almost a relief that he has come and gone, yet a horror to know he's out there still, sleeping under the tobacco roots or nestled in the leaves or hiding in the sewing machines, floating in the diesel tanks or transmission wires or the electrical fields. To know he can be summoned by dirty deeds and transgressions and suffering. To know he he'll just wait for the next full moon.

Puri Dai laments that there was nothing she could have done to fend him off, for the devil-man of the tobacco fields is a hundred thousand times stronger than a wooden puppet. Her girl had a lucky escape. He could have entered through her eyes or her mouth, or even her ear, and would have embedded himself there as the worm embeds in the apple.

53.

When Musselwhite picked me up in the morning, his first words were "Where the hell is that girl?" He kept on hitting me with the same angry question, and I kept saying, "I don't know."

"You know!" he shouted.

"I do not!"

"I'll get it out of you," he shot back. He sped up and went through a stop sign.

"You do not threaten me!" I yelled. I opened the door. "Stop the car." He went faster. "Stop," I said, "or I'll jump out and say you pushed me." That did it. He slammed on the brakes, and I got out.

When I walked into the house—over the polished floors, past the grandfather clock and the mirrors, past the staircase to the bedroom of dresses and Mister Tormentine in the mirror and the other bedroom with its dark curtains—and over to Missus Tormentine, sitting at the kitchen table like it was any other day, I remembered the day this house had been a refuge, right after Missus Tormentine had crashed her car in the ditch and needed my care. I had to remind myself that I was here to collect the money she owed me.

The words of the egg sorters came to me. *She did it on purpose.*

My mother at the supper table. *They've asked for you, Zelda.*

Missus Tormentine was paying attention to her fingernails. As I entered the kitchen, out of my mouth came: "I know what you did. How this started."

She looked up. "How what started?"

"When you drove your car into the ditch back then. It wasn't an accident, was it?"

She smiled. "What do you think?"

"I think it wasn't."

"You'll never know, will you?"

I told her I was quitting. She waved the fingers of one hand in the air so that her nail polish would dry more quickly. Then she held the brush poised over the thumbnail of her other hand. "That's fine," she said. "But you still have some time left." She fastened the lid on her nail polish. "You can stay until whenever the new girl comes, so you can show her what to do. I'll still pay you, but don't expect any perks."

"Sorry," I said. I did not mean it as an apology.

Missus Tormentine looked up. "What about my breakfast?" she said. "And what's with these uncalled-for questions? Yesterday a dead girl and insinuations against my brother, and now this?"

"I'm leaving today. I need paying."

"You used to be so thoughtful, Zelda. Compliant. That really mattered to me. You were coming along nicely," she said, "but now look at you. Insolent doesn't begin to cover it."

She fluttered the fingers of her hand again. "Now," she said, "if you're done with your little revolution, I'll have toast and coffee, please." She opened the bottle and finished her other hand. Two hands in the air, waving themselves dry. Waving one girl out the door, waving the next girl in. Would this new one be sent through the maze? Into the river? Into the jaws of Mister Leatherby and his friends?

"And my wages?"

"Wait." She blew on her nails. When she decided they were dry enough, she reached for her purse. "I need my toast and coffee," she said. She counted out bills.

"There's ten dollars missing," I said.

"Oh for Christ's sake," she said, and rummaged again through her purse. "Never satisfied, are you." She clacked her fingernails on the table, the sound of small knives. "You're like all those girls," she said, "coming here and pretending to work." She threw a ten-dollar bill across the table. "They're a dime a dozen. You're all a dime a dozen. But you. I expected more of you. You were supposed to bring your Gypsy magic into this house. Instead, you brought nothing but misery."

⋆

The devil of the tobacco fields was still with me. He was at my shoulder and in my hair. He woke me in the night. I couldn't shake him. Before anybody else got home, I took Lilly's scissors out to the forest and I cut the beloved emerald dress into pieces. It would never have been free of Missus Tormentine—I saw that now. When everybody had gone to work, I took the pieces, still bright as leaves, and burned them in a fire. I wondered about the dress, if the devil-man had seen it and been drawn to it. Or if he'd seen me as I danced from one side of the building to the other. Had I brought him here? The thought sickened me to the bone.

*

The sun was still low and the shadows bled over the fields when Musselwhite came for Dolores. She was waiting at the front of the motel and wheeled her suitcase to the truck. She turned and limped over to me to put the dictionary in my hands. She kept looking back at us as the truck turned the corner and disappeared. My mother and my aunties went to work. I had nowhere to go. I walked along the road to the place where Dolores had been thrown off her bike. I came back to see a bus waiting in the parking lot. The raklies were being loaded in. They were being taken to another farm. The driver shut the door and pulled out to the road, and I ran after the bus, calling and waving my arms, but it didn't stop. I was filled with an emptiness more expansive than the sky, greater than a black hole. I heard my voice calling her name. *Dolores, Dolores*. Calling for Mercedes, Alma, for all the raklies. Crying didn't fill that vast space. Nothing did. I turned back to the motel. We were alone again.

IV
The lord of the fields

54.

The black hole has so many shapes and so many hunting grounds. It shows up in the darkest times. Its gravity will not let even light escape. Through her closed eyes, Puri Dai sees it across the road. Who needs a telescope when the black hole's in front of me and I can see it without opening my eyes? It sucks in the tobacco field, the silver night leaves, the crickets, the moon. It lowers itself around the scabby white-painted motel and the black asphalt of the parking lot, and around the parking lot's plants: chicory, yarrow, black nightshade, plantain. She sees a cavity, a crater, as if a lake had parted and left a space as deep and black as that of the sky, as if the fields and roads and buildings have disappeared into the black hole that nearly swallowed our girl.

Our girl. She is held down by the grief of losing her friends. She wears her sorrow like a coat so heavy that Puri Dai can see her shoulders sinking under the weight.

55.

Out back, under the grandmother oak, the past days and nights washed through me. They tasted of icy dread. Of blooming nausea. Meat left under the sun: blistering, wafts of rot, maggot nests, flies. My stomach rose. I told myself I'd need four stomachs, like a cow, for the amount of digesting I needed to do. I made myself laugh, but it wasn't happy laughter. It made me think of Dolores, laughing because she had no other choice.

My body couldn't keep still, so I rushed out front to the parking lot, to the road. I went back inside. I made tea I couldn't drink. A sandwich I couldn't eat. I took Puri Dai from her sheet and brought her out to the grandmother oak so I wouldn't be alone. I held her and said, *I don't know what's going on.* I felt her listening. Our arms were tight around each other. I carried her into the forest hush and stood in the cool air. *Smell the green*, I said, and I felt her breathing it in and saying, *This is what you need.*

I'm scared, I said.

Well, no wonder, said Puri Dai. *They're bringing their devilment to our door, and they want to throw you off balance. Don't let them do it, murri shey. If they do throw you off, lean into the falling and let it guide you.*

★

The loss of Dolores haunted me and I could barely eat breakfast. I wished that I'd asked her for a photograph. Or for someone to take a picture of the two of us together. What if over the months I forgot what she looked like?

I listened to Mam and my aunties around the table. Their voices were soft and round and made a blanket around me. Mam poured the tea and said, "What's wrong with you?" I saw from the look of her that she didn't expect me to answer. "Drink your tea," she said, and they went on talking. I drank. Dolores came to me, larger in her absence than if she'd been here beside me.

After a while, we went out back, where Lilly unrolled a length of fabric across the picnic table and laid over it Morning Glory's old green dress, which she was using for a pattern.

Liza May made a face. I felt she was trying to lift me out of my grief. Lift us all. "What is that shitty colour?" she said, sneering at the fabric.

"Don't knock it," said Lilly. We couldn't tell what colour it was supposed to be, because it changed depending on how you looked at it. "It's called revenge," she said.

"It's just ugly," said Liza May.

"That's a start," said Lilly.

"Why are you even doing this?"

"It's for the show at Tormentine's."

"There's a show at Tormentine's?"

"Yes," said Lilly. "This Saturday. You were there when he asked us."

"I don't remember," said Liza May.

"It's happening," said Lilly. "And we're making a ton of money out of it. So don't knock it."

This Saturday? Was there ever going to be another Saturday? Without Dolores or the raklies, there were no days. Time did not move. It hit me then that I would have to stand in that garden by that maze with our puppets, having to breathe the same air as the Tormentines, as Missus Tormentine's brother. I stood up and my whole miserable grieving body was shaking. At first no words came to me, and then something exploded. "He sends Dolores away," I shouted, "and five minutes later we're putting on a show so he and his friends can laugh at us? I won't go! I won't go."

"Well," said Lilly, "that's us told."

"We have to stay away from them," said Liza May. "Zelda's right. I'm not going either," she said. "Them people, they suck the fat and blood from our bodies to oil their tractors."

"That's a bit over the top," said Lilly, "but I have to agree with you."

"They use our muscles and bones to pick their tobacco and sew their leaves." Liza May's voice rose. She said she would not sacrifice Panni Mooi. "They'll kill her."

"Mam, remember how they sent Dolores home," I said to my mother, this time in a quieter voice. "How can we work for people like that?"

Lilly didn't say anything. She had pins between her lips.

Mam said, "This show will give us nearly twice what we've earned all season. We can't not do it."

"The Tormentines and their friends will laugh at the puppets," I said, "and meanwhile our friends are being moved like cattle from farm to farm, and Dolores is gone."

"Yes," said Mam, "I appreciate this. I understand."

I hated her beaten-down voice. The smallness of her. I was angry at everything. A knot formed in my stomach, and my mother was there for me to be angry at. Lilly got up and went inside, and a few minutes later we heard the whirring of her sewing machine. "And you understand too," I said, "that we'll be doing this show while we still carry our sadness for people we lived with and loved." I had never spoken to her like this. I was getting an edge over her and didn't care.

"You've been getting too many ideas from your aunt," said Mam. She stopped and looked at me. "And why haven't you been at work?" Was this her way of trying to distract me? I said nothing about walking out on Missus Tormentine.

Lilly saved me. "She has not been getting ideas from me," she yelled from inside. "Our shey thinks for herself. Not that I always agree with her, Rhodie."

"We already said we'd do the show," Mam said. "We won't go back on our word." I told her I was surprised she'd forgotten we were dealing with people who went back on their word easily and all the time, because words didn't matter to them. But us, our fowki, we had to keep our word with people like the Tormentines, whether we wanted to or not, because if we didn't, they could sideswipe us in the road, throw us away, get themselves other workers who were already waiting in line. It felt to me like the whole time I'd been working with Missus Tormentine, and earlier too, in the tobacco field, I'd had to second-guess what they wanted and what I needed to do to keep them off my back.

All my mother said was "I'm sorry." *Sorry? That's all? That's all you can say?* She didn't ask me again about why I wasn't working.

I told her what Missus Tormentine had said: "She told me to turn Dolores in." I didn't tell Mam about being sent like a rat through her maze, or climbing her treacherous ladder to trim the cedars, or our fancy French restaurant lunch, or that I'd done these things because Missus Tormentine had told me to. And because I adored her, and if she could do them, I could too, in striving to be like her. *To be her*. I didn't say that this desire made it possible for me to think I could play lightly with the lives of others, something I had not done before or since. I didn't tell her that Missus Tormentine was why I nearly got Mercedes drowned. Or about Missus Tormentine's brother and his friends and their so-called picnic, about holding the vacuum cleaner in front of me like a shield, about walking into that house the next day and telling her I'd quit. I was scared to tell my mother these things. She would think less of me. She might possibly hate me.

I yelled at her that she was the one who'd decided to send me to work for Missus Tormentine, even while calling her a tikni parni beng. "That was all about the money, then, too."

"How else are we supposed to climb out of this?" said Mam, looking around the room. "We need this money." I did not tell her about sitting beside Mister Tormentine in his truck, about his heat that almost swallowed me, or about the devil-man of the tobacco fields standing before our door. There were too many things I couldn't tell her. "You have to understand," she said. "We have to do this. We can't back out."

All I could say was "It's you. You don't understand."

There seemed to be nothing more to say, so Mam went back inside, and then I heard the front door slam. She must have gone through to the parking lot, where she was probably pacing back and forth. *Let her stew*, I thought.

I turned to Lilly and Morning Glory, who had just come outside. I was glad of the distraction. With Lilly's hand at the strings in her back, Morning Glory showed her new dress to us. We couldn't see where the colour of revenge started or stopped. She clacked her jaws at us, then opened her mouth in a smile. She and the dress had become one. She showed us the sharp claws of her nails. Her blood-red lips, her painted white fangs.

Liza May got up, nearly tipping the picnic table. She ran crying into the forest. "You can't see, none of you can," she shouted back at us. "You can't see what's going to happen."

Lilly laid Morning Glory across her lap and turned to me. "So that went well," she said.

"How can you be so unkind?" I almost shouted. "You can't blame her."

"No," said Lilly, "you're right."

"It's a horrible situation for all of us."

"Yes," she said. And again, "You're right. Should we go after her?" She looked deflated.

"She had to get away from us. We need to wait."

After a short while, Liza May came back. She'd mostly stopped crying and was carrying a crow in her arms. "It's got a broken leg," she said. She made a splint for the leg and fed the crow from one fingertip. "Thank you," she said to the crow.

★

In the heart of the night I woke, despairing for our family. I went to stand outside the front door. Waiting for the shadow to show itself, to morph into the gliding devil-man. The fields slept and the tobacco plants were still. I looked up at the stars. I thought of Dolores. I thought of the most giant black hole of all: Sagittarius A*, the throat of the sky devouring all matter. Maybe even swallowing the overriding grief and despair of our lives. My mother would never understand its pull. She who put her head down and bent under her work to avoid her life.

The way you talk to your mother, said Puri Dai from the darkness of her bed. *You had no right*. I'd never heard that hard, angry edge in her voice before. She told me it's true that if you take the devil's money, you're in the devil's pocket, but also that we had to earn our living however we could and that meant taking money from devils of all kinds. We exchanged the work of our bodies for their money. *You yourself have done this, so you of all people ought to know*. I was going to answer back, but she told me to go to bed. But my mother was up now too, and she came to the door and put her arms around me. She cried in deep breaking sobs like I'd never heard in all my life.

56.

Her girl has seen the deep mystery of injustice. Puri Dai has felt it too. Them using our kind for hard work or amusement or their own pleasure, tossing us something, anything, to make us stay, because if we want to eat, we need whatever they're going to throw at us. What Zelda still hasn't figured out is that the careless cruelty that was visited upon her has stayed in her body, and because it can't be borne, it leaps out, full force, at the person she loves best. She thinks her mother has never hurt like she hurts now, but if our girl looked hard enough, she'd see the hurt deep down. She'd see the bone-tired woman whose weariness never clouds her daily work. The harvesting, washing, cooking, cleaning. Serving others. Being used under that puro gorjo in her narrow bed, bearing his child in that same bed, saying to him, I won't give you this child who's bigger than my life. Crossing an ocean to begin a new life, to keep working—in orchards, diners, tobacco fields, sleeping in trailers and crumbling houses, doing it all again the next year and the year after and the year after that, the child always by her side. And here's Zelda, holding at bay the disgraces done to her mother. Seeing only a mean list of events. Not a full hard life.

Our girl isn't paying attention. She's already been visited once by the devil-man. He's made her skin crawl and ice slide up her spine. You'd think that would be enough to keep her on her toes.

Don't let him come again, Puri Dai says to Zelda. Never let him close. Never let his hand touch you, never let his breath slide across your cheek, never let him come up behind you to plant the devil's kiss at your ear. Watch out for that kiss, murri shey, it's so sweet and light you won't be able to tell if it's a whisper—or if it even happened at all.

Listen to me, girl. There's been a whole lot of justifying and ranting around here. Some things need to be said. The fog has to be burned off and the air cleared. But do not dump your own garbage on your mother. Do not blame her for your own choices.

57.

It had been almost a week since I'd stood on Missus Tormentine's landing and faced off with Leland Leatherby, but it felt, still, as if it had happened only yesterday afternoon. The four men in their crisp white linen suits, their surly pink faces, the ugliness of their bodies poised to leap at me, the contents of the picnic basket hurled across the floor. I hated how these memories aroused such feelings of violence in me.

Morning Glory sat at our kitchen table in her new dress. I felt her watching me, a half-smile on her lips, as I set out the plates. *Revenge*, her smile said. *You know you want it*. I turned my back. The words from Buddy Watmore's tattoo, *love* and *hate*, slid under my skin. *Revenge* wasn't hate, although it was close. I'd never thought about revenge. How would I hold it? Where in my body? Revenge seemed ugly to me. I'd let Morning Glory carry it for now.

After supper, Mister Tormentine pulled up in his truck and walked into our room without knocking. He stood without saying a word; even his silence was ugly. How had I ever been paralyzed inside his heat? His eyes said, *They oughta thank me they've got this place. It's better than they deserve.* I remembered that gaze from our first day in his hiring shed, him looking through us as if we weren't people but envelopes of skin filled with muscle and bone, a collection of arms and legs to carry out each task he required. It was as Liza May said: his job was to make sure our moving parts worked the fields, the sewing tables, the kiln. He'd calculated how much each hand, and its sinews and tendons, was worth. His list of tasks shaped our bodies, our posture; we stooped, bent down, and rose around his needs and demands.

My mother's eyes were still red.

"Outside." Mister Tormentine nodded at the parking lot.

I heard them talking about the arrangements for tomorrow's show. He lit a cigarette, shifted from foot to foot. He looked over her shoulder, at the roof, at the window, at the trees, anywhere but at her, as if she didn't need to be included in his sight. Her body said, *Yes, Mister Tormentine, okay, Mister Tormentine.* She came inside to get the red curtains and told him where they should be set up for our show.

"And lights," she said. "We'll need lights."

"That better be all," he said. "I don't got time running around after you." Without saying goodbye, he went over to his truck and drove off.

What Puri Dai had said stayed with me. I was swimming through shame. I went over to my mother and told her I was sorry—"I'm sorry, really, really sorry"—and it felt like a small empty thing to say. Her jaw shook and she started to cry again.

My arms went around her. We both hung on, as if we were holding each other up to keep from falling.

"It's late," she finally said. "We need to be rested for tomorrow."

I heard Puri Dai. *You're on a dark walk right now*, she said, *but it's okay, my girl, we'll walk together.* I heard her speak to the other puppets. *We have to do the show knowing full well that they'll come down on us with all they've got. They don't know that we know, so we're ahead of the game. Don't forget this. We have to show them who we are. We have to look beyond the coming days, which are only one obstacle in the larger scheme of things. This is a dark time. But our Rhodie's right. We have to do this.*

Morning Glory said, *This will be our revenge.*

I wouldn't go that far, said Puri Dai. *I'd say it's our truth. Our tatcho kovas. Puppet truth, human truth. It's the same thing.*

Panni Mooi started crying. The other puppets were silent. They must have fallen asleep, for after a long time I heard nothing. Later, in a moment of restless sleep, I overheard Panni Mooi's voice. *Yes*, she said. *Okay. I'll do it.*

★

Early the next morning, Liza May took her crow out into the forest. Lilly found them after lunch and brought them back to our room. I watched as Liza May stroked the crow's feathers, and she asked it what she should do. "I don't want to go near that man's house," she told the crow. "I don't want to see him. I don't want to breathe the air he breathes." The crow leaned into her hand. "That man will breathe his mokkadi air out," she said, "and I'll breathe it in, and his bad air will get into my lungs." The crow made a low hoarse sound. "See?" said Liza May. "Even the crow's telling me not to go."

"Liza May," said Lilly, "if the crow tells you to stay, if you yourself know you must stay, then stay."

Liza May went back out to the forest. She did not yet know that Panni Mooi had agreed to do the show with us. We ate early, because we'd be on the road in half an hour. My mother set aside a sandwich for Liza May, who'd be hungry. Then she grew still. "This is an important show," she said. "The biggest one we've done." It seemed to be the beginning of a speech: a lot at stake, everything had to be right, maybe this would finally tip us over into having enough money for the down payment on a house. Instead, she said that she would not be performing. She paused, then said: "This is not a decision I have taken lightly."

"Bowing out?" said Lilly. "After all this?"

"If I'm in the show I won't be able to keep an eye on things. We're going into the lion's mouth," said Mam, "and I have to make sure we're safe, all of us. Them people, we don't know what they can get up to."

Lilly and I looked at each other, and Lilly shook her head, but I saw that my mother was right. "No, Lilly," I said, "this is the right decision." My mother, she'd keep herself behind things, careful, watching, listening, because anything could happen. I recognized in that instant, even as she stood upright and exhausted before us, how she had always watched over us, and we needed her to do so tonight.

★

Lilly sat the puppets outside, brushed their clothes and their hair, and washed their faces. "Looking good," she said, standing back. "Are we ready?" Mr. Yesterday and Young Chavo gave thumbs-ups. Puri Dai and Morning Glory half-smiled. It was hard to see what Panni Mooi was thinking, even though last night she had agreed. And if Liza May didn't come, what was Panni Mooi to do?

We carried the puppets to the truck. I folded the sheets over their bodies and faces to shield them from the dust. Liza May came running around the side of the motel. She was out of breath. She didn't tell us what had happened to change her mind.

We drove past the late fields and long shadows across the road. Field after field after field of acid green, then other naked fields already harvested, tobacco stalks like flags here and there in the bare earth. The road was dry, and dust rose around us. The sun lowered itself to the distant trees, and then, minutes before we pulled into Tormentine's driveway, it left only a thin burning edge above the branches.

As I stepped out from our truck, what first hit me was the noise of laughter. Almost like the coyotes, they sounded. I wanted to turn around and go back to the safety of our room. I looked over at Liza May. She had already lifted Panni Mooi from her shroud and was holding her tight. We took the puppets in our arms and came around the side of the house to a flash of earrings, necklaces, bracelets, the gleam of gold hair. It was as if many Missus Tormentines had sprouted in the garden. Skin white and polished to a dull rich glow, the air drunk with perfume and smoke, women calling out "honey," and men shouting each other's last names. They exhaled their cigars into the evening air and the smoke filled the garden.

Then I began to see the faces. There was Missus Tormentine talking to her husband. My stomach rose in my throat.

She had on the river-blue dress I'd been wearing when Tormentine had walked into the bedroom. Missus Tormentine's stomach had started to show: it was soft, rounded, a gentle swell. She glanced over at me and then looked away. As if I didn't matter. As if I wouldn't be believed. *Go ahead. Look away.*

Where was Leland? She must have heard my thoughts, because she turned to Tormentine and said in a voice clearly meant for me, "My poor brother felt unwelcome here after being attacked and humiliated by a person we thought we could trust." She caught my eye with a pointed stare.

I wanted nothing more than to leave, but instead I concentrated on picking out individual voices from the commotion. I learned who the mayor was; the gavverbeng police chief, his wife, the hardware store owner, the manager of the car dealership, the bank manager, and too many others. Musselwhite was there too and made a show of turning his back on me. Mrs. Shuttleworth, the jam judge, arrived. We were glad to see her. My mother waved, and Mrs. Shuttleworth bellied over to us with her daughter and husband following. "This is the lady," she shouted to her husband, taking hold of Mam's hand. "The jam lady I told you about."

Mrs. Shuttleworth and her family calmed me down. "It's okay," I said to Liza May, "we're all right. She's our friend." I looked around at the people in the crowd. Maybe they weren't Tormentine's friends. Maybe they were his mirrors. I thought of all the gold mirrors inside that house—the need to see yourself from every angle, and in every light, to make sure you're real.

My mother fussed over the state of the puppets, smoothing their clothes and hair, adjusting the folds in the two long red curtains that had been hung near the pond. The curtains grazed the ground, almost hiding the heavy extension cord that trailed down from the house. Liza May turned to us. "I'll start," she said, looking as if she were about to step off the edge of a cliff. "I'll do it for Panni Mooi. I'll do it for the crow." She asked for the card table and the chairs Mam had requested, and which were leaning against the willow. In her plain clothes, hair pulled back, fingernails bitten, Liza May went to stand before the curtains. She waited. The talking stopped. There was a rustling as people sat. They too waited. A light flicked on and illuminated her clear bare face.

"Act One," she said. "The Great Game." She stood before her audience, and they must have been struck by how ordinary and small she was. I saw her fingers slide into the hollow of Panni Mooi's back, plucking the strings as if playing a harp. Panni Mooi lifted her head, nodded to her audience, turning first to the right and then to the left. The painted tears shimmered in rainpaths down her cheeks. I heard the quiet click of the gears, and then Liza May released Panni Mooi into the air. The audience drew a sudden single breath, and Panni Mooi hung suspended above the ground, her green hair alive as river grass, shimmering, wavelike.

"In the great game," said Liza May, her voice clear and high, "we too easily throw the lives of others into the treacherous waters of the river. Like this," and she flicked her fingers at Panni Mooi, who billowed into the pond, thrashing around in a dance of half-life and half-death, then stepping from the water with yellow scum clinging to the hem of her skirt. "In the great game," said Liza May, "we run through the maze to the point of oblivion, searching for a way out, and when we finally arrive, our clothes are ripped, our hair is pulled, we are in shreds, and our minds have been left behind to wander in them dark tunnels for eternity." Young Chavo twisted and turned, clutched make-believe branches, threw himself against invisible walls, and dragged himself, finally, moaning, to the end of an imaginary tunnel. There was a shudder of laughter at his antics. He dropped to the ground, his body in spasms till it slowed to a twitch and then stopped.

"No," whimpered a woman.

"It's not what you see in the game," Liza May went on, "but what the game sees in you." Mr. Yesterday, the handsome old devil-man, the puro beng, with his five packs of cigarettes and his cloven hooves hidden by shoes, pranced high and dipped low into the light. He sat himself down at the card table and crossed his legs, leaned back, and drew on his cigarette, blowing smoke rings out at the crowd.

"How's he doing that?" I heard somebody say. "The guy isn't even real."

Puri Dai, bent like a fish hook, braids dishevelled, gasping for breath, shuffled over to sit opposite him on the other side of the table. Mr. Yesterday was now the dealer. Leaning even further back at a dangerous tilt, he nodded and winked at the audience. He was going to take the pathetic old girl for a ride. With elaborate twists and turns of his hands, Mr. Yesterday produced a full deck of cards and began to deal. What the audience saw, and Puri Dai didn't, was the great number of extra cards he had up his sleeve. Puri Dai lost four rounds, and Mr. Yesterday was grinning away like nobody's business. He invited the audience to clap and gave them a thumbs-up when they did. Somebody called, "Wipe the floor with her."

In the fifth round, which was the last, Puri Dai held up a face card and motioned to Mr. Yesterday for another. He winked at the audience again and dealt Puri Dai her second, and last, card. Mr. Yesterday had a five, and reached for his own card, which had been laid face down. "Blackjack," somebody hollered from the back. But even with the advantage of all the cards up his sleeve, Mr. Yesterday came up with a total of thirty. Puri Dai held up her cards. Twenty-one. She gave the audience a ghost of a smirk. She straightened herself out, stood tall, holding out her winning cards for all to see. Mr. Yesterday, the puro beng, was so convulsed with rage that he jumped up, tipped over the table, and disappeared in a tower of his own smoke.

"The handsome devil was never seen again," said Liza May, withdrawing behind one of the red curtains.

There was silence from the audience. "Oh man," somebody said. "This is creeping me out." Then someone off to one side clapped, so they all clapped, and then they started yelling their heads off. Liza May was called back for two bows. She turned to us. Her face was flushed. She was smiling and crying. In the darkness she went to the shore of the pond and lay herself down, where she continued to cry, but so quietly that we barely heard her.

"Lilly," said my mother. "You go."

Lilly strode out from between the curtains and somebody yelled, "Wow!"

"Act Two," she said. "The Lord of the Fields." She drew a breath. "A poem.

"The crow's asleep, the owl is still
The sun is sinking over the hill
The wanderer wanders with heavy feet
His eyes are closing, he's falling asleep."

She took a step forward, leaning toward the audience.

"Wherever you walk, wherever you roam

A story of justice to follow you home
A song of sorrow to put you to bed
A white shroud of mourning to place o'er your head
A song to dance to, a song to weep
A flagon of tea to send you to sleep."

At this last line, Lilly gave a knowing smile. The puppets awoke from their slumber, and Morning Glory, in her revenge-coloured robes, strode out between the curtains. Lit from above, she was beautiful and terrible, with her flaming hair and scarlet lips and smouldering green eyes. Lilly reached her hand into Morning Glory's back, and Morning Glory's eyelids fluttered. "Welcome, friends," she said, "and enemies." I heard nervous laughter. She opened her luscious red mouth in a smile and bared her sharp teeth. People drew back in their chairs, and I heard a single intake of breath that rippled from one end of the garden to the other.

Panni Mooi, a solitary tobacco worker, sang to herself as she rode her imaginary bicycle back and forth between the red curtains. She was singing so joyfully and sweetly that she didn't hear Little Chavo roar up behind her, and she didn't know what was happening till he sent her flying off the bike, up into the air and down to the ground, where she lay in a tangled heap. A few people in the audience started whispering among themselves. Missus Tormentine's blue gas-jet eyes were nearly shooting flames, and a woman in the audience cried out, "No!"

As one of his dark deeds, the lord of the fields banished a wounded young woman never to be seen again. Morning Glory brewed a tea of belladonna, the deadliest of nightshades, and made a show of boiling the water and bruising the leaf, dropping it into an imaginary cup. As Liza May gave the cry of a saw-whet owl in the background, and my mother and Lilly started yipping like coyotes, Morning Glory fed the tea to the lord of the fields who, through his greed, had not only sent the young woman from his realm but was plotting to ruin the families of all tobacco workers in the fiefdom. The lord of the fields, lying in his opulent invisible bed, polished off Morning Glory's deadly tea, smacking his lips and holding out the cup for more. Mister Yesterday crawled up to the bed, licking his own lips with his long red tongue, and turned to the audience, giving a great wink and a grin.

It was acted out in a slapstick way, so nobody really had a clue what was going on. They were all laughing. Somebody drew a sharp breath when the belladonna drinker landed choking and twitching on the ground. Morning Glory, teeth flashing, held out the empty teacup for all to see. After a while the mayor called out, "Has that guy croaked yet?" and Morning Glory said, "The last breath has left his earthly body and the spirits are ushering him into the shades."

People were bent double with laughter. The hardware store owner, red-faced, tears running down his cheeks, slapped his thighs and yelled, "You're killing me here." The woman who had called out "No" was still crying. The puppets were done. Their heads lolled; their arms dropped. We carried them, limp, drunk with exhaustion, behind the red curtain.

When the laughter fell away, and there was silence again, I came out to stand before the audience. "Act Three," I said. "Invisible." Thinking of Dolores, of the raklies, of my family, of my life to this point, I sang of the deep river we all must cross. My one voice, love, spiralled down like a leaf from the air to meet my other voice, hate, dissolving in discordant notes in that same air, and my third voice, invisible, flew out in blue notes that rose and fell and rose again into the dark air. The people in the chairs followed my voice with their ears and eyes as it flew through the garden, touching each one, and then, finally, coming back home to rest in my throat. I, Zelda, was no longer invisible. I was seen. Seen as I wished to be seen.

The audience stood as one. People were shouting. A woman with frightening orange hair rushed at me with flowers that she threw into the air. A man shouted, "I'm yours." We were mobbed.

"How do you do all that stuff?" asked the mayor.

"We just set the stage," said Lilly, "and the puppets do the rest."

The mayor shook his head. "Unbelievable," he said. "Unbelievable." He turned to his wife. She was the one who had thrown the flowers. "Remarkable, aren't they, Peg," he said.

More people edged the mayor out of the way. The dentist said I had beautiful teeth, and if I ever needed work done to give him a call and he wouldn't charge me a cent. The gavverbeng police chief reached over and tried to touch my hair, and the woman beside him moved in five inches from my face. "I don't care what they say about you people," she whispered, "I think you're real talented. You should be on television."

Then the mayor cut in again to ask for what he called a "special favour." He started with a sort of apology: "I don't mean anything by it, young lady, and I'm not trying to pigeonhole you," he said, "but your people, you all tell fortunes, right?"

For the first time, with a gorjo, I felt like I could put one over on him, even though I'd never done the dukkering. "You mean, can we all predict the future? Every one of us? Like it flows in our blood?"

The mayor went kind of red. "Well, no, I didn't mean it like that."

"Howard," went his wife.

"I can try," I said, and leaned in and took his hand, frowning over the lines in his palm. I lowered my voice to a breathy whisper and made some stuff up, a drama that rambled a bit, and I couldn't figure out where it was going, so I eventually stopped.

"Unbelievable," the mayor said. "That's exactly what the wife told me last night. Isn't that right, Peg?" His eyes were nearly out of his head, and his wife nodded furiously. He backed away into the crowd, and I heard him telling a group of people that he couldn't believe what had just happened. "It knocked my socks off." He held up his hand. "Look," he said, "I'm still shaking." The people he was talking to craned their necks, trying to see me.

I found Mam and my aunties. We thanked the puppets for telling our truth. We gathered them up; they were heavy in our arms. We carried them to the truck and wrapped them in their sheets.

58.

I wanted to walk for a bit. I wanted to keep on singing. "I'll meet you at the crossroads," I said to my mother, who was talking with Mrs. Shuttleworth about jam and their dislike of commercial pectin. I headed out across the road to the tobacco field to let myself get lost in the star-crazy sky. I felt better. "Dik at the shooting stars," I sang. "Look how beautiful." The stars rained down like tears. I turned around under them and the leaves of the tobacco plants almost grazed my shoulders. I thought of Dolores. Would the night above me reach as far as her garden? If it did, would we be looking at the same stars in the deep dark sky, the kushti kauli ratti? Her hand at one end of the sky, mine at the other, the thread of stars between us. "Dolores," I called. "Are you there? It's me, Zelda. Stay away from the black hole, whatever you do." I started laughing. It felt better to laugh than to cry.

I wandered deeper into the field. The plants were higher here, and I could barely see over the tallest leaves. Soon they'd be harvested and the field would once more be stubble and earth. The stars were falling all over the place. I imagined them dropping into the field. I imagined Dolores being here with me. We'd go down the rows, leaning our heads back as far as we could, pretending to swallow the stars. "Dolores? What do your stars taste like?" And she'd answer that they tasted like corn, or willow-bark tea, or forest mushrooms, or nightshade jam. We'd have a star-swallowing contest, but we'd both win.

She had said that she would write to me. I had never gotten a letter from anyone. I could only imagine the excitement of going to the post office to pick up an envelope with my name and an address written on it. I saw Dolores sitting at a wooden table with the sheets of paper spread out in front of her. I saw the pen in her hand. I saw her thinking about what to tell me. Maybe she'd be sitting in her garden, describing the plants that grew there.

Behind me, a rustling of leaves in the path. "Dolores," I called again. I sang her name over and over.

The air brimmed with nightshade.

A shadow rose. It came between me and the stars.

If only this were Dolores, I thought. I longed for it to be Dolores.

"Hey," said the shadow. "Come here."

It was a man's voice. Was this the devil-man of the fields? My blood froze. I wanted my mother. By now she and Mrs. Shuttleworth might be waiting at the crossroads, or maybe they were still back in the driveway, talking about jam. Had I raised him up, the devil-man, by walking here through his fields, even without a full moon?

"Stop. Wait." I knew the voice. "Hey. C'mere." I knew the shape this voice gave to its words. "Come over here," said Tormentine.

My own voice came back to me, clear like my song. "Get away from me," I said. "Go away."

Tormentine moved closer. "You don't tell me what to do," he said. "These here are my fields. That place you live in, that's my place. The bed you sleep in, that's my bed."

It was as if my feet had been yanked by the current and pulled out from under me.

"I want you," I heard. "*You*. I want you." Voice hot and thick as tar. His hands parted the leaves as if swimming, tobacco stems crashing under his feet. His arms shot out at me and up from behind him came my mother with a two-by-four. She coshed him over the head and he landed out cold on his tobacco plants. We ran.

"We never did nothing," panted Mam beside me. "He was never here."

V
Knives

59.

O my girl, murri shey, I'll ride into the undertow with you, I'll hold you in my arms, and if we're pulled apart—and we will be—the currents will bring us together again, because the water, the panni, the rough raging water always comes back to itself.

The blows have entered her girl's body in ways that even Puri Dai can't fathom. Puri Dai sends out the cry of the loving grandmother.

O my girl, my Zelda, I'm here beside you.

60.

Back in our room, my mother sat on my bed. She had brought me tea. "I seen him from the road," she said. "I seen him going after you." She lifted the cup to my lips. "My own tikni shey," she said, "my little darling girl." She tipped the cup. "Drink," she said, and I drank. She stroked my face. "Beautiful like you were the morning I first seen you in the doctor's house, when he handed you to me and I held you in my arms." She told me how I had cried and cried, and then when she took me and rocked me, I had stopped my crying. Each part of me had been each part of her—our shared blood was the nourishment her body had given me. "My tikni shey," she said.

The doctor had been impatient and wanted to take me from her arms then and there. "You don't want this child," he said. "It's half mine. My wife and I will give it a good home and a good life. Better than you could ever do." Mam asked for some money to support herself over the next days, and he put it into an envelope and gave it to her, only to get rid of her.

"Let me keep her with me, just for this one last night," she told him. "Then she'll be yours, and I'll go away, and you'll never see me again."

"Fine," agreed the doctor, although she saw that he was not happy with this arrangement. In the quiet of the night, she wrapped me in a small cotton blanket, covered my head, gathered her things, and took me through the house and down the stairs, silent past the library, where he was still awake and reading. She opened the front door and left.

"And here we are," she said. "Nothing will put itself between us." She got into the bed beside me and held me as if I were still that little birthling. She stroked my eyelids shut, and I barely noticed when, after a time, she got up and went into her own bed.

★

In the morning, since it was Sunday, we slept late, then laid the puppets out to air under the grandmother oak. We spent the day in the backyard, talking little, dozing. Each time I closed my eyes, I saw Tormentine's shadow, like the devil-man of the tobacco fields, hanging over me. After it got dark, I went to bed. "Don't forget the puppets," I called from my window. Lilly and Liza May, who were still sitting outside, gathered them in their arms and brought them in.

The night closed itself around me, and I was visited by a dream of heavy brown moths, their long tongues entering the luminous night-scented tobacco flowers. The walls of my dream shone. Then a sudden disturbance—was I dreaming an earthquake? I jolted awake to shaking walls and a grinding roar, as if the building were being hit repeatedly by a train.

When I ran to the front window, I saw a car crashing against the front of the motel, pulling out and crashing again. Outside, somebody was dumping something onto the asphalt. I heard swearing. My mother came running and turned on the outdoor light.

It was Missus Tormentine. She was throwing the bodies of dead swans at our window.

"You," she screamed. "You think you won! You did, bitch! You won." There was swan blood on her face and hands and up her arms, smeared across the front of her nightgown, and on our window where the bodies of the swans had struck. "My swans," she moaned. "My beautiful swans. See what the coyotes did to them!" She looked up at us and her eye makeup was streaming down her face. "This is you!" she screamed at me. "This is your work! You sent them." Her empty hands were red with the swans' blood.

"I lost my baby," she howled. "My baby! You poisoned me and my baby with that nightshade shit you forced me to eat! Yes! Forced! And you went and cursed my brother, and he'll never be the same again!" She screamed about me being after her husband and plotting for him to give me a job so I could be near him, and that was why I'd gone to work for her. "Everybody knows," she said. She screamed that I had used magic to make him want me, and for him to follow me into the tobacco field. "He never had a chance, did he?" Because of me, the coyotes had killed her swans, and I'd put a curse on her and her baby to make it end up a clotted red puddle in the toilet. "You will never be blond like me!" she screamed. "You will never be white or have a husband or a house or gold rings. You will have nothing!" She started to sob. She pulled her arms around herself, rocking back and forth. My mother sat her down, and Missus Tormentine said, "Don't touch me, don't touch me," even as she let herself be folded into Mam's arms.

★

We didn't sleep after she left. I heard Liza May whimpering to Panni Mooi, the words piling up and spilling into the air.

"Get me some water," Mam said, stepping out of her nightclothes, which were smeared with blood. I went inside for a pitcher and poured water over her hands and arms. "More," she said, "I'm not clean yet." I went in again for water.

"Get out!" said Liza May, who stood shaking in the middle of the room. "Panni Mooi says get out."

"I have to get my Mam's things," I said. I found a clean T-shirt and a skirt.

"That lady's blood breath is all over you! The swan death is all over you," said Liza May. "Get out!"

"It's Liza May," I said to Lilly and my mother when I went back outside. "She's coming apart."

"No wonder," said Lilly.

Mam was shivering, naked, standing helpless in the parking lot.

"Rhodie," Lilly said, "put your clothes on."

"Yes, yes," said Mam, and she went into our room. She returned wearing an inside-out T-shirt.

Everything slowed down. We couldn't move; we couldn't stop looking at the bodies of the swans heaped under the window.

"Leave them there," Lilly said. "Leave them for the police to see what she did, because them gavvers will surely be here in the morning. Leave them for Tormentine. Let him clean up this mess."

My mother disagreed. "They'll say we done it. We'll be blamed. We have to think of Liza May, who is being most affected by all this." She went inside and I heard the water running. She brought out a pail and soap and a rag, dipped the rag into the water, and sent it from one side of the window to the other, leaving a smear that ran down the glass like pink rain. She threw the water, dark now, into the middle of the parking lot and brought me the pail. It took four pails of water to clean the window. "We're going to bury the swans," she said. She looked over to the east. "The sun will be coming up soon." She went back inside and changed her clothes again.

We carried the swans into the forest. We had only a small shovel to lift them one at a time, and when we untangled the bodies, we saw that there were five of them, and two were cygnets. The coyotes must have eaten the rest.

It felt as if we spent most of the night digging the grave. We placed the bodies of the swans inside and were about to cover them with earth when Lilly stopped and held up her hand. "Wait," she said. "Listen." After a minute we heard a muffled wittering sound, a slight movement, and we saw that one of the cygnets was alive. Lilly freed it and called out to Liza May. "Here's a chiriklo for you," she called. "It needs you." After a long while, Liza May appeared. She took the cygnet, cradled it in her hands, fussed over it, murmuring, cleaning it, and fed water into its open beak, drop by drop.

My mother and Lilly and I took turns gently covering the swans with earth. "All of us must feed our young," said Mam. "As the swans do, so do the coyotes. It's sad that everything has come to this."

Lilly bent and laid her hand on the grave. "May the earth rest light on their bodies," she said.

"May the poor raklie be healed," said Mam. Then, "Dik, see, the sun's rising," and we looked up at the brightening sky. We went inside. Mam made breakfast, but the eggs congealed on the platter and the toast turned dry. The tea cooled in the pot. We couldn't eat. "We need to get ourselves ready," she said. "We're not going to be here much longer."

Later, the police paid us a visit. There were two of them, looming gavvers in cardboard-stiff uniforms. Liza May hid behind the curtain when she saw them coming, and my mother invited them to sit down. They refused, shifting from side to side in their heavy boots. One of the gavvers brought out a notebook and pencil. He looked around at us. "Where were you folks last night?"

His pencil waited nervously in the air.

"Before or after we got back from our puppet show at Mister Tormentine's?" said Mam.

"Ummm," said the gavver, rattling the pages of his notebook.

"After the puppet show we came back and we were here the whole night," said Mam. "Me, my sisters, and our Zelda here. And, of course, the puppets." Mam's voice was high. "Why? Is something wrong?"

The gavver said that Tormentine had ended up in the emergency room with a concussion and didn't remember a thing. "They said at the hospital he was hit."

"What's that got to do with us?"

"They said it was your daughter here who hit him."

"They?" said Lilly. "Who's they?"

The gavver licked his thumb and started going back and forth through the pages. "Ummm," he said.

"Exactly," said Mam. "And who was the witness? He was

not hit by our Zelda here," she said. "Look at the size of her. And you tell me how you can hit somebody who isn't even there." She looked the gavver in the eye. "Our Zelda started back through the field across from their house and never once saw Mister Tormentine. Isn't that so, Zelda?"

The gavver frowned down at my mother, looked at her rough little hands folded in her lap. He turned to me with his eyebrows raised.

"I never saw him," I said.

"Tell me how our girl could possibly knock that guy out," said Lilly. "He's twice her size."

The gavver put away his pencil and notebook. "Don't leave the area," he said, "except for shopping and work." He looked like he'd been told to say that. It was routine.

"We're not at fault here," said Mam. "Just so's we're clear about that."

The gavver switched lanes. "What about the damage to the wall out there?" he said.

"You seriously think we did that?" said Lilly. "You think we'd crash our own truck into the wall? Go check out the truck over there in the parking lot and tell me if you see any damage."

"Well," said the gavver, "we need to get to the bottom of this."

"Yes," said Mam. "You ask Missus Tormentine about that."

We watched them walk out to the police car. Their backs weren't as straight as when they'd first come in. "Gavver-beng," Lilly said.

⋆

We started sorting out what was ours and what was the room's. It took us hardly any time at all. Lilly fried up eggs and tomatoes and bread, and we stopped to finally eat. It was for nourishment and nothing else, because we still weren't hungry. Liza May sat in front of her plate and pushed around her tomatoes.

"Eat," said Mam.

"I can't," said Liza May.

Mam put down her own fork and fed Liza May like a child.

Later, around dark, we heard trucks out on the road. They sounded different than usual, as if there was a kind of method in the way they were paced. The trucks slowed. "Somebody's coming," said Mam. She went to the window. Three trucks were turning into the parking lot with their high beams on, and the light flooded our room. The engines went off; the headlights went out.

"Shut the curtains," said Lilly.

"Shh," said Liza May. She clung to my mother, trying to hide behind her.

It was silent and black and nothing moved. "I can't see anything," said Mam.

"They're coming for us," Liza May whispered. I knew we were all thinking the same thing.

A truck door opened and shut, and footsteps approached across the parking lot. "Hello?" called a woman's voice. "Hello? We need to talk."

"Don't answer," said Liza May. "Don't open the door."

"I'm not a coward," said Mam. "I'm going out."

"I'm going out too," said Lilly. She opened the door and switched on the outside lights. It was the mayor's wife standing there. Her hair shot up from her head like an orange flame. She and my mother stood looking at each other.

The mayor's wife looked unhappy. "You seem very nice and all," she said.

"We are," said Lilly, looking out at the three trucks. "Is that what you and your friends came to tell us?"

"The thing is," the mayor's wife went on, her mouth as dry as sand, "you scare us. The magic and all that. Those puppets. Bringing all that to our doorstep." She swallowed loudly and cleared her throat as if restarting a speech. "Jack Tormentine is our friend. We've known each other all our lives." She was shaking. "He's well thought of in our community." She looked back at the trucks as if for reassurance, and when none came, she turned again to Mam and Lilly. "That girl," she said, pointing at me, "I see her standing right there beside you, that girl tried to set him up for something he didn't do." Again, she glanced back at the trucks. "Your girl there, she sent him to the hospital. He's been nothing but kind to you people. He didn't do anything."

"What didn't he do?" asked Mam.

The mayor's wife seemed to struggle with this. After a while she spoke again. "We don't want any trouble," she said. Her jaw shook. Her hands were hanging on to each other for dear life. "But the thing is. You don't belong here."

Lilly folded her arms. "Who's your posse out there?" she said.

"Oh, they're just neighbours," stammered the mayor's wife. "We don't want trouble."

"Tell them to step out," said Lilly. "If they're not too scared."

"Please, no," went Liza May.

The mayor's wife went back to the truck. We couldn't hear what she was saying. There was another silence that stretched out across the parking lot. The doors finally opened and nine men got out. I saw Musselwhite and the mayor and others who'd been at Tormentine's party. They looked nervous, jutting out their jaws and chests. Some were holding long tobacco knives. They walked together in step, as if they'd been practising. "What is this?" said Lilly. "The tin-pot militia?"

"Now look here," said the mayor, and his wife said, "Howard." She turned to us. "Ladies. We just think it would be better if you left. Moved somewhere else."

"Is that an invitation?" said Lilly. "Can we move in with you?"

"Don't you get smart with us," said the mayor.

"Howard," said his wife.

"I mean," Lilly went on, "your place has gotta be a whole lot nicer than this dump."

"Lilly. Stop it," Mam hissed.

Another truck pulled into the parking lot. Then another. "Get inside and lock the doors," said Lilly.

"There are no locks, remember," said Mam. "He made sure of that." Liza May was sobbing.

Mrs. Shuttleworth emerged from the newly arrived truck with her husband and her daughter. Three women from the egg sorting barn climbed down from the second: I saw Rita Slack, Diane DeVrees, and Coral Peplinskie. In the third truck was the butcher, Willard Crowshank, brandishing a cleaver.

"I thought they were our friends," said Liza May.

Mrs. Shuttleworth came across the parking lot and shouldered up to the men and shouted like the Tillsonburg wrestling champion. She hollered at them to get back in their goddamn trucks and take their sad arses home. "You're pathetic," she said. She hurled a list of names: doughheads, cowards, thugs. Then she turned to the mayor, ordering him to apologize to us. Even at her short height, she managed to loom over him.

I saw the mayor's wife elbow him in the ribs. "Howard," she said. "Say something."

Mrs. Shuttleworth waved over at us. "These here ladies are worth a thousand of youse," she said. The egg sorters brought out Tormentine's eggs and started pelting them at the men, driving them back into their trucks, their faces and bodies and vehicles covered with eggs. The whites slid thickly to the ground and the yolks puddled.

Each truck shuddered out of the parking lot and onto the road. "You haven't heard the last of this," the mayor yelled. I watched his wife bury her head in her hands in the passenger seat.

The egg sorters came inside and made us scrambled eggs from the leftovers in the boxes. They served them with Rita Slack's rye bread. Willard Crowshank sliced a summer sausage, and Mrs. Shuttleworth flourished a jar of her cucumber relish. She bustled, setting out plates and cups and making tea.

"How did you know them people were coming?" said Mam.

"I got big ears," said Mrs. Shuttleworth.

They started gossiping.

"Did you hear about what happened to the Tormentine lady's brother?" said Rita Slack. "He can't get it up no more." She gave a loud laugh.

"Just as well," said Coral Peplinskie. "You know he's been doing it with her."

"Oh, come on," said Mrs. Shuttleworth.

"It's true," said Rita, "on both counts. My cousin Doreen's the receptionist at Doctor Brink's and he left the door open and she heard everything. Totally dead you know where. It just happened a week or so ago."

That would have been around the time of Leland Leatherby's so-called picnic. Had I scared him that badly with the vacuum cleaner? I said nothing.

They started to laugh, and I joined in—but why were we laughing? Was it right to rejoice in the calamity of another, even a monster like Leland Leatherby? But we couldn't stop. It got louder, more raucous, until the laughter turned into tears, and then we were shaking and crying into our food. "Eat," said Mrs. Shuttleworth. We ate in silence, and when we were finished, they cleared the table and washed the dishes for us.

Mr. Crowshank brandished his meat cleaver. He offered to sit on a chair outside the door all night, and he looked like he really wanted to stay.

My mother called him brave but said no, that we needed to get on with things.

After they left, Liza May went out back and vomited. When she returned, her face was clammy and white.

"Come, come, my tikni chirikli," said Mam. She rocked Liza May till she was calmer. "That's right," said Mam. She led Liza May out to the shed. "Dik, look," she said, opening the door, "here are your birds, ready to sleep. Your birds who need you to keep them safe."

Outside in the dark, we took a moment to hold each other as if we were in a sinking boat. We held the puppets too, because we knew they also felt the terror, even though they were safe under the grandmother oak.

We packed the rest of our belongings. It took a long time because our hands felt half-frozen. Our eyes couldn't see our own things in front of us; we saw only the men and their trucks.

"Can we please get out of here tonight?" begged Liza May.

"No," said Mam, "in the morning. Mister Tormentine needs to pay us." We argued with her. We said she should listen to Liza May. We said if this wasn't an emergency, what was? We told her the money didn't matter. "No," said Mam. "I'm getting what's owed us." We finished packing and didn't fall into our beds till late. "Oh," Mam said much later, half asleep. "We forgot the puppets outside."

61.

At first, I didn't understand why the truck visit took me back to my childhood. I would have been six; I remembered it being the end of March, during a late snowstorm. Mister Halliday and his oil truck came to the house we were renting. It was to be the last visit of the season. His hose spiralled through the falling snow into our oil tank. We watched him in the drifts outside our house, dancing back and forth to keep warm. He had nostrils like two burnt squash seeds. They exhaled a white mist. I didn't like seeing something so private coming out of his body. Mam, who smoked at that time, blew her cigarette smoke out the kitchen window. Her hair fell down her back in a coiled braid.

When the tank was full, Mister Halliday knocked at the door, a kind of secret or joking knock, followed by two sly taps like punctuation marks. I saw how his nostrils flared when Mam opened the door to pay him. His nostrils were like dark tunnels; I could picture anything crawling in or out. Then he lifted a corner of his mouth, and it was like he was speaking to her privately, without words. I remember how he leaned into her. His hand went out toward her body, but when he saw me, he pulled back. He said something under his breath. I remembered hearing the word *dirty*. I remembered my mother folding back into the shadows while he stood there shaking his head. His look said more than words, although I couldn't read the expression.

At the end of April, we went to Mister Halliday's gas station to fill up our car. Missus Halliday came out to pump our gas, and my mother stepped out of the car to say hello. Missus Halliday's mouth opened in a smile and inside was an astronomy lesson—dark, endless, with teeth like haphazard stars.

When she was finished filling the gas tank, she pulled out the nozzle. She didn't turn it off and the gasoline ran down my mother's skirt and legs. "Sorry," she said, still smiling. It was Mam's summer skirt, frayed at the hem. Missus Halliday raised the nozzle and I saw the cool gas spray Mam's blouse, which had plastic buttons that were the same blue as the overheated sky. Missus Halliday looked at Mam's blouse. Mam put her hand up to the buttons. I saw that two were open.

I looked up. Mister Halliday was standing at the upstairs window. He tilted back his head and opened his mouth. He made a slow zero with his mouth and kept looking as Mam tried to do up the buttons on her blouse with gasoline all over her fingers.

The zero of Mister Halliday's mouth grew. Mam paid for the gas. She drove home with the gasoline evaporating all over her legs and her blouse. I watched her jaw shake as she tried not to cry.

Lying in bed, I saw the overlay of these events, one on the other, quite clearly. It was the unexpected quiet assault, first at the hands of the Hallidays, and then the Tormentines, and now the locals and their trucks. It made me wonder how many more such violations, quieter, more vicious, I hadn't registered, or that I'd simply buried. I heard the wittering of the cygnet in the shed, where Liza May had settled it with the crow. I heard Liza May whimpering in her sleep.

62.

Puri Dai stirs to the sound of footsteps. Sneaky, they are. They're coming around the side of the building, slow and careful, and she isn't fully awake. Coyotes, she thinks. They must smell Liza May's crow, or the cygnet. She falls back asleep.

Then sits up. The feet are trampling the night-blooming tobacco, and it's the perfume of crushed flowers that warns her.

Sisters, brothers, wake up, she says. The puppets, half asleep, stretch their arms and legs.

What's going on? says Mr. Yesterday.

I don't know.

They sit themselves up slowly.

Where's all our fowki? asks Panni Mooi.

Inside, says Puri Dai. We have to get into the forest, she says.

No, we have to go to our fowki, says Panni Mooi.

The forest is closer, Puri Dai says.

She hears a voice. "I think I see something," says the voice. It belongs to a man.

"Ssshhh," says another voice, also a man's.

There's a cracking of twigs, then silence. Nothing moves. The puppets retreat silently into the trees. Morning Glory climbs a leafy maple. Puri Dai takes Panni Mooi back between the low hills of the dump.

I want Liza May, says Panni Mooi. I want to go back.

You stay, says Puri Dai. You're staying with me. Panni Mooi shakes her head and whimpers.

With his two hands, Mr. Yesterday makes a cradle so that Young Chavo can step up to the first branches of the maple.

I'm scared, says Panni Mooi, and she releases Puri Dai's hands from around her waist. I'm going back. I have to find Liza May.

No, says Puri Dai, it's too far. You have to stay here.

Young Chavo steps into Mr. Yesterday's hands. He climbs. Panni Mooi reaches the tree and seems immobilized, crouched at Mr. Yesterday's side. There are no more footsteps. The cautious rustling of mice and voles returns. The saw-whet owl makes its trilling call deep in the forest.

Whatever it was, says Morning Glory, it's gone.

No, says Puri Dai. It's waiting. Once again, she tries to coax Panni Mooi back to the low hills of the dump. Do I have to come over there and get you? she threatens.

I want Liza May, says Panni Mooi.

What's your problem? Morning Glory asks Panni Mooi. She sounds impatient.

Panni Mooi, says Mr. Yesterday, also impatient. Get up into the tree.

Young Chavo has reached Morning Glory, who is already among the highest branches. She calls to Puri Dai and Panni Mooi to join her. Get up here, she says.

They settle and wait, Panni Mooi still shivering at the base of the tree, Mr. Yesterday still waiting for her foot to step into his hands.

Puri Dai begins to move through the low hills of the dump, intending to bring Panni Mooi back by force. She pauses at a rip in the air.

Then it happens. Seven men move through the trees, over the grasses and ferns. In their hands they carry tobacco knives. Puri Dai sees Musselwhite. She sees Leland Leatherby, behind him the owner of the grocery franchise, the owner of the car dealership, the lawyer, the mayor, the deputy mayor, but she has never seen the tallest, coming now around the corner of the building, the man with the clouded face, cigarette in one hand, tobacco knife in the other, the man whose shoes are too tight, slit open at the sides. Puri Dai feels a shiver down her wooden spine.

The crow wakes, ruffling its feathers, and flies through the shed's broken window at the men, pounding them with its wings. The men wave their arms to ward it off, but it keeps coming. Leland Leatherby falls to the ground, covering his head with his hands as the crow beats and pecks and tears, and he crawls whimpering back the way he came. The crow follows him.

The others carry on. They work quickly, these humans do. They work without sound. They're over at Panni Mooi, lifting her by her neck, and Panni Mooi's little blue mouth opens in a thin dry scream that freezes the forest. Liza May, goes the scream. Why does Liza May not hear? The scream stops Puri Dai in her tracks. She looks at her feet. Will you move? Will you move? she tells them. I have to get to her, I have to get to Panni Mooi, but her feet refuse to listen, rigid and frozen by the dump's low hills.

Musselwhite's hand clamps over Panni Mooi's mouth. The knives rise and fall. Through the plunging arms of the men, Puri Dai sees the frantic reach of Panni Mooi's fingers. Musselwhite swears. "The little bitch bit me," he says. Her fingers move more weakly, like river grasses pushed in the current, and then they stop. After seconds, she lies shredded on the ground. The men crush her under their boots, and Puri Dai hears the cracking of wood. The painted wood who is Panni Mooi.

Go to her, go to her! Puri Dai tells her frozen legs.

The men stop. "Did you hear that?" says one.

"Yeah."

"Quick," says Musselwhite, "before those bitches in there wake up."

Then they're swarming Mr. Yesterday, ripping the mechanisms and gears and strings from his body like innards from a chicken. Even in pieces, Mr. Yesterday strikes back. The knives rise and fall, the men heave their breath.

"There's three more," says Musselwhite, panting.

Puri Dai is stuck in a trance. Before her wooden eyes the men seem to have shed their skins, and she sees the bitterness of their childhood selves, lonely, discarded, crushed, knocked around by parents or other kids, which now drives the shame and rage from their bodies with each lift and plunge of their arms.

From her perch, Morning Glory comes alive.

"Another one up there," says the owner of the car dealership. "It's on that branch, can you see it?"

The tallest reaches up and takes a swipe at Morning Glory with his tobacco knife, but she surprises him, dropping like a bobcat onto his shoulder, drilling her fingers into his eyes, sinking her fanged teeth through the skin of his neck. Her blood-red smile never leaves her lips.

Puri Dai again speaks to her frozen legs. Run out there to my beauties, she begs, I have to save my beauties—and in that instant, her legs give a jolt, taking her over the hillocks of the dump. Her white hair comes loose, a web that catches Musselwhite. He trips and flails in the tangle. The tobacco knife slips from his hand. Up close, his eyes roll back, his mouth is a hole. She wants to feel pity—smells his terror, sees his arms shield his head. His hands grab at the mist of her hair. She stoops for the tobacco knife and flies at the other men. They've seen her coming and are now stampeding over each other trying to get away. She hears their boots scuffling in the dirt. A hand trampled, the crunch of bone. She swings the knife and it pierces the back of the tallest man, the devil-man himself. He doesn't bleed. From his open back spews a dark mist.

The murderers leave. They crawl as one, panting and pawing through the dirt. She doesn't hear their truck start or leave. They must have parked somewhere up at the road so as not to draw attention to their arrival.

The pieces of Panni Mooi and Mr. Yesterday lie scattered on the ground.

I did this, says Puri Dai. Me, the grandmother, the protector. I did not protect them. If only I'd made them all come with me into the forest, if only I hadn't frozen, if only, if only.

What she has done cannot be undone. It is unforgiveable. She should have forced them to hide.

Throw me into the fire, she says. I'm no longer fit to walk among my beauties.

Puri Dai has seen many things. She knows what was done to the old ones. To their fowki. The violence of these deaths, carried out so quickly and quietly, blooms inside her. In her limbs, the hollow of her body, in the levers and gears and strings of her core.

She stands over Panni Mooi and Mr. Yesterday. She says a prayer. May the earth lie light on their bodies. On the bodies of all who have gone before. May their memories be blessed by the moon and the sun and the air. Remember the plants and waters and all beings. Remember the moths. They always come toward the light, even through the darkest veil.

63.

I thought I heard a sound in the night. A small thin scream. A mouse, maybe, caught by an owl. I thought I heard Puri Dai—I thought I heard her calling. But I'd been struck down by a dark sleep, and though I heard *save them, save them,* I imagined it was part of a dream in which we were being saved by Mrs. Shuttleworth and the egg sorters. I didn't have any reason to connect those words to the puppets.

We went outside in the morning to collect them, and the first thing we saw was Mr. Yesterday at the bottom of the tree, his innards and mechanisms torn out, arms and legs and head battered and thrown across the ground. We couldn't recognize what was left of Panni Mooi. All that remained were her tears. Morning Glory's arm was slashed, as was her forehead. Young Chavo and Puri Dai were unhurt. Liza May, shaved down to a ghost, poured Panni Mooi's tears into a cup.

We gathered the remains, folding their sheets around them. We carried them out to the back of the truck and laid them down, then sat in the backyard, unable to speak. Everything had lost its meaning. The green forest before our eyes belonged to another world. Not to this one—this world was a fog with sudden edges. One foot over the brink and you fall off.

"For heaven's sake, Rhodie, can we not just get out of here?" said Lilly. "Forget that parno beng and his money."

My mother backed down. She looked like she was going to cry again. She said that she was deeply sorry. That she'd brought this upon us.

As we were carrying the last of our things out of the room, Tormentine drove up. We looked to see if he was alone or if he might have a convoy behind him. He got down from his pickup and shouted from the middle of the parking lot that we had wrecked his community. He shouted that we were finished. That we were lucky to get out of here alive. He came closer, red-faced and shaking. His voice rose and he sounded like the coyotes. I couldn't make out all his words; it was as if he were shouting at us through a fog. Would it ever disperse? Was the fog inside me?

My mother walked over to Tormentine. Her shoulders squared against him. She told him to pay what he owed us. I heard her say, "Now. Pay us now." A new fog of words formed around me. Through it I heard "not a goddamned cent from me," and Lilly's voice saying "employment standards branch." They counted out loud what he owed. Lilly took a step forward; my mother took a step forward. Tormentine swore. He backed up, stumbled over the flowers growing out of the cracks in the parking lot's pavement. He crammed his hand into his pocket and a fistful of bills flew into the air. I watched them flutter to the ground. Mam bent to pick them up, counted them and rose, waiting. I heard "not enough" in her quiet voice. Tormentine seethed and pulled out more bills, this time slamming them on the hood of his truck. Mam counted again. She raised her eyebrows at his raging. I heard again "not enough," and he swore at her and yanked out more bills and slammed those onto the truck as well.

My mother counted all the money twice, wetting her finger between each bill. She counted a third time, even more slowly. A roiling sound came from Tormentine's throat. From my mother I heard "compensation for our puppets" and "what your people did." He boiled over. Through the fog, his feet went up and down on the asphalt, and his eyes whirled. His mouth made a giant dark hole, and sound shot out. We watched. This time the money came from his wallet. It was fat with bills. Mam counted again.

She said "five dollars too much" and tucked the extra bill into his shirt pocket. I saw a diplomat's smile on her face. Tormentine unleashed a torrent of new words. I heard "don't you touch me with your dirty little fingers," I heard that we were stealing the shirt off his back because that's what our kind do. I heard "typical." I heard "you people. Filthy, conniving." He said those words, the words gorjos use to diminish us, to try to make us feel like dirt in the road or garbage in the ditch, "Gypsies, you goddamn dirty Gypsies," but in that moment we looked at each other and knew, even after all that had happened, that we'd never felt more clear or whole, and for a moment, the fog began to thin.

"That little bitch over there," he yelled, pointing at me. "She thinks it's funny." I watched his spit cascade into the air. "Look at her! She's the one who started all this." He said because of me Missus Tormentine had run off to Hamilton to live with her goddamn brother. He said we tried to kill her with that nightshade plant I told her was jam but it was really poison, and how we'd put a curse on his unborn child. He said we'd covered up for that girl he had to return, that Mexican.

"Guatemalan," said my mother.

"Dolores," Lilly added. She said loudly and more clearly, "*Dolores*. The Guatemalan tobacco worker."

Strangely, that stopped him for a second. "Well," he said. "Whatever. Who gives a shit." He returned to his rant, going on about us stealing tobacco leaves from the drying sheds, saying Musselwhite would back him up.

Lilly just laughed. "We never chorred nothing off of you," she said, "except maybe your manly pride." Then she added, "So-called."

"Even his truck looks angry," Mam said as he drove off.

"Dik at them balls hanging off his trailer hitch," said Lilly, and we all started to laugh. We laughed till our bodies bent over and our stomachs hurt and tears poured from our eyes, and even then, even with the flaying of Panni Mooi and Mr. Yesterday new and raw in our blood, we couldn't stop.

VI

They always come toward the light even through the darkest veil

64.

In the close nest of Annie's house, Liza May's voice drifted downstairs. "The fields under his cloven hoof, the tobacco fields, they found her. They found her," she breathed. "And oh, what they did to her."

We ran up into the room.

"Liza May," we said. "We're here."

"They're coming, the devil-men are coming through the dark, and I can't run fast enough." Her voice like a bird startled in the night.

"Liza May, Liza May."

"I can't run fast enough," she said. "I can't with their knives. With their knives."

"It's all right, Liza May."

"As if they were cutting me," she said. "The men came to look for me, and they came at me."

We sat beside her, stroked her hair. At first, she shook, and her eyes looked down a tunnel we couldn't see. I took her wrist, so brittle and easy to snap, I thought. The bones of her spine curled like a fallen rope. Her hair a nest.

Lilly and I each took an elbow and helped Liza May stand. She put one foot forward as if gauging the ice at the edge of a pond and then brought the other foot to meet the first, sliding herself forward in a kind of shuffle. Her eyes stayed on the floor. All we heard was the effort of her breathing and the drag of her feet on the floorboards. Moving seemed to take a great effort. "They're coming," she whispered again. "See—the tobacco fields. The devil-man gliding on his cloven hoof. He's bringing the men; them other men." Her voice was thin as dry earth, and her tongue rasped over her lips to wet them.

"Nobody's coming, Liza May," we said. "It's just us here." We spoke our names aloud. She whispered them back to us as if they were words in a new language. "You're not alone," we said.

"Alone?" she went. "Is Panni Mooi alone?" She fell into frantic whispering. "Panni Mooi wanted me. I see the men and what they did to her." Liza May lifted her head to look at me. Her eyes were dark holes. "They're the night," she said, "and Panni Mooi wanted me, and she was so afraid, she wouldn't hide. She came to get me." Liza May lifted her arm and pointed. "See," she said, "out there. The devil-man, he glides, and Panni Mooi wanted me, and here are the night and Panni Mooi. Now I see him with the men, I see what they did to her." She turned from me to Lilly. Her voice got louder and faster. "The devil-man, he's in the night, and Panni Mooi wanted me and she was so afraid that she wouldn't hide but wanted to come for me."

All I could say was "We're here."

"Here? You're here?"

"Yes."

"You're here," she said. "You're here."

"We're here, little chirikli," said Lilly. "Our little bird."

When we reached the top of the stairs, Liza May stopped. "Too far," she said, "too far down there." She shuffled herself around and we walked her back to bed.

Annie called from downstairs. "Is it okay to come up now?"

"Liza May," said Lilly, "can Annie come up?"

"Yes." Liza May looked as if she didn't know what she was agreeing to. Annie came into the room with a cup of tea and a child's book of bird pictures.

"Look, Liza May. Here's Annie."

Liza May peered at Annie. "Annie," she said. "Here's Annie."

Lilly held the cup to her lips. "Drink, Liza May." Liza May drank, loudly slurping the tea.

We turned the pages of the book. "Dik, Liza May. Birds. What's this?"

"Swallow," she said. "Owl."

We turned the pages.

"Heron, swift, house finch," she said, and stopped.

We laid her down on the sheet and she turned to face the wall as we stroked the back of her head and her shoulders. "Crow," she said. "Where is the crow?"

"Crow's downstairs."

"Leg," she said. "His leg is broken."

"His leg's getting better," said Lilly.

"And the cygnet?"

"Yes, the cygnet is fine."

Even after Liza May's breathing slowed and she slept, we kept watch. After a while, she sat up and called, "Panni Mooi," and lay back down again.

★

We couldn't get away from Tormentine's death-motel soon enough. They put Liza May in the back with me, and she held the shreds of Panni Mooi tight against her body as we drove. "Are they following? Are they following?" she asked, craning her neck to see the road as it spun its dust behind us.

"Nobody's following," I said. She kept asking the same question and I kept giving the same answer.

Annie was waiting in front of the bookstore. Safe. We were safe. She led us upstairs. Oh, the cleanliness and brightness of the rooms. Sunlight lay across our beds, real beds with sheets from Annie's cedar chest—the sheets smelled like the cedars that grew behind her bookstore.

We took turns sleeping in the bed across from Liza May, because she woke often in the night, calling out for Panni Mooi. For two weeks we were occupied with her care: feeding her, bathing her, showing her the bird book. Nothing else entered our world during that time. Eventually, her torrents of words slowed, and a day came when she began to return slowly to us. Soon she was getting up by herself to walk to the top of the stairs. One day she said, "I can do it now," and she went downstairs into the bookstore. We felt a weight had been lifted from our shoulders.

65.

My beautiful friend Zelda: Greetings from your dear friend Dolores. I hope this letter reaches you and finds you well! I write from our garden, where we have been harvesting our corn and potatoes. I tell my family about our suppers with you and your mother and aunties, cooking and eating together and laughing almost always. I tell them about the puppets and the joy they brought us. At night we sit outside looking at the sky and talk about my brother, knowing he is up there with his beloved stars. At those times, I also think of you. The situation here is not good. There were massacres in two nearby villages. The army sends its death squads to do this. I wish I had better news to tell you. But in our house, we try to be as happy as we can. My mother likes to sing and tell stories, which keeps our spirits up. Our hens have hatched thirteen chicks, and our neighbour's cat is about to have kittens, so there is much excitement about these new lives.

When Annie first put the envelope in my hands, I rushed upstairs to share the news with Liza May but realized I couldn't read the letter. Liza May was asleep on her side of the room and woke long enough to say, "Stop talking," which I took as a good sign.

Annie, whose Spanish was good—though she still needed a little help from the dictionary—translated each word as I sat by her side in her downstairs office.

Dolores's letter stayed with me. I wanted to reply, but there was no return address on the envelope. Maybe it wasn't safe for them to receive letters. I thought about their terror being so much greater than ours, but I also saw how Liza May suffered in a way I could have never imagined. I remembered Lilly telling me, after one of Liza May's nightmares, how grief and horror are passed down through our bodies, from grandmother to mother to daughter, and so on, so that even though we think we can't remember the past, our bodies don't forget. She told me that their past was our present, woven into our cells and tissues, and they grew into each other and couldn't be separated.

In a way, it was fortunate that I didn't have an address for Dolores. I didn't want to tell her what had happened after she'd been sent back, especially about the puppets, and how we'd fled, shaking and crying, to Annie and the safety of her bookstore. I didn't want to tell her about our friends being taken to another farm. I desperately wished for Dolores and her family to appear on Annie's doorstep one day. I went to sleep that night telling myself a story in which they stood with their suitcases on the sidewalk, and we opened the door in the morning to see them waiting there.

During those first weeks with Annie, we were able to begin the work of sifting the dark events from our lives. Liza May, though, she still couldn't do it, even though she improved each day. What was left of Panni Mooi lay in a box under her bed. My mother had tried to coax Liza May to put her elsewhere, saying that Panni Mooi's remains were too close and her spirit was drifting up into the bed, which was unhealthy for Liza May. Liza May went into another rant, and Mam withdrew. After this, Liza May started sliding again, and she got on my nerves with the endless tossing and turning at night. She was her own ghost.

In the meantime, we fed the crow. Lilly removed the splint and the crow was able to walk. The cygnet was another matter. It was growing quickly, so we ended up giving it to a customer of Annie's who already had a pond with two swans.

66.

At last. At last, Puri Dai and Young Chavo and Morning Glory are freed from the trunk to sit in the garden. The crow has come to perch on Puri Dai's shoulder, and the puppets comfort each other. They try to talk about that tragic monstrous night but can barely find the words. It had all happened so quickly: a cascade of knives, blood, accusations, the scuffling of the men's bodies across the earth as they crawled back to their truck. Puri Dai laments that she could not stop the horrors from unfolding.

The crow waits for Liza May at Annie's back door. He would have flown to her bedside, guarded her, sung her crow songs, but the humans stopped him from entering the house. The crow says to Puri Dai, Wait and see, one of these days she'll be reborn as if hatched from a crow's egg, and people will bring her their birds: birds with broken legs or fractured wings, suffering from incurable ailments, dying of grief or broken hearts. Liza May will take them in her hands and give them what no other human can give.

I know this, says the crow, from my own experience. That girl will grow old surrounded by birds.

Puri Dai says, That girl will be saved by birds.

67.

We were sitting in the backyard one morning when Liza May came into the garden, fully dressed. She had brushed her hair. When she saw the crow, she called out and the crow hopped onto her arm. "Crow," she said, "you remember me." We ate around the table. It felt as if we were almost whole again, with her sitting here among us.

The night terrors receded. She hardly woke shouting or screaming anymore. After what seemed to be the final nightmare, my mother brought out the box from under Liza May's bed, and when Liza May wasn't there, we opened it to look at what was left of Panni Mooi.

"It's good she can't see this," said Lilly, touching the scattered pieces.

Mam said we would heal Liza May as she healed her birds, but she wouldn't be as she was before. "We can't go back to what we once were. Them days are gone." She put the box of

Panni Mooi's fragments back under Liza May's bed.

Mam asked Liza May, "Are you ready for us to put Panni Mooi together?"

And each time Liza May said, "Not yet."

★

I had just finished helping Annie shelve books when it came to me that I should fix the bicycle. That thought took me instantly back to the night at the side of the road, Dolores lying in the ditch and me screaming her name, trying to bring her back.

Before supper my mother and I went into the garage and brought the bicycle out to the driveway. I didn't know where to start.

"I don't know how to fix bikes," I said.

"I bet Annie has a book about that," Mam said.

The bicycle stayed in the driveway for days, leaning against the garage, until I finally went out to visit it again. The more I looked at it, the more the bike became a thing of mystery. One morning, as I was running my hands over the bent wheel, a truck pulled up in front of the abandoned storefront across the street from Annie's bookstore. It was Harry, the farmer who had run over Missus Tormentine's dog. "You again," Harry said, and he came over. He asked about the bicycle, and I told him that seeing it brought back a terrible memory. That it wasn't just a bicycle but a part of my shared life with Dolores. He walked around the bike, poked it here and there, and finally said: "I can help you."

Harry showed up with various tools. He said we needed to fix the brakes and the gears. The front wheel wasn't true, which he told me meant it wasn't straight, and this would have been caused either by the truck hitting the bike, or by the bike falling with great force into the ditch.

As we worked, I told Harry about Dolores. About how we'd found the bike back at the motel, about Dolores's family garden, about the harvest, about the chicks that had hatched, about her mother who told stories and sang and made them laugh. Then I told him why the mother sang, and why they had to keep laughing. I told him about the brother, about the death squads and the two villages. "Oh, jeez," Harry said.

He talked about his family. "It's nothing like what happened to your friend," he said, almost apologetically. He told me about his brother who was in a home after a fall at work. "He can't feed himself or walk or talk," Harry said. "He can't roll himself over in bed, so he has to be turned all the time. He's a big guy, and it takes three people to turn him." The fall happened two years ago, a week before Harry and his brother were to go hunting.

Harry returned a few days later with a new wheel that he'd found in his barn. I thanked him and helped him put it on. I learned how to adjust the seat. I liked watching him work. His hands, with long fingers and veins across the backs and up his wrists, were careful and deliberate. He showed me how to oil the gears and the brakes, and finally he said, "How about you take her for a spin." I couldn't forget Dolores flying into the ditch, and everything that had followed unrolled before my eyes.

"I don't think I'm ready yet," I said, and I think, after hearing Dolores's story, Harry understood. He seemed to be that kind of man.

It occurred to me that after helping fix the bike, he might not come back, but then I saw him again outside the hardware store. I asked how his brother was. A useless question, I thought, and Harry said, "The same."

I found myself asking if he wanted to come into the backyard, where I knew my mother had brought out tea. Seeing Harry, Liza May ran for the protection of the doorway, saying, "Is he one of them people coming to get us?" She waited there till Harry stood up to leave. I walked him to the gate and felt I needed to explain to him why she feared him. I told him what the gorjos had done to our puppets, and the nightmares that had been caused by the attack.

★

Mrs. Shuttleworth's cousin, Ace Musselwhite, was a real estate agent, and he took my mother and Lilly to see a house outside town. The owner, a widow with no family, had died, and Ace told Mam the house was going for next to nothing. Among other things, it needed a new roof. Mam said she'd have to think about it. Ace Musselwhite phoned the bookstore twice a day, and she figured he really wanted to get the house off his hands. Still, she told him the same thing every time: "Let me just think about it."

With us, she went into more detail. There was a front porch where we could sit after supper and watch the fields across the road, a small barn for future hens and Liza May's rescued birds, an abandoned vegetable garden still growing asparagus and rhubarb at the far end, lilac bushes up to the front door, a good well, an almost-new septic system, and many trees: elms, maples, pines, and others she couldn't identify, as well as a small orchard. The fruit trees would need pruning and the garden tilling, she said. The one thing missing was a tangle of black nightshade vines, but that didn't mean there weren't any growing nearby, and she would keep looking. The land bordered on a forest at the back, and maybe there would be owls at night.

She said the house needed a lot of work, including painting, and when she took us there, we'd see the peeling wallpaper and understand what she meant. She described a front hall as wide as the dining room. Windows on all sides looking out over the garden, the orchard, the forest, letting in the sun. She couldn't stop talking.

Eventually, she took out her many coffee tins of money and we counted. Annie's dining table was heaped with bills, and two card tables were brought from the garage for the piles of change, which we sorted and put into paper rolls. Annie took her to the bank to open an account, even though Mam didn't like the idea of the bank. We weren't used to them. Why keep your money where you can't see it or get your hands on it? She met with the bank manager and shook during the visit, and didn't understand anything that he said. Such an experience was frightening to her. Four days later she met Ace Musselwhite, and the house was hers. She spent that evening in tears.

★

The bike was finished, the gears and brakes oiled, and there was no longer any reason for me not to ride it. Harry came to see me off. I was unsure at first, but he said, "You can do it," and then, when he saw I was still hesitating, he said, "Do it for your friend." Yes. For Dolores. At first I wobbled slowly down the street, Harry cheering me on, and then I waved, turning a corner, imagining Dolores beside me, and I headed out along the dirt roads. Each evening I rode further, and I found myself going through tunnels of trees, late light streaming through the branches, or past tobacco fields, now only a few with plants left to harvest, the others with bare stalks waiting to be plowed under for the next year.

68.

Puri Dai's eyes follow Zelda as she gets up from the table. Supper is over, the women are all leaning back happily, hands on their stomachs, teacups drained, eyes half closed. In the garden: the low sounds of birds getting ready for night. She hears her girl wheel the bike out to the sidewalk, and then Puri Dai is alone with the rest of her family. Zelda doesn't know it, but one of these days, she's going to be dunked in the waters of the fast-moving river and find herself at the door of kingdom come, and then she'll rise again, washed clean of all those mokkadi fowki, clean under the moon, and she'll be with her own fowki once more. Puri Dai knows this, and she waits.

69.

Late September, the first cool night, with sharp-scented aster and goldenrod in the wind. A stain of light still lay in the sky. I'd biked further than usual and found myself back along the river road where I'd first been taken by Missus Tormentine. The shoulder narrowed where the road met Tobacco River, and I slowed. The river was wider here, deeper and raging. I didn't know whether to go back to that place where Missus Tormentine had coaxed me out to the current, and where I'd nearly drowned Mercedes.

I heard the truck before I saw it. It picked up speed as it came up behind me. The driver gunned the engine. I heard the roar of the truck hugging the curve of road, I saw the beer bottle fly out ahead of me and hit the gravel. I felt the hot breath of the truck beside me. It was only seconds—I was lifted into the air, and I soared, the sky at my feet.

Maybe he didn't know it was me. Maybe he did. My body flew into the shore's shallow waters. I tried to move but couldn't. My hands felt my ribs, my arms. Maybe something was broken. Something was always broken somewhere. The Tobacco River sucked me into its current. I saw Puri Dai and Panni Mooi, Morning Glory and Young Chavo and the ghost of Mr. Yesterday, I saw my mother and Liza May and Lilly. As my head went under and my mouth took in the river's water, I saw their linked arms, their long strides as they moved into the waves, and I was able to lift my head and breathe. Here was Puri Dai. With one hand she held my head and with the other she pulled me out. *Take my hand, girl. That's right. Not far now, nearly there. That's right, my beautiful shey.*

The driver stepped on the gas and the whole truck shuddered and skidded, somersaulting over the shore and into the river. Face at the window, mouth a cave. As the truck sank, I saw the balls, the dark pink balls, rise to the water's surface and detach themselves from the trailer hitch, rocking in the current as they were carried away.

Jack Tormentine, going to meet the black hole that swallowed all light, swallowed even gravity, so that nothing could ever claw its way out. Tormentine spiralling into the black hole in the bari kauli ratti, the giant black night.

70.

Will this never end? Puri Dai says to herself. Her girl, her Zelda, comes to her just before dark, and she sees her quite clearly, even though Puri Dai is with the others in the back garden. Zelda had gone off on her bicycle. The crow is agitated, digging its claws into Puri Dai's shoulder, and she turns to him and goes, Will you cut that out? The crow looks at Puri Dai and says, I see her. She's not here, but I see her.

Puri Dai sees her now. A terrible vision. She finds she is not consumed by fear, not frozen to her chair in the garden, but is over at the river. How did she get here? She reaches out her hand and pulls her girl from the water. She sees ambulance lights flashing on and off. She sees the people standing over her Zelda's body, her girl flat on the riverbank, not moving. A man is bent over her working at her body, breathing into her mouth. Puri Dai shakes Zelda. Wake up, girl, wake up, and she plants the ancestor's kiss on Zelda's chalk-white face. Wake up, girl, my beautiful darling girl, wake up, my tikni shey.

Zelda's eyes are open. They're covered with a film grey as fog, and they don't appear to be seeing anything. Is there life in those eyes, those green-as-leaves eyes? I'm here, says Puri Dai through her tears. Zelda keeps looking at nothing. Not just at nothing, but through everything to a great nothingness. Is she staring into the black hole? Has she been tipped over the event horizon into the place of no return? Come back, darling girl, come back, says Puri Dai.

The paramedics carry her girl's body to a stretcher and load her into the ambulance. O so tikni and small she is, like a twig under the blanket, all strapped in, the oxygen mask on her mouth and her dripping hair all over the pillow. The ambulance tears off, siren blaring. Puri Dai tries to keep up, goodness knows she tries, but she's too ancient. She returns, exhausted, to the garden, where the others are sitting around the table eating ice cream and drinking their tea. She tries to tell them, for the life of her she tries to tell them, but the words don't come out. The crow tries to tell them, but they can't hear, and they just sit there talking and telling jokes, finishing their ice cream, drinking their tea, drinking their tea while Puri Dai sits inside her wooden body, crying for her girl.

71.

A light was in my eyes. It shone down at me from a great height. I thought it was the light you see as you leave this world. Then a face came between me and the light, and a kind, blurry woman in white asked my name and what day it was, my address, my birthday, and if I knew where I was. Before I could answer, the light faded, and the woman's voice said from a great distance, "Stay with us."

Stay? Stay where? In this echo chamber, with its rushing and beeping and clanging? Is this what it was like to be carried from one world into the next? Busy voices? The humming rushing symphony of noise? I wanted to say stop, but then everything went black again, and I saw before me the four hundred billion stars of the Milky Way, and then, finally, Sagittarius A*, the black hole at its heart. The massive black hole, the rotational centre, held out its arms to pull me in.

Here was the light shining over me again, and I dropped. I was in the nightshade now, the nicotiana, the night-flowering tobacco sending its jasmine scent into the air, the long threaded tongues of the hawk moths entering each bloom, the tobacco fields green by day and silver by night, the belladonna of the lord's cup, the berries of black nightshade dropping from the vine, the smell of earth, of the flowers, of the fields.

I heard a commotion and someone said a name that I thought was mine. When you're on your way to the other side, do you still have a name? How did I know this name? "Zelda, Zelda," said the voice. "My Zelda." I saw my mother before me, and then the black returned. Her cries grew thinner; they drew back like a wave from a shore. Shore. Had I been in water? I was caught midstream in a current between here and there. Where was here? Where was there? "Stay with us, dear," said a woman's voice. "Stay."

★

For what seemed an endless time, my eyelids were the sky and the Milky Way slid from one side of my vision to the other. Then one day I was lifted and carried from place to place. Later, I felt a bed beneath me, and I was lying on my back, and the sun streamed behind my closed eyes. The sheets smelled of cedar and the air around me smelled of tea. I opened my eyes. The tea was beside me in a cup on a table and I saw the steam rise into the air. I saw a glass of water. A roll of bandage. At the far side of the room, a chair. Someone was sitting in the chair. Puri Dai was sitting in the chair. Someone was humming nearby. It was Lilly.

"I saw the Milky Way," I said, "inside my eyelids."

I told her I was going to go to a school that specialized in stars. "A university. I'll be an astronomer. Like Dolores's brother." She thought I was joking, maybe still feeling the effects of what she said was my near-death experience, and she laughed out loud. I didn't think it was funny. "We come from the stars," I said. "Everything does." I looked across at Puri Dai and she nodded in silent agreement. At that moment, stars filled the room, even though it was daytime.

72.

There's my girl, says Puri Dai. My girl made of stars. We're star people, so when Zelda says this aloud to her auntie, Puri Dai agrees. Too bad Lilly has to laugh, but Puri Dai understands there are many ways of knowing different things. We come from the stars and we'll return to them, to the kushti kauli ratti, the good black night. We'll join together with its constellations and galaxies. We'll be the tiny scattered vibrations that wheel in from outer space and we'll ride round and round in the pure airless dark just as the wheels of the vardo go round and round on the lungo drom, the long road that takes us from here to there, from there to here. The road, our own road, unfurls from the morning through the day into the night and back to the dawn. My Zelda and I, we will always be part of each other. We'll know each other in a new way. My girl and I, we'll carry each other as we whirl through the dust and brilliance of galaxies.

73.

Dear Zelda: The situation here is very tense. Because of my brother, they are watching my family. My sister was to start university, but my mother said no, they are killing and disappearing students. We have been advised to apply for asylum in your country, because your government is accepting refugees. My cousin who is a lawyer is helping us with this. In the meantime, please give all our love to your family.

★

A second letter followed in a week.

My dear Zelda: My brother's friend came to see us and said we are on a list, and that we have to leave within 48 hours. We are giving the hens and their chicks to our neighbour.

We're going to Mexico. All our documentation will be processed there. I am frightened. I feel bad that we have to leave my brother's telescope, because aside from his clothes and books, it's the only thing we have left of him. But we can't bring it with us. I will bring his astronomy book and his green sweater.

★

These letters were read to me by Annie, who visited my bedside to translate them. My mother brought me bowls of soup and changed my dressings, first on the side of my head, then my ribs and my arm. Under the cast my leg was unbearably itchy.

Who knows what would have happened if somebody hadn't been driving by when I was thrown into the river? The person who'd found me on the riverbank said it was a miracle I was alive, and the people at the hospital also called it a miracle, and my mother didn't tell them that we didn't believe in miracles. I remembered nothing of that night after pulling myself out of the water, although I could have sworn Puri Dai was there with me. They told me an ambulance had come to take me to the emergency room, and that the police went knocking on Annie's door looking for Mam—the same gavverbengs who'd tried to accuse us of coshing Tormentine in the tobacco field.

I didn't like the crutches, especially going downstairs. I could have been a circus performer, swivelling on the root of one crutch at a great height, lowering my good foot to the next step, and swivelling again. I heard Lilly and my mother calling me. "Where are you? Do you need help getting down?" My descent was sluggish and exhausting, and I could not summon the energy to answer them.

When I finally arrived at the garden, I set the crutches by my chair and sat, breathless, stretching my legs and looking out at the remains of Annie's late-summer flowers. Lilly was gathering asters and black-eyed Susans into a bouquet, and my mother sat, head back, eyes closed, face to the sun. Annie was reading the paper. Everything around me comfortable, normal: the air hummed with bees and the late whine of insects, as if no terrible thing had ever happened or could happen here.

Annie straightened. "My God," she said, frowning at the newspaper. Her glasses dropped from the end of her nose. "You need to see this." She held out the inside page with its headline. *Beloved farmer dies in tragic accident.* There was a picture of Mister Tormentine looking too handsome, and another of Missus Tormentine at the funeral. Even with the veil covering her head, I knew how she'd be: face and body held stiffly in a silent rage. Lilly told me I should go straight to the reporters and tell them what had happened that night, but I said nobody around here would believe me. Why should they? I wasn't one of them.

The next week my mother and Lilly started booking shows. They said the puppets would not return to the tobacco fields but instead would visit new places: libraries, schools, community centres, the nursing home, the art gallery in Hamilton. It was too late for the fall fairs, but Mam said she'd book these for next year.

*

Our new house was only a short drive from Annie's, ten or so minutes. The crow, who hadn't left us, rode beside Liza May in the truck's bed.

I caught the first glimpse of the house as we came down the driveway, past a mailbox and a dense screen of willows, and through a lilac grove. I imagined spring blooms hazing across the branches, bouquets on our kitchen table.

The house was painted a periwinkle blue, and was peeling in places, and framed by a white-painted porch with sagging steps and a door with a long window and glass panels on either side. Wild grape vines had wound themselves across the windows, and when my mother turned the key in the lock and opened the door, we entered a half-lit hush, the fragrance of buried wallpaper and wood. It was a kind, comfortable smell. Mam was smiling and crying at the same time.

We followed her along the creaking wooden floor to the back of the house, where a second porch opened off the kitchen. Trees, a barn, a plot of earth for a garden, and beyond the yard, a forest. The crow flew off and came back with a small hinge, and later a bottle cap, dropping them like offerings onto the porch railing.

Upstairs were five small bedrooms, each with its own faded, peeling wallpaper. Someone had placed pails under blisters in the ceiling where rain had come in. I thought of the leaking blue bedroom at Missus Tormentine's house.

"Is this going to get fixed?"

Mam seemed irritated by my question. "Ace is taking care of it," she said.

Finally, we moved in. We carried the puppets: Puri Dai, Morning Glory, and Young Chavo first. Two boxes carried the remains of Panni Mooi and Mr. Yesterday, and we set these in front of the mantelpiece. We opened the box with the fragments of Mr. Yesterday.

"He's beyond saving," said Mam.

Lilly went into the kitchen and made tea, and we sat around Mr. Yesterday's box, finally able to mourn him. The next night we had a party and invited our friends: Annie, Harry, Mrs. Shuttleworth and her family, Crowshank the butcher, and the women from the egg barn. The crow sat on Liza May's shoulder, and we lifted the puppets in our arms and did a little dance around the yog, the first fire at our new house.

★

Our new house. Our house, even though a bit of a wreck, had an innocent beauty. It felt as if good lives had been lived here. The living room and kitchen smelled faintly of black tea and wood smoke, and whiffs of old glue and wallpaper clung to the walls. I liked the light that flooded the rooms, and the kitchen with its many cupboards and battered harvest table in the middle. The insides of the bedroom closets had been painted white and held no secrets. Our jars of jam were lined up on the cellar shelves.

Yet for me the house still wasn't enough. The life I wanted would not fit inside its walls. Even so, over the next weeks, as the weather grew cool and the nights longer, I settled within it. The mailbox was its heart: that's where my longing lived. I went down the driveway past the lilacs every morning to check for letters from Dolores.

Every day Liza May collected the crow's gifts on the back porch railing: a key, a rusted screw, a dead vole.

The morning came when I opened the mailbox and saw an envelope with my name written on it. The letter was in Spanish, with English copied below in Dolores's handwriting.

Dear Zelda: The embassy gives us ministers permits and we will come to Toronto maybe in a month. With love, Dolores

I stood at the mailbox and read and reread the letter. I closed my eyes and saw Dolores in our backyard, lighting the fire, cooking with us in the kitchen, the dictionary on the table. Dolores with her mother and her sisters, the kind ones and the angry one, the sadness of the ghost brother in the air around us. I saw us looking at the night sky, naming the constellations. I ran inside with the letter.

"They're coming!" I shouted. I showed them the letter.

My mother right away started talking about what to cook.

"But they're not even here yet," I said. "Who knows when we'll see them?"

"We'll make a fire and grill sausages," Mam said over me. "We'll catch a rabbit and make a stew. We'll make pies with our own apples."

"Mam, they don't get here for a month." I went to bed thinking of Dolores. Of our new lives.

★

I was in a dream in which I walked into a house. I soon saw that it was our house, but different, as places often are in a dream. "I'm home," I said in the dream, and I must have spoken aloud, because my voice woke me. I sat up. "Home," I said aloud. I didn't trust that word *home*. It felt like a kind of suffocation: fluffy curtains and floral room spray and cakes made with pink food colouring perched in the middle of the table, like you'd see in a magazine. I'd never believed in the idea of home, aside from the place where you ate or slept in at any particular time. For us, it had always been bare rented rooms, trailers, farmhouses, half-broken quarters allocated when working on farms. These places had seemed as if they'd be absorbed into thin air after we left. Here, now, in each room, I could touch the plain sensible walls and feel the solid floor under my feet.

I sat in the dark and saw this house as my own version of home, different from my mother's: a stopping place on my road, an atchin tan to which I'd return again and again. I thought of my old territory of Invisible, the land I'd carried both inside and out, and how it was now an unnecessary skin. Standing in my bedroom, looking out at the trees of the night orchard, I discovered that I'd sloughed it off.

★

My mother found the Grade 8 teacher who had put on the art exhibit at the fair. Mam and Lilly went out for the afternoon and came back with the drawing of the two women sewing tobacco leaves. They'd bought it for five dollars, and the girl who made it had signed her name on the back. "That's my friend Laird's daughter," said Annie when she saw it. The drawing was even more delicate than we remembered, with strands of the women's hair stuck to their faces as they worked, the veins of each tobacco leaf standing out, and even darker veins on the backs of the women's hands. It was as if the plant veins and human veins were sisters engaged in the same work of moving life from one place to the other.

74.

At the local high school, I explained to the guidance counsellor that I'd only reached Grade 10. They said I could go to night school, even though the semester had started three weeks ago. You can catch up, they told me, but it might take two or three years to graduate. I asked for information about studying astronomy. They were patient with me, explaining that it might be covered briefly in the night-school science courses, but for serious study I'd have to go to a university.

I went away with my first five textbooks, which were used and dog-eared and had notes in the margins, but they were like five new worlds to me. The smell of the paper reminded me of Annie's bookstore. I'd start classes after I'd told my mother, which I feared doing: she would think I was abandoning her. Breaking us apart.

I turned the pages of the books, looking at diagrams of triangles, petals, roots, frog innards, and mysterious mathematical symbols, and imagined how much more I'd know after

I'd read to the last pages. In one textbook, I found directions for making a telescope, and I took over the kitchen table. The telescope was simple, made with a cardboard mailing tube, a smaller tube, and two magnifying glasses of different sizes. You could move the narrower tube back and forth inside the bigger one, depending on what you wanted to look at and how close you wanted it to be.

"What are you making?" said Mam.

"A telescope."

"Where'd you ever learn to do that?"

"Just from a book."

"What book?"

"One from Annie's."

I felt Puri Dai's wooden eyes at my back. *Quit with the lies. All we want here from now on are tacho kovas: only true things. Tell her. Tell her the truth.*

Lilly drove me to the hardware store to get magnifying glasses. It took two days to make the telescope, and then I brought it outside at night to explore the sky. Harry came over and we looked at the almost-full moon. "Going to be a hunter's moon in the next couple of days," he said.

He helped me hang the bicycle on the back wall of the barn. We stood back to admire the bike, now more a work of art than a wreck. It bore the wounds of impact, its front wheel folded into a half-moon, the frame twisted in upon itself.

⋆

Tell them, said Puri Dai. *Tell them about this school business.*

She and Young Chavo and Morning Glory were waiting on the bench in the hall as my mother folded the red curtains.

Tell them, Puri Dai said again. *Tell them so they can get used to it. Tell your mother.* I looked over at Mam. I figured she already knew something was up.

"Mam, I'm going to night school," I blurted. "Starting next week." She stopped folding. She stood with the curtains in her arms and didn't move. I said I wanted to study astronomy at a university someday, but that was a long time off.

Liza May said: "We can't go to universities."

Lilly said: "Of course we can."

It was another minute before my mother spoke. "You'll forget our ways. They won't matter to you," she said. "You'll go away from us." I told her I'd never been closer to her or to my aunties. "It's time we were on the road," she said to Lilly and Liza May, and then turned to me. "You needn't come," she said pointedly. They took the puppets and the red curtains out to the truck. "We'll be back late," she said.

I'd hurt her again—a new, different hurt—with my desire for learning. After they left, I cleaned. I scrubbed floors and walls, washed windows, turning out every cupboard and drawer. It was night when I heard the truck pull into the driveway. I went out to help bring in the puppets. My mother wouldn't look at me. "I'm still going to night school," I said to her back. "It's no big deal, everybody does it. It's half an hour away. I can walk."

"Okay," she said. "Okay. Do what you want."

"You'll be great," Lilly said. "You'll kick their arses."

You can do anything, murri shey, said Puri Dai as I carried her into the house.

When the puppets were safely inside, we went out back. The moon was so bright that it made the stars disappear. Through my telescope we saw shadows of craters, mountains, waterless lakes.

"I want to study the stars and all that out there," I said.

"Okay, okay," went Mam. It was the only response she was able to give.

"What about the puppets?" said Liza May. "Who'll look after them when we're gone? Who'll do the shows?"

I had not thought about the puppets. I had not thought about my mother and my aunties being gone.

"You'll have time to figure that out," said Lilly.

My family, the ones of flesh and the ones of canvas and metal, paper and glue and wood, they were the beginning of my road, my drom. I turned to look at the past, turned again to look at what was to come. In the winter, or maybe the spring, Dolores and I would see the sky together. We'd stand under the kauli ratti, the beautiful black night. I'd maybe know a few more things about stars, and I could tell her what I'd learned. I'd have to fold the puppets into this new life, but I did not yet know how I would do it.

75.

It was the time of migrations, of turning inward, shutting down. Birds gathered in the trees, then tore off as one to fill the sky. Mornings, we were awakened before sunrise to a cacophony of song. The air coming through our open windows was cool and crisp, accompanied by the beginnings of that smoky autumn aroma. Crows too were gathering, and Liza May determined it was time that her own crow should return to its world. The crow must have sensed this as well, because whenever she went outside, it lifted from her shoulder and swooped up to the air above us before gliding into the forest behind our house. The crow wouldn't forget, though; we knew it would return from time to time with small gifts placed on the railing of the back porch: shiny things or dead offerings. As I watched it disappear through the trees, I imagined myself flying off, returning, flying off, returning. I tried to imagine what gifts I'd bring. A real telescope? Stories about the Milky Way, black holes, galaxies?

★

Liza May put down her fork and out of the blue said she wanted to bring Panni Mooi back to life. *Life.* We had not spoken about Panni Mooi since leaving Annie's. My mother started to make a list of materials, and then a plan formed. This was to hide the trembling of her jaw and the tears that had begun to gather in her eyes. The faster she talked, the more the tears welled, spilling over her eyelids and down her face. I could see that all the changes in our lives had overwhelmed her and she'd come a bit undone: she who had cared for us, held us together, now needed to be held. Lilly and Liza May comforted her, speaking to her in quiet voices.

"All that other stuff is behind us now."

"Look at our lovely house. It's what you dreamed of."

"We'll be whole again, like Panni Mooi. Changed, but whole."

On the weekend, out in the garden, we began to build Panni Mooi a new body of wood covered with layers of heavy paper soaked in a paste of flour and water. Each layer was left to dry in the sun, so that three days after we put on the final sheets, moulding them to the built-up shell underneath, Panni Mooi's body was hard as bone. Then we fashioned her upper arms and thighs of cloth, stuffing them with straw, and attached them to her body. Lilly carved her hands and her lower legs and feet from lengths of soft pine.

Her head was difficult, particularly her nose and ears and lips, her cheekbones, eye sockets, her chin. We needed to get her face exactly right. Her expression should be of sorrow and wonder, said Liza May. The building of her face required an underlayer of leather and many layers of paper and glue, and even though smaller than her body, her head took longer to build and to dry.

Within a week, her face was ready to paint. "She's still got to have tears," said Liza May. She was the one to do the painting. Panni Mooi's cheeks were more flushed, her eyes brighter, and her lips curved at the edge of a half smile. Blue transparent tears ran down her face.

Days later, we laid her, dry now, face down on the kitchen table. The cavity of her back was exposed. We worked over her and in her, like doctors performing an operation. Lilly and Harry had made the miniature gears and pullies that were housed in the back of her body, and these we connected to her wires and strings. Liza May and Mam pulled them gently, first opening her lips, then raising her eyebrows, making her frown. She was not quite the same being, but the heart of her was there, shared with the heart of the old Panni Mooi. Liza May braided her hair and varnished her tears. We all knew, without saying it aloud, that by making Panni Mooi anew we were rebuilding our own lives.

At night my mother came to sit on my bed. She took my hand. "Murri shey," she said. "I was wrong. Nothing will put itself between us."

The shadows climbed my wall. Downstairs, Liza May and Lilly were talking, drinking their tea in the kitchen. The last tea of the day. I heard the rattle of the cups settling down from time to time in their saucers. There was a silence, then a flurry of words, then silence. A completeness entered this silence. It was Panni Mooi made whole. It was more than Panni Mooi. It was a grace, a cleansing. The mokkadi, the defiled, swept away and balance restored. This was the code of our fowki. Balance restored through each simple act.

I heard their footsteps as they came up the stairs, first Lilly's, then Liza May's, lighter, quicker. I heard their low whispers.

"Good night."

"Night."

I thought of night and its meanings. A time, a place of stars, a darkness, a leave-taking. I heard the doors of their rooms open and then quietly shut. The house was settling into sleep. I looked at the silver pool the moon sent across my bed. I looked at the backs of my hands for signs of Buddy Watmore's ghost tattoos. They had faded into insignificance.

My mother pulled the sheet up to my chin. I was in one moment the tikni shey held close as Rhodie rushed past the doctor into the night, and in the next moment the young woman who would take five textbooks to school and from their pages the deepest mysteries would unfold.

76.

Puri Dai the grandmother speaks, her voice a bright ribbon unspooling in the air. How beautiful and light you rise, murri shey, through the dark and fog and the caves inside caves, your clear eyes skimming the lungo drom.

Puri Dai's sitting at the kitchen window: her girl has brought her here on the way out to the clothesline with the wet laundry. Her wooden eyes watch Zelda hang the sheets and nightgowns and pillowcases. Her eyes see the rocks that ring the yog. They see the wooden chairs around the rocks, the ring of maples around the chairs. Rings around rings around rings. The barn's further back under the elms. A place for Liza May's birds, because birds will come. The patch of black earth for the garden and its dream of carrots, beets, lettuces. The forest.

This is our world, says Puri Dai.

Nights are cold now. The creaking floorboards of the bedrooms, the wind seeping under the doors, the steaming kitchen. Zelda and the three sisters are folded in, cooking suppers, shaking out blankets and unpacking sweaters, socks, long underwear. They wear their coats now when they sit out at night around the yog, eating rabbit stew that sends its hot breath into the air. In the next weeks, the frost will overtake the fields and ditches. In the weeks after that, the snow will come. Blizzards will batter the house. All white except the sky full of blowing snow and stars in the kauli ratti, the beautiful black night.

After the winter, after the ice and snow sink into the roots and tunnels and underground streams, green life will erupt, a sprouting haze pushing itself up through the earth, leafbuds forming along the tree branches. The yarrow, plantain, the horsetail, St. John's wort, evening primrose, blue-flowered chicory, broad-leafed furry mullein—all the healing medicines will unfurl at the edge of the forest and in the meadows and the gravel along the sides of the roads.

Our sheets and pillowcases and nightgowns billow in the wind. They spin somersaults on the clothesline, the nightgowns leaping as if inhabited, occasionally resting.

Last night, out at the yog, there was talk of planting an oak in the spring. A small granddaughter oak, a future grandmother. It should comfort Rhodie that her Zelda will return sometimes to sit under its branches. Puri Dai, who never ages, will sit beside her, or perhaps in her lap, as they send each other their wordless words, and the nightshade, the dark bright nightshade, teems around them.

Acknowledgements

Deepest thanks—

To author, colleague, water sprite and dear friend Nina Munteanu, who said to me one day, "Why don't you write your family stories into a novel?";

To my sister-in-arms, author, poet, storyteller and harpist Frances Roberts Reilly, for her constant and warm support, beginning with her praise for my short story, "Nightshade," which planted the seed for this novel;

To Ursula Pflug, my initial guide and brilliant mentor in the early development of the manuscript;

To lovely and generous author Caren Gussoff Sumption, for permission to use the incisive words from her short fiction "Climacteric," first published in *Luna Station*, March, 2025;

To my daughters Zoe and Riel, who played endlessly with our grandmother puppet, infusing her with new life;

To my amazingly supportive partner Eric Mills; and

To the team at Assembly Press: Leigh Nash, my editor extraordinaire, whose clear vision, insights, and wisdom were invaluable; Andrew Faulkner and Debby de Groot for their enthusiastic encouragement, guidance and support; and Greg Tabor for his gorgeous cover design.

I'm deeply grateful to the ancestors:

Grandmother Lizzie Lee, aunties Lilly and May, and the fragments of their stories that inspired me;

Father Leonard Hutchinson, who taught me to tar a roof, build a table, and lay a floor, and who with Grandfather Birchony built the puppets that filled my childhood;

Sister Rhoda, who brought stories from cousin Iris in England: the family's travelling years in Lancashire, the fairs, the carved and painted horses, and the vardo (caravan) whose walls shimmered with mirrors; and

Brother Bobby, for the stories of our family as they entertained at the garden parties of wealthy farmers in the 1920s southern Ontario tobacco belt.

Finally, I wish to thank the Government of Ontario and the Ontario Arts Council for their generous financial support through the Literary Creation Projects (Works for Publication) grant.

Photo credit: Ingrid Mayrhofer

Lynn Hutchinson Lee is an award-winning author of Anglo-Romany descent on her father's side. Her short fiction has been published in *Room*, *Wagtail: The Roma Women's Poetry Anthology*, and elsewhere. An excerpt from *Nightshade* won first prize in the 2022 Joy Kogawa Award for Fiction and was shortlisted for the 2022 Swedish Writers' Festival Prize. In 2023, *Nightshade* was shortlisted for the Guernica Prize. Her flash fiction won the Editors' Choice Award in Guernica's *This Will Only Take a Minute*. Her novella *Origins of Desire in Orchid Fens* is published with Stelliform Press. Lynn writes in Toronto, cooks for friends, feeds birds, and gets lost in her garden.

Printed by Imprimerie Gauvin
Gatineau, Québec